ONE OF OUR KIND

ONE OF OUR KIND

A NOVEL

Nicola Yoon

ALFRED A. KNOPF
NEW YORK | 2024

THIS IS A BORZOI BOOK
PUBLISHED BY ALFRED A. KNOPF

www.aaknopf.com

Library of Congress Cataloging-in-Publication Data
Name: Yoon, Nicola, author.
Title: One of our kind : a novel / Nicola Yoon.
Description: New York | Alfred A. Knopf, 2024.
Identifiers: LCCN 2023031557 (print) | LCCN 2023031558 (ebook) |
ISBN 9780593470671 (hardcover) | ISBN 9780593470695 (ebook) |
ISBN 9780593688434 (open market)
Subjects: LCSH: African American families—Fiction. | LCGFT: Novels.
Classification: LCC PS3625.O5375 O54 2024 (print) | LCC PS3625.O5375 (ebook) |
DDC 813/.6—dc23/eng/20231023
LC record available at https://lccn.loc.gov/2023031557
LC ebook record available at https://lccn.loc.gov/2023031558

Jacket images: Shutterstock
Jacket design by John Gall

Manufactured in the United States of America
First Edition

TO ALL OF US

"A long leash is still a leash."

—OCTAVIA BUTLER, *Patternmaster*

"Definitions belonged to the definers, not the defined."

—TONI MORRISON, *Beloved*

PART ONE

"It really is beautiful here," Jasmyn says, looking out of the passenger-side window. Here is the Black history museum with its massive roman columns and grand staircase. Next door, the manicured sculpture garden is populated with statues of W. E. B. Du Bois, Marcus Garvey, Stokely Carmichael, Malcolm X, and, of course, Martin Luther King Jr. A block later the Liberty Theater, with its ornate rococo stylings, comes into view. Enormous posters announce the dates for December's *Nutcracker* performance. Beautiful Black ballerinas star in every role from the Rat King to the Sugar Plum fairy.

Her husband, Kingston—everyone calls him King—takes a hand off the steering wheel and squeezes her knee. "Been a long time coming," he says.

Jasmyn smiles at his profile and rests her hand atop his. God knows he'd worked hard enough to get them to here. Here being Liberty, California, a small suburb on the outskirts of Los Angeles.

She turns her eager gaze back to the sights of the downtown district. They pass Liberty Gardens with its bountiful variety of cacti and succulents. On a previous visit, she'd learned from the entrance plaque that desert flowers have unique adaptations that allow them to extract the maximum amount of moisture possible from their parched environment. Jasmyn told King she felt a kinship with them because of the way they found a way to thrive despite hardship.

"Bet they'd prefer if it just rained a little more," he teased.

"Probably," Jasmyn said, and laughed along with him.

They drive by the aquatic complex, and then the equestrian center, where she sees two young Black girls, twelve or thirteen years old, looking sharp in their riding jackets, breeches, and boots.

Finally, they begin the drive up Liberty Hill to the residential section. They'd visited Liberty three times before, but Jasmyn is still awestruck and, if she's being honest, a little discomfited at the sheer size of the houses. Why call them houses at all? Modern-day castles are what they are. Expansive lawns and landscaped hedges. Wide circular driveways, most with fountains or some other architectural water feature. Multiple cars that start at six figures. They pass two parked pool service vans and another for tennis court maintenance.

It's hard for Jasmyn to believe that everyone who lives here is Black. Harder to believe that, in just one month, she's going to be one of the Black people who lives here. The Jasmyn that grew up fighting for space in a cramped, one-bedroom apartment with her mother, grandmother, and older sister couldn't have imagined she'd end up in a place like this. That Jasmyn would've thought this kind of living was only possible for the rich white people she saw in TV shows.

But here she is, driving by these outrageously colossal homes, on her way to her *own* outrageously colossal home.

King turns down their soon-to-be street. It's a week before Thanksgiving, but a handful of the houses already have Christmas decorations up. The first has not one, but two enormous Christmas trees on either side of the lawn. Both are flocked and decorated with crystal snowflakes. Closer to the house itself, spiral-strung lights ascend to the top of their fifty-foot-tall palm trees. There are wreaths in every window and a more elaborate one hanging from the front door.

But it's the house half a block later that makes Jasmyn ask King to slow down and pull over.

"These people aren't playing," King says.

The house has three separate displays, all of them animatronic and so realistic Jasmyn does a triple take. On the left side of the driveway there's a nativity display complete with bowing Wise Men, baby Jesus in a manger, and two angels with wings beating lightly. On the right, there's an elaborate Santa's workshop display featuring Mrs. Claus and her helper elves wrapping a tower of presents. The final display is on the roof. Santa, resplendent and jolly, is poised for takeoff in a life-sized sleigh, complete with rearing reindeer led by Rudolph.

But the most incredible part to Jasmyn, the part that makes her smile wide, is that all the figures are Black. Santa and Mrs. Claus. The angels and the elves. Baby Jesus and the Three Wise Men. Every one of them, a shade of brown.

"Just beautiful," she says.

She's seen Black Santas before, of course. For the last two years, she's made a special effort to seek one out for their six-year-old son, Kamau. And to this day, she still remembers the first time she ever saw one. She'd been nine and overheard their neighbor telling her mother about it.

"I hear they got themselves a Black Santa down at the mall," the woman had said.

Jasmyn begged her mother to go and meet him. The following weekend, along with every Black family in the neighborhood, they went. The line was long and her mother was mad by the time they got to the front. But Jasmyn sat on Santa's lap and asked him for the thing she thought a Black Santa would understand: money. Money so her mother didn't have to work two jobs. Money so she could have her own room and not have to share the living room with her sister, Ivy. Money so they could afford a house in a neighborhood that was less dangerous. It didn't occur to her to ask for one in a neighborhood that wasn't dangerous at all.

Six weeks later her grandmother died and left Jasmyn's mother enough money to quit one of her jobs for a few months. Her sister dropped out of high school and moved in with her older boyfriend. "God works in mysterious ways," her grandmother always said. It seemed to Jasmyn that Santa did, too.

King leans closer to her so he can get a better view of the display. "We definitely making the right move, baby," he says.

He says it because at first, Jasmyn had taken some convincing.

Liberty is something more than a neighborhood and less than a township. According to the brochure, it's a community. A gated, outrageously wealthy, and Black community.

"A Black utopia," King had said when he first told her about it. "Everyone from the mayor to the police chief to the beat cops to the janitors, all Black."

"How can they keep it all Black legally?" she asked.

Kingston eyed her like she was naive. "How many white folks you know want to move into a predominantly Black neighborhood?"

She conceded the point.

"It's a place where we can be free to relax and be ourselves," Kingston said.

She was skeptical still.

"There are no utopias," she told him. Certainly not for Black people and certainly not in America. Not anywhere in the world, if she was being real. She reminded him that Black utopias had been tried with little success before: Allensworth and Soul City, for example.

"This one will last," he'd insisted.

And she'd wanted him to be right. Wanted to live in a place surrounded by like-minded, thriving Black people. A place with wide, quiet streets where their son could ride his bike, carefree, with other little Black boys. A place where both King and Kamau would be safe walking around at night. She imagined them going for a stroll on some cold evening, both of them wearing hoodies. She imagined a cop car pulling alongside them. But this cop car had Black cops, and they were slowing down just to wish them a good evening.

But Liberty's wealth got under her skin. Would she fit in with rich people, even if they were Black? Would she ever get used to being wealthy herself? And worse than that insecurity was this: she didn't want to turn into one of those bougie Black people who forgot where they were from—and the people they came from—as soon as they got a little walking-around money.

"Baby, what are you talking about?" King had asked. "We haven't lived in the hood for a minute now," he said.

They'd argued in the kitchen of their two-bedroom apartment in the mid-city district. The neighborhood was working class, with quite a few older immigrants, their first-generation kids, and, of course, Black people. It wasn't rundown by any means and it certainly was better than Compton, where Jasmyn and King had both grown up. Still, there were homeless tents every few blocks or so. Some stores were still boarded up from the protests against police brutality a few summers before. The public school they sent Kamau to was decent but didn't have nearly enough Black teachers. Living there made Jasmyn feel like she'd come far from where she started out, but not *too* far. She still felt a part of the pulse of the Black community in LA.

King had been more upset by her resistance than she'd expected. "You're a public defender. You do more for our folks and our community than most people, for God's sake," he'd said.

"That doesn't mean I can just up and abandon them," she said.

He stared at her, mouth hanging open for a few seconds, before saying anything. "How is it abandoning? It's not like you're leaving your job. I'm talking about moving to a place with *only* Black people."

Jasmyn knew her resistance was more emotional than logical, but she couldn't shake the feeling that she'd be losing some part of herself if she moved.

It'd taken an incident with a white cop later in the spring to finally convince her to move.

"We should get going or we'll be late," King says now, and starts the car up. "We got the interior designer at ten and the landscape architect at eleven a.m."

Jasmyn nods. "Maybe we should come back tonight with Kamau so he can see those animatronics lit up and moving," she says as they pull away.

King squeezes her hand. "Good idea."

"Can you imagine his little face when he sees all this?"

King bulges his eyes out, imitating the funny face that Kamau makes when he's amazed by something. They both laugh.

Jasmyn rolls down her window and sticks her arm outside, letting her hand ride the air currents the way she used to as a child. She takes a long breath. Even the air in Liberty smells different, crisp and new. They pass two more Black Santas. A young couple walking with their toddler son and a dog waves to them as they drive by. Jasmyn smiles wide and waves back. In a couple of months she and King and Kamau will be the ones waving to someone new in the neighborhood. Maybe they'd get a dog, too, once they were settled.

She rests her hand on her stomach. It'd taken them years longer than they'd planned to get pregnant again, but their second son is just seven months away. That Liberty, this place of Black splendor, will be all he knows fills her with pride. She imagines that growing up, surrounded on all sides by Black excellence, will plant a seed in both his and Kamau's hearts. It will help them both flourish, secure in the knowledge of their own beauty and self-worth.

Jasmyn reaches across the console and squeezes King's thigh. "You were right, baby," she says. "This is the right move."

COMMENTS 1378

In response to our article "Liberty: The Creation of a Modern Black Utopia"

The Los Angeles New Republic *is committed to publishing a diversity of voices. We welcome your on-topic commentary, criticism and expertise. This conversation is moderated according to the* Republic's *community rules. Please read the rules before joining the discussion.*

- **WHITE LIBERAL IN NYC**
  I am an older White liberal living in NYC and I have been a steadfast champion of civil rights practically my entire life. It never fails to surprise me how short-sighted Blacks can be, even a high achieving one such as Mr. Carlton Way undoubtedly is. Would the great Martin Luther King Jr. approve of this so-called utopia? I daresay he would not. He would call it what it is, a dystopia. Mr. King wanted us to unite! White, Black, Brown, Yellow, Red, Purple, Whatever! All peoples together. A community like Liberty is taking us backwards not forwards.

- **DMN666**
  LMFAO. Why stop there? Why not go all the way back to Africa? Good riddance is what I say.

- **BLACK AND CURIOUS IN SF**
  How do they decide who is Black? Does Mr. Way do it himself? Is there genetic testing? Is it the one-drop rule or the paper bag test?

- **ARTHUR BANE**
  I am well aware that this will be a minority opinion in this "news"paper, but Liberty sounds idyllic. Maslow's hierarchy of needs includes (among others) safety, belonging and love, esteem, and self-actualization. America

has a long and atrocious history of denying these basic needs to its Black citizens. Why shouldn't they carve out a place for themselves?

- **FED UP IN MISSISSIPPI**
  Another day, another article about the Blacks and their discontents. Don't you people have more important things to write about?

- **PROFESSORGAYLE**
  Historically, all utopias have failed.

PART TWO

I

The first thing Jasmyn notices about the older Black woman on her front doorstep is that her hair is *relaxed*. Not *natural*. Meaning that every six to eight weeks or so the older woman goes to a hair care salon and sits in a chair while a hairdresser applies a chemical that some people—Jasmyn among them—call "creamy crack" to her hair. The chemical transforms her natural, kinky, and beautiful hair into bone-straight locks.

Jasmyn studies the woman's hairline. It's funny how much hair can tell you about the kind of person you're dealing with. To Jasmyn's mind, using creamy crack is a sure sign of being an unenlightened Black woman. She finds that the practice is more common among the older generation. They steadfastly believe that taming their supposedly wild hair will make them more respectable.

Even her own mother hadn't been immune. Right after Jasmyn graduated from college, when she decided she didn't want her hair relaxed anymore, her mother warned her off.

"Let me tell you something," she'd said. "Nowadays, you young ones think times have changed. You think you can be Black as you want, but I'm telling you, your *white* bosses will judge you behind your back. To your face, they'll say how nice your hair is. Meanwhile it's the girl with straight hair or the weave getting promoted. You mark my words," she said.

That had been one of the last conversations they had. Her mother had a heart attack and died a few months later.

Jasmyn feels the familiar grief as an expanding thickness in her throat like she'd never again take a full breath. Even then she'd known that her mother was trying to protect her, trying to make life easier for Jasmyn than it had been for her. But she also knew that nothing changed if someone didn't change it. She'd stopped relaxing her hair and grown out her Afro.

And those bosses her mother had talked about? They had no choice but to promote Jasmyn. She was excellent at her job.

Jasmyn touches her short Afro and pulls her eyes away from the woman's hairline. She reminds herself not to judge the older woman too harshly. She came up at a different time.

"I'm Sherril," the woman says. "Think of me as your one-woman welcome committee." Her smile is innocent and broad. Jasmyn can see all there is to see of her elaborately white teeth.

"Well, thank you," says Jasmyn. "I don't think I've ever been personally welcomed into a neighborhood before."

Sherril waves her off. "I'm sorry I took so long to stop by. I know you all have been here for at least a couple of weeks now." Her accent is southern, Mississippi maybe. "We like to let folks know they're right where they belong."

There's no denying the kindness of the gesture. Jasmyn feels a slight wash of shame over the way she'd judged the other woman. Not for the first time, she reminds herself that Black people exist on a continuum from Uncle Tom to Black Panther. Some folks come to enlightenment later—sometimes much later—than others. Some folks never get there at all.

"Would you like to come in?" Jasmyn asks.

The woman shakes her head and Jasmyn watches her hair pendulum around her face. Not a curl or a coil or a kink is anywhere in sight.

"Maybe another time," Sherril says. "Besides, I'm sure you have a world of unpacking to do."

She doesn't correct Sherril's assumption. Despite the fact that they've been here for only two weeks, they're already settled in. King had hired a moving company that did it all: packed up their old apartment and unpacked and moved them into their new house.

"I stopped by to give you some welcome to Liberty treats," Sherril continues.

She hands Jasmyn two boxes. The first is a simple cardboard one with what looks like shortbread cookies.

"I made them myself," Sherril says.

"Thank you. This is very nice of you," says Jasmyn with a smile. "Funny enough, these are my son's favorite. He'll devour these in one swoop if I let him."

The second box is larger than the first and tied with fine gold ribbon. *Liberty Wellness Center* is embossed in cursive across the lid.

"Oh, you didn't have to do this," Jasmyn says.

"Of course I did, sugar," Sherril says and smiles. "Go ahead and open it up."

The box itself is exquisite: teal blue, velvet soft, and shimmering. Aspirational packaging, the advertisers call it. It smells faintly herbal. Jasmyn tugs at the silky ribbon. Inside, she finds a small bouquet of sage and lavender twigs tied together with gold thread nestled against white satin. Below the bouquet, there's a dark blue silk sleep mask and a heavy black card with gold printing. At first Jasmyn thinks maybe Liberty has its own credit card, but when she turns it over, she sees it's a membership card to the Wellness Center. Next to the card are delicate glass bottles with facial cleansers, toners, and moisturizers. All the product names are French and written in cursive so ornate, they're barely legible. Combined with the sumptuous blue and gold of the box and ribbon, the whole package is definitely reminiscent of eighteenth-century European royalty. Jasmyn traces a finger over the looping letters, slightly frustrated that, even here in Liberty, Eurocentric standards of beauty and luxury reign.

Still, it is a beautiful package and so thoughtful of the other woman to bring it to her. Jasmyn says as much.

"Self-care is important," says Sherril. "Everybody needs an escape from the world every once in a while."

Jasmyn nods, though she doesn't much agree. There's always so much work to be done, especially for their community. Community care *is* self-care.

Pregnancy heartburn kicks in and Jasmyn rubs at her stomach. "Take it easy in there, sweetie." She smiles up at Sherril. "This one got me burping."

"You're pregnant," Sherril says. She takes one step back, and then another, as if this discovery is unexpected and, somehow, alarming.

"Fourteen weeks along." Jasmyn waits for the woman to ask the usual questions: *Is it a boy or a girl? Have you already chosen a name?*

But the questions don't come. Sherril looks at her stomach for so long it makes Jasmyn think maybe she has some tragic maternal history. Maybe she hadn't been able to have children of her own. Or maybe she lost one to gangs or to police violence. Or maybe she was simply lamenting the passing of her childbearing years.

Sherril's eyes drift up from Jasmyn's stomach to her breasts and up to her trim Afro. "That's quite a shirt," she says.

Jasmyn checks to see what she's wearing: a T-shirt with a raised fist and the words *Black Power* in cursive below.

"I didn't know they still made those," Sherril says.

Jasmyn frowns her confusion. Of course they do. Why wouldn't they?

"Well," Jasmyn says. "Thank you so much for these. I can't wait to eat the cookies." She stacks the gifts against her stomach.

"Yes, it sure was nice to meet you. Welcome to the neighborhood again and be sure to visit us up at the Wellness Center." Her eyes drop to Jasmyn's stomach again. "It'll do you a world of good, especially in your condition."

Jasmyn smiles and promises she'll visit just as soon as she finds the time. Which will be never. She'll never have the time for something so extravagant and so fundamentally unnecessary. Not when she could be using all that time and money helping people less fortunate than herself.

Jasmyn walks them out to the driveway and watches as Sherril makes her way to her car. As she opens the door, sunlight flares in the side-view mirror, haloing her hair, her face. It has the effect of making her look paler than she had before. Jasmyn squints, trying to see through the light to what's really there, but Sherril closes the door. The side mirror shifts and the illusion is lost.

Jasmyn walks slowly back to the house. A fine shiver feathers its way across her skin. She frowns up at the sky, searching for something to explain her sudden chill, but the spring sky is a wide-open expanse of cloudless blue. Still, the air feels charged and full somehow, as if it's readying itself for a release.

Back inside, she rubs her hands up and down her forearms to warm them. What was the silly thing her grandmother used to say about goosebumps? That it meant someone had just walked over your grave. The first time she'd said it, Jasmyn was just a little girl and she'd cried, inconsolable. She remembers Ivy making fun of her tears and her mother scolding her grandmother for "putting morbid nonsense into the child's head."

Jasmyn huffs a laugh at the memory and shakes off the odd feeling of foreboding. She replaces the lid and reties the bow on the Wellness Center package. It really was thoughtful of Sherril to bake cookies and bring welcome gifts. No one had ever stopped by with presents in her old neighborhood. Truth is, she didn't even know the names of any of her old neighbors.

She texts King and tells him about Sherril's visit.

They really do believe in community here, she types.

Just make sure you save me some of those cookies, he texts back.

2

"You better not be tracking mud all over my brand-new floors," Jasmyn says to Kamau when he comes into the kitchen from the backyard.

He gives her a sheepish look with those big brown eyes of his and then turns right around to go take off his Nikes outside on the deck.

"That's more like it," Jasmyn says when he's back.

"Sorry, Moms."

"It's all right," she says, and opens her arms. He dives into them for a hug. "Which freckles should I kiss today?" she asks.

Kamau grins and makes a big show of thinking hard about the decision by stroking his chin in the same way King does.

Jasmyn laughs. They play this kiss-the-freckle game at some point every day. Sometimes he chooses the delicate spray across the bridge of his nose. Other days, he picks the constellation on his left cheek or the small sprinkling just under his right temple.

Today he picks his cheek. Jasmyn gives him three nuzzling kisses before hugging him close and holding on to him a little tighter than she normally does. She knows she needs to go easier on him. It's hard to be in a new neighborhood and at a new school trying to make friends when you're six years old. Hell, making new friends is hard for her, too, and she's thirty-six.

He slips out of her arms. "Can I get a snack?" he asks and runs over to the pantry.

He's small for his age, short, and a little too thin. King worries about him being tiny, doesn't want him to get bullied. But Jasmyn thinks he'll hit a growth spurt soon enough. He and King are so much alike physically, same slightly too-big ears and perfect eyebrows. She has no doubt Kamau will end up being over six feet tall just like his father.

Jasmyn watches Kamau grab a bag of chips and sighs. No matter how small he is now, she knows it won't be long before he's *perceived* as being grown. She'd read more than one study that said cops overestimate the age—and, therefore, underestimate the innocence—of Black children by about four years. Instead of Kamau's height, what King really needs to be worrying about is giving Kamau the Talk. He needs to talk to him about how to deal with the police harassment that will inevitably come his way. If he'd already given it to him, Kamau would've known not to say anything to the cop who pulled them over last spring.

It's not often that you recognize the moment propelling you from one kind of life into another while the moment is still happening. But for Jasmyn, the traffic stop was one such instance, and she'd felt her path shift.

It was late afternoon on an unexpectedly cool spring day. The three of them—Jasmyn, King, and Kamau—were driving home from the annual children's Easter party that King's new job put on. Even though he'd been working as a venture capitalist at Argent Financial for about three years, Jasmyn still thought of his job as new.

Every year, the company hosted a catered family brunch, complete with the Easter bunny, multiple chocolate fountains, egg decorating and story-time stations, and a massive Easter egg hunt. It was over-the-top and, Jasmyn was sure, far too expensive. Still, Kamau loved it, which meant she loved it, too.

She'd been leaning back against the headrest with her eyes closed when King said, "Oh shit." The note of suppressed terror in his voice bolted Jasmyn upright. A siren sounded. In her side-view mirror, she saw the reds and blues flashing.

"Ohhh, Daddy said a bad word," Kamau said in the delighted and superior way children use when they catch their adults doing something wrong.

"Hush up, baby," Jasmyn said. She used her gentlest voice.

This wasn't their first time being stopped by a cop, but it was their first time with Kamau in the car.

King turned to look at Kamau in the back seat. Then he looked at Jasmyn for a long second.

She read his fear, reached for his hand, and squeezed. "You got this," she said.

"Maybe he'll be Black," King said.

They watched and waited, but the cop who emerged from the car was white.

King rolled down his window and put his hands on the steering wheel, in plain sight. His grip was so tight that his knuckles blanched. Jasmyn wanted to reach out and touch his hand or hold it—something, *anything*—to relieve the clawing fear invading her throat. But what if the cop deemed her movement suspicious? She could picture the incident report. *Suspect moved in a threatening manner.*

She wondered if she should record. Sometimes, video was the only way to get justice. On the one hand, she knew the law, knew she had the right to do so. On the other hand, recording the cop might antagonize him and lead to an escalation. In the end, she kept the phone in her lap and recorded voice only.

The cop arrived at the window. His eyes ransacked the car's interior before resting, finally, on King.

He asked for license and registration. He asked if King had had anything to drink and where they were coming from and headed to. King answered the questions as if they weren't presumptuous, rude, and completely out of line. *A kids' Easter party, Officer. Home, Officer. Nothing to drink, Officer.*

The cop explained that the car's registration sticker had expired. He went back to the patrol car to run their plates.

How many times had Jasmyn reminded King to replace the registration sticker? Three times? Four? And now look. Still, she didn't bring it up. He was surely feeling bad enough.

"How you doing back there, baby?" she asked Kamau.

"I need to go pee," he said.

"Can you hold it for Mommy?"

"OK," he said. "But I really need to go."

It took ten minutes for the cop to come back. Before he could say anything, Kamau blurted: "My daddy said a bad word."

The cop's head swiveled to Kamau. "Oh, he did, did he?" His voice had a drawl in it.

Jasmyn froze. In her mind, she saw all the possible paths leading out from this one. The one where her husband's and child's bodies lay riddled and ruined on asphalt. Down another path, her body joined theirs. Down another, only Kamau is murdered. Down another still, he is orphaned.

She felt, in that moment, a profound powerlessness, the certainty that the trajectory of her life was not up to her, not really.

Jasmyn studied the cop's face, watched him decide what path her life would take.

He smiled. "Sometimes daddies say the wrong thing. You have to forgive us," he said. He looked back at King. "I have a little boy, too." Then he straightened, handed King his license and registration. He rapped the roof of the car. "Get that sticker updated," he said, and walked away.

That night she and King fought. "When are you going to talk to him about cops?" Jasmyn asked. She was upset that Kamau didn't already know not to say anything to a cop unless he absolutely had to. It didn't matter that he was only six.

"Why can't we just let him stay young and innocent for a while longer?" King wanted to know.

She'd jabbed a finger at him then. "You saw how close we came today. You know how that could've ended. You can keep him innocent *or* you can keep him alive. Those are the choices. *You,* more than anybody, should know that."

She knew she was wrong to say it even as she said it.

King's older brother Tommy had been killed by a white cop when he was just thirteen. Talking about what happened to Tommy wasn't something they did. His death was a wound in King that had never scabbed over, much less healed.

Jasmyn apologized. She blamed her insensitivity on how afraid she'd been during the stop. She'd kept apologizing until the hardness in King's eyes softened. After a while, he forgave her.

A couple of weeks after the traffic stop, King had come to her again about moving to Liberty.

It was the fourth time he'd asked in six months. Each time Jasmyn had put him off, saying that she was happy where they were and that she didn't want to upend Kamau's schooling. King pointed out that she didn't particularly like Kamau's school. Still, she'd said, stability was important. The third time he asked, she used all the same excuses and added that it was much too rich and bougie.

"Rich, bougie, and Black," King counterargued with a smile.

After the incident with the cop, he asked again for the last time. "All the cops there are Black," he'd said.

"Not all Black cops are good cops, baby," she said.

"Yeah, but they're less likely to harass you just for being Black, right?" he said, and she'd had to agree with that.

She'd been about to launch into her usual counterarguments when he pulled her into his arms and rested his forehead against hers. "Baby, I couldn't live if something happened to you or Kamau. Not after Tommy." His voice was small and so young, as if time had collapsed and he was still trapped in the immediate aftermath of Tommy's death. "It's my job to keep you safe. To keep both of you safe," he said. "Let me do my job."

Jasmyn hadn't realized he was crying until she felt his tears against her cheek. In that moment she decided. She loved him too much to deny him something that meant so much. Maybe being in Liberty would help soothe the part of King where Tommy's loss remained fresh.

"OK, baby, we'll move," she'd said. "OK."

≈

Now Jasmyn presses a hand over her heart and does a slow turn around her brand-new kitchen. The linoleum gleams. The white marble countertops are cool beneath her hand. She has one of those moments where the life you imagine for yourself and the life you actually live crash into each other. What to make of the bright line connecting the moment with the cop to this moment right now?

"Moms, can I please watch TV?" Kamau asks.

"Yes," she says, "but only for half an hour and then—"

"You have to go and do something else," he says, singsonging the end of her sentence with a wide smile.

Jasmyn laughs. "Get gone before I change my mind about how much time you have," she says.

She watches as his skinny little legs propel him down the hallway. He holds his bag of chips high in the air, like it's a prize. A small laugh bubbles up and out of her and she presses a hand to her lips. Sometimes it feels as if her love for him is too big for her body to hold. She almost calls out to tell him not to run, but she stops herself. In her head she can hear King telling her to just let him be a little boy. Maybe King is right. At least here in Liberty he has more of a chance to be just that.

3

"Hey, baby," King says from her office doorway.

Jasmyn holds a hand up for him to wait so she can finish rereading the police report. It's her third read through and she still hasn't found any inconsistencies she can exploit. She sighs and massages the tight muscles in her neck. There's no way around it. She's going to have to advise her client to take the damn plea. No way can she prove that the cop hit him first.

She closes her laptop, looks up, and gives King her full attention. He's leaning with his shoulder pressed up against the doorjamb. In their old apartment his solid, six-foot-four-inch frame would've completely filled the doorway. In this house, though, he has plenty of space.

He looks tired, the kind of tired he always looks when he gets home from mentoring Terrell at Mentor LA, a local charity that pairs adult volunteers with at-risk youth.

"How was it?" she asks as he comes around her desk.

Instead of answering, he leans over for a kiss. She tilts her face up to meet his and holds his face in her hands. Kissing him hello is one of the best parts of her day. He smells green, like something fresh and familiar she can't quite place.

King leans down farther and kisses the swell of her stomach. "How's my boy doing in there? Quarterbacking?"

It's their little joke. Unlike Kamau, who barely kicked in utero, this baby *moves.* She knows King is hoping their second child will be more like him personality-wise—outgoing and sports-loving. Kamau is more like her, quiet and bookish.

"He threw a few passes," she says.

King straightens and then half sits against the edge of her desk. "Terrell's parole officer called me," he says.

"He back in?" Jasmyn asks even though she can guess the answer.

"Got him for possession with intent to sell," King says.

She slaps the arm of her chair. "Shit."

"Calm down, baby," King says. "It's not a death sentence. He'll be out again."

"But he won't be the same. Prison makes you hard. You know this."

She's seen it so many times, the way prison kills the spirit. No, not every time, but most. King says prison isn't a death sentence. But there's more than one way to die.

King closes his eyes and pinches the bridge of his nose.

Jasmyn shifts her chair closer, wraps her arms around his waist. She knows how responsible he feels for the boys he mentors. Knows that Terrell landing back in prison is going to wound him for weeks.

"You know one of the things I love most about you?" she asks.

"Tell me," he says, voice quiet.

"How deep you feel things. I know this is not easy for you."

He rubs her back and she tightens her arms around his waist.

"Kamau get to sleep all right?" he asks.

"Fell asleep at seven thirty on the dot." That's when it occurs to her to wonder where King has been all this time. "If Terrell is back in jail then why are you home so late?" she asks.

"Went up the hill to check out that Wellness Center," he says.

"You went to the *spa* after you heard about Terrell?" she asks, pulling back.

In King's place, she would've spent the rest of the evening at Mentor LA helping out in some way or looking for someone else to mentor. God knows there's no shortage of boys who just need for someone to see their worth and believe in them despite their circumstances. At the very least, King could've gone to see Terrell and told him he'd still be there for him when he got out.

A kind of wariness settles on King's face. "Something wrong with me going to the spa?" He wipes his hand over his freshly shaved head.

Jasmyn still hasn't gotten used to this new style. She misses the nice, big Afro he used to have. Right before they moved to Liberty, he buzzed it all off.

She opens her mouth to respond but closes it again, not wanting to get into an argument. So he took a night off to go to the spa. There were worse things than that. Besides, she knows the Terrell thing hit him hard.

"Nothing wrong with it," she says, leaning into him. "Now I know what you smell like: cucumber and mint."

He laughs. "It's nice up there. Got some great facilities. Fitness center, pool, Jacuzzis, steam rooms. A whole heap of treatments. Very impressive." He rubs his head again. "We should go together."

She smiles and makes a noncommittal sound.

He pushes himself off the desk. "How much longer you working for?"

"Twenty minutes?"

"Make it ten and there's a root beer float in it for you. We can watch some late night."

Jasmyn laughs and rubs her stomach. "Me and this wild child you got in here will take that deal."

Fifteen minutes later, she settles down on the couch next to him, root beer float in hand.

This room, the family room, is her favorite. She remembers touring the house with the realtor for the first time. Jasmyn had asked why there were three living rooms. The woman explained one was a family room, another was the formal living room for entertaining, and the final one was a den. All Jasmyn could think was that she now had to buy three sofas. The house was more than they needed. How was she supposed to furnish it all? That's when King had stepped in and taken care of everything by hiring designers. By the time they moved in, the entire house was furnished and decorated.

"How's that float treating you?" King asks.

Jasmyn slurps her response.

He laughs and plays with the controls on the remote.

The TV is King's favorite thing in the house. It's a ten-foot projection screen that descends from the ceiling with the press of a button. Another button press closes the window shades and lowers the lights in the room.

King powers up the screen. He kisses her temple and settles back into the cushions, looking satisfied and less tired than he had been before.

"Sorry about Terrell," Jasmyn says, feeling the need to say it just then.

"I tried my best," he says.

She rushes to reassure him. "Oh, baby, I know you did," she says "I know."

King scrolls through the TV menu until he finds the show he wants to watch.

For a few minutes, Jasmyn pays attention. The host begins his monologue by making fun of the racist president and his latest antics. The studio audience laughs. King does too. His teeth shine bright white in the glow from the screen. Jasmyn supposes she should be laughing as well, but she doesn't find it funny. To laugh at something repulsive, even if it was a mocking kind of laughter, is a kind of softening, an incremental step toward acceptance. Before you knew it, the repulsive thing seems less so.

King shifts and pulls her in close. "We got it pretty good, don't we, baby?" he says.

Jasmyn smiles and rests her head against his shoulder. He still has that green, fresh-from-the-spa smell, but she tries not to let it bother her. "Yeah, we sure do," she says.

4

"Where should we eat?" Jasmyn asks King as they're driving through downtown Liberty on their way to brunch. Instead of sitting up front next to him, she's in the back with Kamau. Earlier he'd complained of being lonely. She'd patted her stomach and reminded him he'd have a brother in a few months.

"But that's too long," he'd said.

They drive by the Jamaican food place where they'd had lunch on their first visit to Liberty. The food was excellent, with authentically spicy jerk pork. On that visit, she and King laughed about the "Caribbean" place they'd gone to in Santa Monica years before. Not a Black person in sight, not at the tables and not in the kitchen. The jerk sampler they'd gotten didn't have salt, let alone any other kind of spice.

They pass by two barbershops and two hair salons and two nail spas, a place devoted to eyebrow waxing, another dedicated to body sculpting, all of them impeccably upscale. She compares the street to the ones where she grew up. Missing are the wig shops, check cashing places, corner stores that sell everything from loosies to tampons, Chinese restaurants with bulletproof glass. Mercifully, there's no expectation of danger built into the DNA of the design here.

Again, Jasmyn remembers the first time they toured potential homes. The real estate agent had been a woman with pale brown skin and short wavy hair. She spoke in the bright, peppy way of someone trying to sell you something. She'd driven them around Liberty and explained the town's two distinct residential areas. The first was in the Flats, closest to the downtown area. By Liberty standards the houses there were modest, priced in the high six figures. The other residential area extended up from the Flats to the gated community at the top of the hill, close to where the Wellness Center dominated the skyline. The agent took them on tours a quarter of the way up the hill where the homes started in the low seven-figure range.

The house they eventually chose was the third one they saw.

"It's practically new," the agent said. "You'll be happy to know—should you select this wonderful property—you'd be only the second family to call it home."

Jasmyn had been surprised they wouldn't be the first. The house certainly seemed like it was brand-new. "When was this built?" she asked.

They were all standing in the bright white kitchen. King turned the faucet on and off to check the water pressure. He opened and closed the cabinets. Jasmyn had never even seen a kitchen so large and beautiful. Could it really come to be theirs?

The woman consulted her clipboard. "Construction was completed in January of last year."

"So the other family lived here for less than a year?" Jasmyn asked. That was surprising. "What happened? They die or something? Don't be letting us move into no haunted house now," she joked.

Both King and the agent laughed at that.

But Jasmyn wanted an answer. "Seriously, though, do you know why the other family moved away so quick?"

The agent looked down at her clipboard as if the answer were on there. "I'm not sure," she said.

Jasmyn didn't miss the evasiveness in the woman's voice. Maybe she was just being a good agent and protecting the privacy of her clients. Jasmyn let it go.

Later, King said he'd noticed her nervousness, too. "Probably didn't want to scare us and lose out on the commission," he said.

The next morning they'd made the offer on the house. By the evening, they were proud owners of a six-thousand-square-foot, multistory house with six bedrooms, five bathrooms, a gourmet chef's kitchen, and a generous backyard with mature fruit trees and an Olympic-sized pool and Jacuzzi. And, of course, three living rooms.

≈

Now as they pull into the traffic circle that borders the huge and immaculate central park, Kamau points outside the car window. "What are those people doing?" he asks.

Jasmyn looks. A group of ten or fifteen people are doing some sort of exercise in a small clearing between the trees. They're wearing gray sweatshirts with *Liberty Wellness Center* stenciled across the back and matching spandex pants.

"It's called yoga," she says to Kamau, even though it doesn't look like any kind of yoga she's ever seen.

She recognizes the couple leading the group. "Don't they live a few houses up from us?" she asks King.

He nods. "Angela and Benjamin Sayles," he says. "Nice people. Both of them are plastic surgeons. She specializes in burn victims and he does some sort of reconstructive surgery. They're part of the group that helped found Liberty in the first place."

Jasmyn watches them shift positions, pointing their legs toward the sky. How is it that she and King now live next to people—*Black* people—with enough money and pedigree to found entire neighborhoods?

When she and King first met, he was a history teacher at Martin Luther King High School in Compton. In those days, they couldn't even dream of living in a neighborhood like this. Not on her public defender's salary and his teacher's one.

But one day he'd taken an online class so he could understand how their retirement money was being invested. One of his teachers, a Black man named Carlton Way, took King under his wing. He said King had a brilliant analytical mind. He'd made sure King applied for, and got, a full scholarship to do an online MBA. As soon as he graduated, King gave up teaching and went to work for Argent Financial, Carlton's company. In three years, he worked his way up to junior partner at one of the biggest venture capital firms in Los Angeles. It was Carlton Way who told King about Liberty in the first place. It turned out that creating Liberty had been Carlton's idea. He'd recruited a few of his wealthy friends as founders and together they'd made Liberty into a reality.

Jasmyn had met Carlton only once, soon after he'd taken an interest in King. He'd taken her and King to dinner at the most expensive restaurant she'd ever been to. Aside from the decor and atmosphere, she knew it was expensive because the menu had no prices listed. Also, the three of them were the only Black people there, including the waitstaff.

The main thing Jasmyn remembers about Carlton is how comfortable he seemed in his own skin. She'd never seen anything like it, certainly not in someone Black. He had the sturdy and effortless confidence of a wealthy, white politician. Was it his extravagant wealth that gave it to him? There was something gilded, something robber-baron-esque about him. Jasmyn couldn't decide if she admired it or was repulsed by it. Still, the thing she remembers most about that evening was how badly she'd wanted to make a good impression on Carlton for King's sake.

King pulls into a parking spot right in front of the French bistro he's been wanting to try. For the rest of the morning, Jasmyn can't help but compare her experiences here in Liberty with the world she knew before. The restaurant is bustling, but not packed. The hostess greets them with just the right amount of friendly professionalism and seats them quickly. Their waiter is prompt and attentive. She and King don't have to stew at being ignored in favor of a white couple, as has happened to them at restaurants so many times before.

The food is delicious. Even Kamau, who's normally picky, likes his meal. They have a wonderful time. On the drive home, Jasmyn sits up front and holds King's hand.

They pass by the park again. The yoga people are no longer doing their poses. Instead, they're sitting on their knees in neat rows on the grass. From where they are in the traffic circle, Jasmyn can only see their backs. The man she'd noticed before—Benjamin Sayles—is standing at the head of the group sweeping his arms in, up, and out, like he's conducting an orchestra.

Jasmyn looks on, bemused. "Are they singing?" She doesn't take her eyes off them as King steers the car around the circle. Finally, their faces come into view.

They aren't singing. They're laughing. Their heads are tilted back, and their eyes are half closed, and their mouths are wide, and their teeth are bared.

Jasmyn slaps King's shoulder harder than she means to. "King, look," she says, pointing out at them.

"Jesus," King says, rubbing at his shoulder. He looks to where Jasmyn pointed. "What on earth is going on there?"

Jasmyn opens her window. At first, she hears nothing beyond the usual street noises. But then the sound reaches her: laughter so loud and brash and raucous, it's almost vulgar.

The hairs on the back of her neck stand up. She stabs at the button to close her window. "The hell was that?"

King shakes his head. "No idea." Then he chuckles. "Some type of meditation? People will try anything."

"You see they're wearing Wellness Center clothes?" She looks over at King. "That the kind of craziness they get up to up there?"

"Wouldn't catch me doing any of that ridiculous nonsense," King says, laughing.

Jasmyn laughs now, too. They really do look ridiculous.

"Can we go get some ice cream?" Kamau asks.

"We have ice cream at home, buddy," King says as he turns them onto their street.

Jasmyn looks back, trying to catch a final glimpse of the laughing people. Just as she does, they slump to the ground in unison, like marionettes whose strings had abruptly been cut.

BLACK BUSINESS INSIDER: "PROFILES IN BRIEF: CARLTON WAY"

Who is Carlton Way?

Born in the Bronx, New York, Mr. Way, 56, put himself through MIT, graduating magna cum laude in chemical engineering. He subsequently earned an MBA from Stanford, becoming the youngest African American ever to graduate from their storied program. Following stints at Goldman Sachs and Morgan Stanley, Mr. Way founded his own firm, Argent Financial, specializing in investments in lifestyle products. He is also a co-founder of Liberty, a thriving, entirely Black Los Angeles suburb founded on the principles of Black excellence.

Net Worth

Per *Forbes*, Mr. Way is worth an estimated $3 billion.

Personal Life

Born to public school teachers, Mr. Way had an early life marked by the tragic loss of his father to a police-involved shooting. He is unmarried and has no children.

Notable Philanthropy

Since 2017, Mr. Way has paid the loans for the entire graduating class of Howard University, an HBCU (Historically Black College or University) in the United States. In an interview, Mr. Way said he wanted the graduates to be "unshackled from the chains of financial slavery."

5

The news alert pings Jasmyn's phone as she's walking Kamau into school the next morning. She glances at the screen. *Breaking News: Black man dies, child injured during officer-involved shooting in Los Angeles.*

"Jesus Christ. Please don't tell me they shot a child," she mutters out loud without meaning to. She starts to click the link, but then doesn't. Better for her to wait until Kamau is tucked away in class.

Kamau tugs on her hand. "Moms, you're not even listening," he says with his mad face on.

Jasmyn looks at him and wants to smile. His mad face is especially cute. The way he scrunches his little nose up tight and pushes out his lips reminds her of when he was a baby. She wants to scoop him up, cuddle him close, and keep him safe.

"I'm sorry, baby. Say it again. Mama's listening."

He pouts a little more but repeats himself anyway. "Nico wouldn't let me hold his comic book."

"Remind me who Nico is again?"

"I said that already," he whines. "He's in my class."

"All right, calm down," she says and kisses the top of his head. "Why don't you tell me all about Nico and this comic book."

By the time they get to his classroom, Jasmyn has agreed to buy the new Miles Morales *Spider-Man* comic for him.

On her way out, she runs into the principal.

"Mrs. Williams, lovely to see you," he says, holding his hand out for a shake.

Ordinarily, she'd be happy to see the man. He has a confident, no-nonsense air and a smile that puts her at ease. Now, though, all she wants to do is to leave the campus so she can read the news about the shooting. Not knowing the details makes her feel unsafe, like a fault has developed underneath her feet and she's no longer sure where to stand.

Jasmyn bites the inside of her cheek and tells herself to be patient. "Lovely to see you as well, Principal Harper," she says and shakes his hand.

"I believe you met my wife, Sherril, a few weeks back. She's Liberty's one-woman welcome wagon."

"Oh, yes, I did. Please thank her again for those cookies. They were delicious. Kamau devoured them."

He laughs. "I'll ask her to bake some more."

"No, it's OK. I wasn't trying to—"

"Believe me, it's no problem at all," he says, waving her off. "Speaking of Kamau, I have to say, he's adjusting very nicely, better than we could've hoped given the mid-grade transfer." He taps his nose and leans in slightly. "I have a feeling for these things and I can tell that he'll thrive here."

His words are a balm and Jasmyn feels some tension leave her shoulders. "I'm so glad to hear that. I've been worrying a little."

"That's only natural," he says. "But now you can set that worry aside."

"Thank you," she says, surprised at the depth of her relief and gratitude.

"No need to thank me. 'It takes a village,' as they say." He holds out his hand for another shake. "Well, I'm sure you have a busy day. I won't keep you."

As soon as she's outside the school gates, she plucks her phone from her purse. There's another breaking news alert. It turns out there's cell-phone video of the shooting.

"Jesus Christ," she says aloud to no one. Her scalp prickles hot and then cold and hot again. Her dread is crushing and, too, so familiar.

She opens the article as she walks. It starts with a bold-faced warning: **This video contains graphic content. Viewer discretion is advised.** Will there come a day, she wonders, when these videos don't even have a warning? When they are so commonplace that they're no longer shocking?

At first the article is everything she's come to expect from incidents like these. White cop. Traffic stop. Dead Black man.

But then she gets to the part about the child, and Jasmyn is only able to process the most basic details.

Girl.

Four years old.

Collapsed lung.

Critical condition.

MLK Hospital.

Mercy Simpson.

Her name is Mercy Simpson.

Jasmyn flashes back to the incident with the cop in the spring. It could have turned out so differently. It could've turned out like *this*.

She presses a hand to her chest, wanting to push down the bile rising inside her. The back of her throat burns. The baby kicks, as if he can sense her distress. Jasmyn pulls her eyes up from her phone to check where she is. It's still morning. She's still on the sidewalk in the bright sunshine outside her son's school.

She's still here, in America.

According to the article, the dead man's name is Tyrese Simpson. His girlfriend, Lorraine, was in the car with him. She's the one who recorded the video. Mercy Simpson is their daughter. The police say

Tyrese was reaching for a gun. Lorraine says he was unbuckling his seat belt. The police are promising a thorough investigation. They're asking for patience and calm.

It's all Jasmyn can do not to fling her phone across the street. How dare they ask for patience and calm? How dare they ask for anything at all?

She scrolls to the video at the beginning of the article and clicks the link.

The first image Jasmyn sees is of the cop's face, pale and hard, hovering in the driver's-side window. The little girl, Mercy Simpson, is crying in that inconsolable way four-year-olds do. Lorraine shushes her, calls her "sweetie," tells her they'll be home soon. Jasmyn hears the slight tremble in Lorraine's voice as she tries to hide her terror from Mercy. She pitches her voice high, gives it a soothing singsong quality. It's the tone every parent uses when they're afraid of something but don't want their child to be afraid of it, too. Jasmyn recognizes Lorraine's tone because she's used it herself on Kamau.

Tyrese asks why he was stopped, but the cop doesn't answer. Instead he asks for license and registration.

The camera falls over and gets obscured by something that Jasmyn guesses is fabric. Lorraine was probably trying to hide the fact that she was filming. Next, there's a shot of the glove compartment being opened.

Jasmyn pauses the video to gather herself for what's coming. Once, when Kamau was little, about three years old, she'd been watching cartoons with him. King came into the room and, for some reason or another, paused the TV. Kamau immediately began crying. When they asked why he was upset, Kamau explained that the characters in the show were very hungry and just about to eat, but now that the TV was paused they'd have to be hungry for longer and their tummies would hurt. Jasmyn had wanted to laugh at his absurd sweetness, but she stopped herself because Kamau had his serious face on and she didn't want to belittle his feelings. For him, the characters on TV were real. When you paused it, you paused their real lives.

"So what happens when you turn off the TV?" Jasmyn had asked.

"They wait for us to come back," Kamau said.

Jasmyn started to explain but King put his hand out to stop her.

Later, King said: "No harm in letting him believe it. Let him have his innocence for as long as he can."

Now Jasmyn's finger hovers over the PLAY button. She wishes Kamau's sentiment had been right, that if you paused the video, you paused the life. That if she doesn't press PLAY then Tyrese and Lorraine and Mercy will be safe. But it's not the witnessing that makes it real. These things—these murders—take place whether you watch them or not.

She resumes the video.

The cop asks Tyrese to step out of the car.

Tyrese asks why and Lorraine does too.

Mercy Simpson wails even louder.

The cop realizes he's being filmed and tells Lorraine to stop.

And then, chaos.

The camera tumbles to the ground, filming only the roof of the car. The audio is still recording. It's hard for Jasmyn to make out the words because Mercy Simpson is crying at the top of her lungs, but she catches most of it:

Why I can't record? It's my right to record you.

Put your hands where I can seem them!

Why you can't see them? They right here!

You asked him to get out the car!

I can't see your hands!

They right here!

And then the shots, like small bombs exploding. Like lives exploding.

One. Two. Three. Four. Five.

And then Lorraine is screaming and the cop is swearing. But it's Mercy Simpson's sudden shattering silence that undoes Jasmyn.

She presses the phone against her chest, squeezes her eyes shut. "Jesus Christ. Jesus Christ."

"Honey, are you OK?" a woman's voice asks.

At first, Jasmyn doesn't realize the woman is talking to her, but the voice comes again, closer now.

"Do you need a tissue?" the woman asks.

Jasmyn touches her face and understands that she's weeping. She takes the tissue, dabs at her face. "Thank you."

"Of course," says the other woman. "Is there anything I can do to help?"

"I'll be all right in just a minute. Just a minute." She takes a deep breath and then another.

"Please, take all the time you need," the woman says.

A few more seconds pass before Jasmyn can compose herself enough to really pay attention to her Good Samaritan.

The woman is pale brown with loosely curled black hair—a 3B curl pattern if Jasmyn had to guess—and dressed in a lavender pantsuit. A little girl, a miniature version of her mother, stands next to her.

"Why don't you run into school from here?" the woman says to her daughter.

The little girl's face lights up in delight at the prospect of half a block of independence. "Bye, Mama. I love you," she says and skips away.

Jasmyn protests. "Thank you, but you didn't have to do that," she says. "Go ahead and walk her in."

The woman just smiles and then guides Jasmyn from where she's standing in the middle of the sidewalk to the sidelines.

Jasmyn feels the eyes of other mothers and fathers on her as they hurry by.

"Please tell me what I can do to help," the woman says.

Jasmyn holds her phone aloft. "I watched the latest shooting."

The woman's eyes register nothing.

Of course, Jasmyn thinks. She doesn't know yet. The news only just came out.

"There was another shooting," she says, voice shaking. She presses her nails into her palms and wills herself to be calm. "They killed him. They almost killed his daughter, too. She's in the hospital fighting for her life."

"Who killed who?" the woman asks. Her curiosity is small and mild.

"I'm sorry, I'm not doing a good job explaining."

Jasmyn's eyes fill with tears again and she dabs at them. Now she feels vaguely like an army chaplain charged with delivering the worst news. Impossible news. *Your child—the precious thing that is you and not you, the thing that is your beating heart made flesh—is gone.* Who, Jasmyn wonders, called Tyrese Simpson's mother and father to tell them that their son was dead? Who is caring for Lorraine while her child struggles for air through punctured lungs? Who breathes for Lorraine?

It's this last thought that allows Jasmyn to pull herself together. This news will be as hard for her Good Samaritan to hear as it was for Jasmyn. She offers the news carefully, threading a poisoned needle.

"The cops killed another Black man last night. His daughter was in the car with him and they shot her, too. His girlfriend got video. I was just watching it. His name was Tyrese. His little girl's name is Mercy." She holds out her phone for the woman to take.

Understanding blooms in the other woman's eyes. "Oh no," she says. "I don't watch those. It's much too much for me."

Jasmyn raises her eyebrows and sweeps a reassessing gaze over the woman. That 3B curl pattern might be a 3A and she really is a very pale brown. Her makeup is impeccable, a palette of blushing pinks and gloss like a freshly misted orchid.

Of course Jasmyn has met her type before. She's one of *those* Black people, too delicate to face up to the world we live in. The kind that looks away and pretends that if she can't see the world's violence against Black people, it isn't happening. Jasmyn has never understood, or agreed with, that way of being. She always clicks the headlines. She always watches the videos. Why should she feel safe and comfortable when yet another Black man is dead? No. It isn't OK to look away. She always watches. Bears witness.

"Is there anything I can do to help *you?*" the woman asks. She offers Jasmyn another tissue.

Jasmyn waves the offer away, not wanting to take anything else from the other woman. She inches her shoulders back and stands taller. "I'll be all right in a minute." She wipes her face with the tissue she's already holding. It comes apart in her hands.

It occurs to her then that she's doing the thing King sometimes accuses her of doing: judging other people and finding them lacking. Just because this woman doesn't watch the videos doesn't mean she doesn't care. After all, here she is, offering care to a stranger. Jasmyn feels a compulsion to connect with her beyond this moment of comfort. Maybe it's because she's still raw from watching the shooting. Or maybe it's because the woman is Black, too, and therefore must—in some essential part of herself—understand how Jasmyn feels, because she's feeling it as well.

"Actually, I will take that tissue if you don't mind," Jasmyn says. She rolls her shoulders, trying to loosen them, trying to give the woman a second chance.

The woman hands her the entire packet. "You keep it."

Jasmyn thanks her and wipes away her remaining tears. "I'm Jasmyn, by the way," she says. "My family and I just moved here a month ago."

"Oh, yes, the newcomer. You're going to love it," the woman says with genuine enthusiasm. "I'm Catherine Vail."

Jasmyn doesn't miss the way Catherine says *the* newcomer instead of *a* newcomer. This is what happens when you live in a small community, she supposes. Everybody gets up in everybody else's business.

They make small talk. Catherine's job is an unusual one. She's a speech and dialect coach for actors specializing in accent modification. She's divorced, with full custody of her little girl.

"Listen," Jasmyn says. "I hope this isn't presumptuous of me, but do you want to exchange numbers? I'm sure there'll be protests tonight at city hall and vigils at the hospital." Most of her friends and some of her coworkers would be going out to one or even both. "We could meet up somewhere downtown if you want."

Catherine hesitates, and Jasmyn thinks that maybe she'd judged her correctly in the first place. She *is* the type that looks away. But then she says, "Of course," and enters her number into Jasmyn's phone.

"Well, it was lovely meeting you. I hope your day gets better." Her voice is a placid lake, cool and serene.

When Jasmyn texts Catherine later in the day to ask if she wants to attend a vigil in front of MLK Hospital, the woman declines, saying she can't find a babysitter. Jasmyn stares at the text for a few seconds. People lie all the time to get out of things they don't want to do. Maybe Catherine Vail can't find a sitter, but Jasmyn's gut says the woman simply isn't interested in protesting or in being vigilant. But, again, maybe she's jumping to conclusions too quickly. She sighs, puts her phone away, and gets back to work.

≈

The vigil is small, only about a hundred or so people, mostly Black women. They congregate in a parking lot across from the emergency room. Someone hands out tea candles and someone else says the Lord's Prayer. After a while, a woman starts singing "Amazing Grace." Her voice is resonant and clear, like struck crystal. One by one, everyone else joins in and Jasmyn imagines for a moment that their combined voices make it to Mercy Simpson's ears and give her some small comfort.

"How was it?" King asks later when Jasmyn climbs into bed.

She takes a few seconds to settle into the soft warmth of the sheets before answering. "You know how it is," she says on a sigh. Over the course of their relationship, she and King have gone to quite a few vigils together. They always left feeling angry, energized, and comforted in equal measure.

"Want me to massage your feet?" he asks.

"You're a godsend," she says, and unearths her feet from the covers.

King's hands are magic, stretching her toes and digging into her aching arches. When he's done, he peppers her stomach with small kisses. "My boy is getting bigger every day," he says.

"Baby's first protest," Jasmyn says before cringing at how morbid a thing it is to say.

"Jesus," King says. He pulls away and props himself up on his pillow. "Sorry I couldn't get out of my meeting and go with you," he says.

"It's all right, baby," Jasmyn says. "You know I understand." She shifts closer to him and throws a hand across his stomach. "Let me tell you about this woman I met at school this morning." As she describes her encounter with Catherine Vail, Jasmyn realizes it's still bugging her.

"I told her all about what happened, how they killed Tyrese and about Mercy being in the hospital and it didn't seem to affect her. She didn't get angry, didn't get sad, didn't get anything."

"Maybe she's just tired," Kingston says. "Maybe she needed a day off."

There are no days off, is what Jasmyn thinks, but does not say. "She looked richer than rich. Some folks get a little money in them—" she begins.

"And forget where they came from," King says, finishing her sentence for her. He looks at her. "Baby, you need to stop worrying. That's not going to happen to us," he says.

"All right, all right. I know I'm worrying for nothing."

King turns off his bedside lamp. "Come closer," he says, and stretches out his arm so she can tuck into his side.

"There *was* one nice moment at the vigil," she says. "We all sang 'Amazing Grace' together. It almost felt like we were in church."

"Incredible," King says, softly.

She tilts her head to look up at him. "The thing I always come back to is how resilient we are. I mean, after all Black people have been through, all we're still going through, we find some kind of way to keep on going."

"Gospel truth," King says.

Jasmyn sighs, settles her head back down on his chest. "I just love us."

King leans in and kisses her temple and then her cheek and then her lips. "I love you," he says.

"I love you, too, baby," Jasmyn says back.

She closes her eyes and falls asleep thinking about how she'd held hands with strangers and swayed in the dark and sang her resistance. About how Black people, *her* people, could find a way to make any place holy.

Excerpt from *Black Excellence Magazine*: *Catherine Vail, Accent Whisperer to the Stars*

Mrs. Vail, who originally went to Hollywood to become an actress, quickly found she had a facility for accents.

"I grew up in suburban Ohio, but most of the roles I was offered called for an 'urban' accent. Of course, what they meant is they wanted me to sound as if I was from the hood in New York City. Funny enough, it never occurred to them that being from the hood in Southern California, for example, sounds much different than being from the hood in the Bronx. On one particular set, I helped a fellow actress, who was also Black, to perfect her AAVE (African American Vernacular English). One thing led to another and here we are."

Indeed, Mrs. Vail has made quite a name for herself coaching Hollywood A-listers to deliver authentic-sounding accents. Most of her work, though, involves accent reduction—removing specific regional patterns from speech. Commercial casting directors prefer "standard American English."

"What's funny is that no one actually speaks standard American English. It's this made-up dialect that you only learn through professional training. A person's accent tells you so much about them. An accent is an amalgamation of sounds based not only on where you've lived, but your race and class as well as the people you've known. I find it interesting that the industry prefers us to sound like we're from nowhere in particular."

6

Jasmyn sighs and turns on their fancy new espresso machine to make herself a decaf. She has work to do tonight and needs to at least pretend she's having caffeine. For the third night in a row, King's at the Wellness Center. Ever since the disappointment with Terrell going back to jail, he still hasn't chosen another boy to mentor. Jasmyn has been trying to give him time to recover, but two weeks have gone by already. How much time does he need?

She remembers when she first found out that King volunteered with young Black men who needed looking out for. They'd been trying to schedule their third date. Jasmyn suggested dinner on a Tuesday, but King turned her down because he had his weekly Mentor LA meeting. She'd been so impressed with his dedication to their community that she'd texted one of her girlfriends. "This one might be a keeper," she'd said.

It's true that mentoring is a lot of work, with daily check-ins via text or email or phone, weekly in-person meetings with your mentee, and bimonthly field trips. And the work itself, trying to keep the kids in school and on the straight-and-narrow path, wasn't easy. Most of the kids had hard lives that made them hard as a result. Most were in the program reluctantly. Some were even there involuntarily as part of a plea deal or parole.

The machine beeps and Jasmyn pushes a button and watches her cup fill up. Upstairs at her desk, focus comes slowly. She circles her thumb around the rim of her mug. All she can think about is the boys King could've been helping these last two weeks. The boys who are being swallowed whole by the system while he's recovering. The boys who are going to end up needing her public defender skills.

She works for longer than she originally intended to. It helps her feel better, as if she's picking up the slack for King while he gets himself together enough to get back to volunteering at Mentor LA.

It's 9:30 p.m. by the time she's ready to call it a night. King still isn't home.

Jasmyn: What kind of wellness takes all night?
King: Ran into some people here
King: Tell you about it later

Jasmyn leans back in her chair and sinks into her social media feeds. The police chief in the Tyrese Simpson case has released Tyrese's priors. Standard operating procedure for those racists. Muddy the waters. It shouldn't matter that Tyrese had a few drug possession charges on his record. The truth of the matter is that he was executed for the crime of being Black. The truth of the matter is that his little girl is still in intensive care for the crime of being Black. She thinks about Kamau safely sleeping in his bed just down the hall. Will his children or his children's children have to endure a world this cruel? God, she can't bear the thought. She has to believe that all the work she and others like her are doing will make a difference in some distant future, even if she won't be alive to see it.

She slips into bed at 10:45 p.m. Still no King. She's too irritated to even text. She'll talk to him about how much time he was spending up there later. She'll make him recommit to the Mentor LA program. Make him sit down with Kamau for the Talk.

≈

The glow coming from King's side of the bed wakes Jasmyn up. It takes her a good ten seconds to work out that the light is from his laptop and that it's the middle of the night: 1:13 a.m. according to the clock on the night stand.

Jesus, is he looking at porn right now? That would be the last straw for him this evening. All her earlier irritation floods back. "Why the hell are you on the computer at this hour?"

King jumps. "Shit. Guess time got away from me."

Jasmyn folds her hands across her chest. "Guess it's a pattern tonight." She watches him scour her face and sees the moment he realizes how annoyed she is.

He nudges her with his shoulder. "I'm sorry I was so late, baby," he says. "Forgive me? I promise it won't happen again."

"Better not," she says, not quite ready to let it go yet.

King starts to close the laptop, but Jasmyn pushes herself up to seated and stops him with a firm hand.

She peers at the screen. "Houses? How you looking at real estate at one a.m.?"

The laptop light makes his overnight stubble glint silver. He runs his hand down his mouth and chin. "Got to talking with some people about the property values around here. They're incredible. Good as any white neighborhood. Better."

The house he's looking at is in Beverly Hills. The price is around what they'd paid for theirs.

Jasmyn frowns. "Why are you looking at that? Don't tell me you're wanting to move to Beverly Hills."

"What? No. I'm just comparing what we got to what they got. Check it, our house is just as nice as this one and it costs about the same," he says. "That means our property values are good." He sounds just as excited as when he was first trying to convince her to move to Liberty.

"Our house is even nicer because it's here in Liberty," Jasmyn says.

"True dat," he says.

This time when he tries to close the laptop, she lets him.

After the lights are out, King spoons her from behind, wraps his arm around her belly, nuzzles at her neck.

"Don't even try it. I'm still pissed at you for coming home so late," she says, but without much heat.

"I think I know a way to get you un-pissed," he says.

Jasmyn can't help smiling at the tease in his voice.

He nibbles at her ear and slides his hand across her breast, playing with her nipple until her breath hitches.

"How'm I doing?" he asks.

Jasmyn moans softly. "Hush up and keep doing that."

King chuckles in her ear. "Yes, ma'am."

He's gentle as he always is, gliding worshipful hands over the swell of her stomach and down her thighs. He feathers kisses onto the nape of her neck in the exact spot that makes her needy. She pushes back into him and surrenders to the pleasure, to the miraculous joy of being known and loved, to the joy of loving and knowing in return.

Afterward, right as she's falling asleep, she thinks again about the shabby one-bedroom they lived in when they first moved in together. It was barely big enough for two, but they loved it. Jasmyn took it as a testament to their love that they didn't mind always being on top of each other.

"King, you remember our old place, over on Stanley?"

He yawns into her hair. "What? The roach motel, you mean?"

"It wasn't that bad," she says even though he's right. It *was* that bad. They'd had roaches. Rats, too. And peeling paint in the bathroom. And the smell of grease and spice that lingered, left over from the previous tenants.

King chuckles. "It's just the sex making you sentimental," he says, and kisses her neck.

She smiles in the dark. He's right about that too.

Still, she misses that old place. She misses their old lives in the sharp way you miss things that are taken away from you. Except that old life hadn't been taken away. They'd given it up willingly. And things are better for them now. So why does she feel such loss? Life is all about trade-offs, Jasmyn thinks. You give up some things to gain other—better—things.

7

Just as Jasmyn is pushing through the playground gates, a woman—Jasmyn recognizes her as one of the preschool teachers—pulls her aside. She's dark-skinned and beautiful with a wide-open face and a huge Afro. She's wearing bright red lipstick, large gold hoop earrings, and more bangles than Jasmyn would know what to do with. Her clothes are colorful, like the rainbow lorikeets she and Kamau feed whenever they go to the zoo.

"Are you Kamau's mother?" the woman asks.

"Yes," Jasmyn says. She glances over to where he's chasing one of his friends across the Astroturf.

The woman beams and pulls Jasmyn into a hug. She even rocks them side to side.

Jasmyn disentangles herself as gently as she can manage.

The woman laughs. "Sorry, sorry, couldn't help myself. I'm Keisha." She presses a hand over her heart. "I can't tell you how nice it is to meet you."

"It's nice to meet you too," Jasmyn says, keeping her voice polite enough not to be rude, but cool enough so the woman doesn't hug her again. Not that she has anything against hugging, but hugs are intimate, and not something she feels comfortable doing with a stranger.

"Heard you were having a hard time last week," Keisha says.

"I'm not sure I—"

"The Mercy Simpson shooting. Catherine Vail said she found you 'distraught and sobbing' in front of school last week." Keisha uses her middle fingers for the air quotes.

Jasmyn is too confused to laugh at the fuck-you quotes. Had Catherine gossiped about her? But she'd been so sympathetic.

"Let me let you in on a secret," Keisha says. "You can't confide in that one."

It's the way she says it that lets Jasmyn know that Catherine Vail hadn't just gossiped about her. She'd mocked her.

Jasmyn touches her stomach. "These pregnancy hormones got me crying." The thought of that woman laughing at her behind her back is humiliating. More than that, it's infuriating. Her first instinct about her had been right after all. She *was* one of *those* Black people who didn't see the value in solidarity. But then what was she doing here in Liberty?

Keisha waves her hand. "Listen, I'm with you. Those videos hit hard if you have a real working heart. Unfortunately our Catherine Vail doesn't have one of those. Some of the folks around here are only interested in themselves." Keisha leans in closer. "You want to meet up for drinks later?"

Jasmyn studies Keisha. One of the necessary skills of her job is the ability to spot a liar. This woman doesn't seem like one. With her big Afro, her loud clothes, and her louder laugh, she seems a damn sight more authentic than Catherine Vail did.

"Come on, come on," Keisha prods. She points at Jasmyn's stomach. "Don't worry, I'll drink for the three of us." She throws her head back and laughs with raucous enjoyment.

Jasmyn can't help her grin. She *likes* this woman and her take-no-prisoners attitude, her honesty, and her directness. Keisha could have kept Catherine Vail's antics to herself, but instead she took the time to warn Jasmyn about the kind of person she was dealing with. Jasmyn appreciated her for it.

"All right," she says. "Drinks sound great."

"Fabulous!" Keisha says, clapping her hands together. Then she winks. "And don't worry, I won't hug you for so long next time."

Jasmyn touches her face, embarrassed. "No, it's just—"

Keisha laughs and winks again. "It's OK. I get it. Twenty dollars says you never had sex on a first date either."

Jasmyn guffaws. If it weren't for the size of her belly, she would double over with laughter.

"I know I'm a lot to love," Keisha says, deadpan. "Let's say six o'clock? That way I can get home and wash the smell of these children off of me. No offense to your Kamau. I'm sure he smells lovely."

"No, he smells pretty bad."

"I know that's right," Keisha says.

On the drive home, Jasmyn goes over their conversation in her head. Keisha had been right. She'd never had sex on a first date, though, with King, she'd come pretty close. The memory of pushing him out of her apartment so she wouldn't be tempted to attack him and take all his clothes off makes her laugh.

"Moms, why are you laughing?" Kamau asks from the back seat.

Jasmyn smiles. "I think I made a friend today, baby," she says.

LIBERTY DAY SCHOOL

STAFF BIO: *KEISHA DAILY*

EDUCATION

Spelman, BA Early Childhood Development

WHY LIBERTY DAY SCHOOL?

It's a place where I get to teach the next generation of Black kids how to be resilient and authentic.

WHAT IS THE ONE THING PEOPLE WOULD BE SURPRISED TO LEARN ABOUT YOU?

I am the fastest knitter you ever met. No, really.

FAVORITE QUOTE

"I'm rooting for everybody Black." —Issa Rae

8

"Go ahead and fill that sucker up all the way up to the brim, sunshine," Keisha says with a cackle.

The handsome young bartender pouring her wine does as she asks and then winks. After he moves away, she turns back to Jasmyn. "I do believe that toddler is flirting with me."

Jasmyn laughs. All day she'd been looking forward to these drinks. So far she hasn't been disappointed.

Keisha wiggles her ring finger. "Think I should tell him I'm married? And not just married. Married to a *woman*." She cackles again, but Jasmyn can sense her watchfulness. No doubt she's trying to suss out any homophobia.

Jasmyn empathizes. She knows what it's like, always having to check what kind of waters you're swimming in, knows how tiring it is to have to keep your shoulders up by your ears in anticipation of the next inevitable slight. And Keisha has it even worse than she does. She has to deal with homophobia on top of all the other things.

"Nah, let the boy hope," Jasmyn says. She sips her virgin margarita. "What's your wife's name?"

"Darlene." The relief in Keisha's eyes is obvious. She unlocks her phone and shows off their wedding photo.

In the picture, Keisha and Darlene are standing at a floral altar in a park somewhere. Keisha's Afro is pulled into a high pouf and she's wearing a two-piece white velvet suit. She's mid-laugh with her mouth wide open. Jasmyn can almost hear the bright happy sound. Darlene, her wife, is the kind of beautiful that you can't help but stare at. She has dark brown skin, wide doe eyes, high cheekbones, and a short Afro. She's wearing a cream silk sheath dress. Unlike Keisha, she's not laughing, but the smile on her face is radiant and full.

"You both look gorgeous and so happy," Jasmyn says.

Keisha tells her that they met on a dating app. They've been married for six years and they recently started thinking about having kids. They moved to Liberty just four months ago.

"It's the kids thing that made Darlene want to move here," Keisha says. "She got this bug up her ass about what kind of environment kids should be raised in. Then it was Liberty this and Liberty that. Swear to God, I moved just to shut her up." She says the last part with a smile and Jasmyn can see how much she loves her wife. Keisha's one of those people for whom teasing is a form of affection. "Anyway, much as I bitched about it, she was right. It's nice to be surrounded by so much melanin."

They spend a laughter-filled hour chatting. Keisha tells her the best places to go shopping for comfortable shoes, the best place to get "a strong, no-frills cup of coffee and a regular glazed donut," and the best place to get whiskey "after you get that baby out into the world."

From there, they move on to gossip. Keisha hasn't made any close friends since she moved to Liberty, but she has funny stories about some of the over-involved parents she's met at school. "Just because these people have money, don't mean they have sense."

"Oh, this I have to hear," Jasmyn says, leaning in.

"Well, I know about at least two affairs happening as we speak."

"Nope, nope, nope," says Jasmyn, shaking her head.

"Yup. And then there's the mom who emailed the entire school a rant about her husband that she meant to send to her divorce attorney."

"No, shut up, that did not happen," Jasmyn says with a laugh.

Keisha presses a hand to her heart. "Swear to God it's true."

"Now I know who to come to when I need some gossip."

"Stick with me," Keisha says. "I got you."

Eventually they get around to the Wellness Center. "You been up there?" Keisha asks.

Jasmyn hesitates. The smart thing would be to just say no and not confess her true feelings about spas and self-care and "wellness" culture in general. She likes Keisha and doesn't want to offend her in case she's one of those wellness types. On the other hand, it'd be nice to find a true friend here, someone who sees the world the way she does.

She decides on the truth. "Who has time for massages and all that? I'll rest when the work is done." She emphasizes "the work."

Keisha's eyes light up. She slaps her hand on the countertop. "Exactly," she says. "That is *exactly* how I feel. We got so much work to do." She runs a finger up and down the stem of her wineglass. "Darlene loves it up there. Can't get enough." She says it quietly, like she's confused by it.

Jasmyn thinks about how much time King has been spending at the place. She wouldn't say he loves it, though. He's just taking some time out.

Keisha finishes off the rest of her wine. "I knew I'd like you as soon as I heard Catherine bad-mouthing you."

Now they're getting down to it. "What exactly did she say?" Jasmyn asks.

"It doesn't matter what she said," Keisha says. "You know her type. Her only activism is on social media and only on MLK day and only his nonconfrontational quotes. Got no love for Malcolm or Stokely." She rubs a finger across her forearm. "All skinfolk ain't kinfolk."

"Gospel truth," Jasmyn says and nods. There are even Black folks who call themselves Republican. Some of them have enough self-hatred to support the current racist administration. These are the same people who bring up "Black on Black" crime whenever there's a police shooting.

They never bring up "white on white" crime even though white people commit crimes against one another at the same rate as Black people.

"Tell you what, it's not just Catherine, either," Keisha says. She signals to the bartender that she needs a refill. "Some other folks around here need to take a good look in a mirror and realize they still Black."

Jasmyn leans in. "What does that mean?"

"Just look around, count how many relaxers you see. And all the wigs. Notice none of the wigs are 4C wigs, though."

Jasmyn scans down the bar and then the rest of the restaurant. By her count about half the women have what she'd call Eurocentric hairstyles.

"When Darlene and I first moved here, I tried to find us a local Black Lives Matter chapter or any other kind of organization to join, but I couldn't find a thing."

Jasmyn raises her eyebrows. "You'd think there'd be one around here."

"That's exactly what I said to Darlene," Keisha says.

"Huh," Jasmyn says, considering. "Well, you know how folks are. They get so busy with the day-to-day living—jobs, kids, house, and all that—they forget to carve out time to give back to the community.

"Ha! You're more generous than me. I just think people are lazy," Keisha says, laughing.

Jasmyn smiles but shakes her head. "It's just inertia. Most folks need a little extra push to do the right thing. We need to make it easy for them." She leans forward. "Why don't *we* start a BLM chapter?" she asks. One of the lessons she wants to model for Kamau as he grows is that sometimes you have to create the world you want to live in.

Keisha looks at her. "You'd really be up for all that in your state?"

"I'm pregnant, not dead," says Jasmyn, laughing.

Keisha leans in, suddenly earnest. "For real, though, you think we could start one?" Keisha asks.

Jasmyn reaches over and squeezes her hand. "Of course we can start one. Together we'll find ourselves some recruits. Around here, it will be easy."

9

The recruiting doesn't start off as well as Jasmyn expected it to. On the Tuesday after she and Keisha had drinks, she'd tried to sign up the neighbors five houses up the hill from her own, the Wrights.

The husband answered the door. His name was Anthony. He looked like a young Denzel Washington except taller and at least two shades paler.

He recognized her immediately. "Jasmyn, right? Regina and I have been meaning to stop by and give you an official Liberty welcome, but you know how the time goes," he said. "Come in, come in."

Their foyer was grand, a large circular space with white marble walls, ornate gold sconces, and an enormous crystal chandelier.

The smell of lavender was so overwhelming, Jasmyn pressed her fingers against her nose.

Anthony laughed. "You'll get used to it," he said. He pointed out that the sconces doubled as diffusers emitting puffs of mist. "Lavender has natural soothing properties. You should feel your shoulders start to relax down any moment now."

Jasmyn smiled, apologetic, and pointed down at her stomach. "Sorry, this little one is making me sensitive to smells."

"No worries. My wife was the same," he said and waved her off. "Isn't it funny how fundamentally having kids changes you?"

"It's wild," Jasmyn agreed, appreciating how gracious and earnest his comment was.

She spent a few minutes getting to know a little about him. He and his wife were both defense attorneys, though, unlike her, they worked in private practice. They had three kids, all boys, and their youngest was four months old. They'd been in Liberty for just under a year and loved it so far.

"We should get our families together," Jasmyn said. He struck her as down-to-earth and she liked how easily and often he smiled. "Better yet, let's get ourselves sitters for the kids and go on a double date."

Anthony chuckled. "Yes, absolutely to getting sitters. Let those kids be someone else's problem for a night."

He invited her into his sitting room but she declined. "I should be heading home and I don't want to take up too much of your time," she said. "I stopped by because Keisha Daily—do you know her? She teaches preschool at Liberty Day—"

"Yes, I know Ms. Keisha. My middle one is in her class. She's terrific."

Jasmyn smiled, proud of her new friend. She made a mental note to pass Anthony's praise along. "Well, she and I have been discussing the need for a Liberty chapter of Black Lives Matter." She'd paused there, hoping he'd smile and agree right away so she wouldn't have to give him the full-court press. He did neither, and she wasn't sure what to make of the impassive way he looked at her, arms folded.

She took a breath and barreled on. "Of course, you know about the Mercy and Tyrese Simpson case. And I don't have to mention all the others." Again she paused, expecting him to shake his head or suck his teeth, anything to express his anger and disgust over those brutal and senseless deaths.

He remained silent and his face registered nothing.

Jasmyn concentrated on keeping her confused emotions off her own face. This wasn't how she'd thought these recruiting encounters would go. She'd anticipated that they'd be more conversational. She'd expected mutual commiseration.

Disconcerted, she dug her nails into the palm of her hand. "The only way for us to protect ourselves is to organize. We need people lobbying lawmakers, donating to causes, getting the word out, and getting folks involved. Imagine how much good a Liberty BLM chapter could do. We have so many prominent Black people with clout and expertise and money."

Anthony Wright's countenance was still strangely blank. He reminded her of what it was like talking to Catherine Vail after the Mercy Simpson news first broke. Would he mock her after this encounter the way Catherine had?

Still, she wanted to give him the benefit of the doubt. She smiled, trying to make it sincere. "Well, that was the end of my little pitch," she said. "What do you think?"

Finally, his facial expression changed and he chuckled. "Well, that is certainly a well-crafted argument," he said.

By then Jasmyn couldn't help the frown that overtook her face. He'd complimented her even as he remained noncommittal. Her tongue was dry in her throat. She thought about asking for a drink of water, but she wanted to know his answer first.

Before he could give her one, a woman's silhouette appeared at the end of the hallway. "Darling, come and meet our neighbor," he said.

The woman drifted over and slipped an arm around her husband's waist. Regina Wright was even paler than her husband. Her hair was wrapped up in a towel so Jasmyn couldn't tell whether she wore it natural or relaxed or in some other way.

The smile she directed at Jasmyn was wide and welcoming. "So nice to meet you," she said.

Again, Jasmyn explained the reason for her visit. She felt vaguely like she was delivering closing arguments for a case she'd already lost.

The laughter of small children emanated from somewhere deep within the house.

"I'm afraid we wouldn't have time for anything like that," Regina said. Her smile was still so wide and so welcoming.

"Our lives are already full," Anthony explained.

Jasmyn considered trying to convince him. Certainly, he'd seemed nice enough before she started her pitch. But now neither he nor Regina seemed persuadable. Could she talk them into making room in their busy lives for this work? They thought they didn't have time, but she was willing to bet they had less important activities they could cut out of their daily routine. And once they started down this path, their lives would feel full in the most rewarding sense. She just needed to convince them to take the first step. Maybe she could tell them that it was precisely *because* of their children that they needed to make time. They needed to fight for a future where those little Black kids could be safe.

Jasmyn took a breath, ready to try again, but Regina spoke first. "We're so sorry to have wasted your time," she said. Her voice was apologetic but it was also resolute.

Jasmyn swallowed her words and her disappointment. She understood in that moment that Anthony and Regina Wright could not—would not—be convinced. She touched a hand to her still-dry throat. No matter, she thought. Things were better this way. She wanted their chapter to be full of people committed to fighting for the cause in the same way she was. She didn't have time for people she needed to strong-arm. Jasmyn thanked them both for their time and left.

The following night she'd tried again with a house one street over. A boy, maybe fifteen or sixteen, answered the door. Jasmyn asked to speak with his parents, but he said they were up at the Wellness Center and wouldn't be home until much later.

"Your folks spend a lot of time up there?" she asked him before she left.

He shrugged. "They spend all their time there," he'd said.

Now here she is trying once again at the home of Angela and Benjamin Sayles, the plastic surgeons. She remembers seeing them doing their weird yoga in the park. Hopefully they weren't as out there as it'd made them seem. King had said they were nice people, that they had helped Carlton Way found Liberty in the first place.

A woman, wearing an honest-to-god traditional black-and-white maid's uniform with brown stockings and orthopedic-looking black shoes, answers the door. She's older, probably in her late fifties, with medium brown skin and a short Afro.

"Good evening, Mrs. Williams. How can I be of service?" The woman curtsies and dips her head in a small bow.

Jasmyn is no longer surprised that so many people seem to know her name, but she is surprised that the woman curtsied and bowed. Her mouth drops open slightly. What on earth is happening here? She almost barks out a laugh at the over-the-top absurdity of it all but stops herself. The other woman is most definitely not joking.

"I was hoping to speak with the Sayles," Jasmyn says.

"And are they expecting you, Mrs. Williams?"

Jasmyn suspects the other woman knows very well that they're not expecting her. "No, I just thought I'd drop by," she says, feeling slightly chastised. "And you can just call me Jasmyn."

"Of course, Mrs. Jasmyn."

That's not any better, but Jasmyn decides not to push further. She doesn't want to get the other woman into any kind of trouble. Most likely the Sayles instructed her to treat their guests like they're royalty.

Still, though, it makes her uncomfortable to be deferred to in this way, especially by an older Black woman. This woman should be spending her time baking cookies for her grandchildren, not playing maid for rich folks. This entire exchange reeks of money. Jasmyn feels implicated, sullied somehow, in the starkness of the inequality.

"If you could wait here, Mrs. Jasmyn. I'll check to see if they're receiving guests this evening."

Good lord, what kind of people have a housekeeper they make dress in uniform and say things like "receiving guests"? Does she even want bougie people like this joining her Black Lives Matter chapter?

While she waits, Jasmyn takes a look around the foyer. It's grander than the Wrights', but similar in a lot of ways. A lot of marble and gold and crystal. Even the diffusers on the wall are the same, but the scent of lavender is less overpowering here. The decor reminds her so much of the Wrights' that she wonders if they all shop at the same place or what.

The housekeeper returns. "The Sayles can see you now."

It's all Jasmyn can do not to roll her eyes at the ridiculous pretentiousness of it all.

She follows the woman down a richly decorated hallway with textured blue-and-gold wallpaper. Evidently, both Angela and Benjamin went to Harvard Medical School. Jasmyn laughs a little at how enormous the gilded frames holding their diplomas are. Guess they don't want anyone to miss them. She slows her steps to read the ornate script. *Magna cum laude* for both of them.

"*Wow,*" she mouths, impressed despite how ridiculous she already thinks they are. She knows firsthand how much work it must've taken, both intellectually and psychically, to graduate with such high distinction. How much institutional—not to mention interpersonal—prejudice had they dealt with at a place like Harvard?

Still, do the frames need to be so big? Are they simply proud or are they trying to impress, maybe even intimidate their guests? From what she's seen so far, it's probably a bit of both.

The rest of the walls are lined with awards and newspaper clippings. There are even *painted* family portraits. Who gets themselves painted instead of photographed in this day and age?

They exit the main house and walk past a teal-and-white-tiled pool, complete with a waterfall and two hot tubs; an outdoor kitchen and bar with a built-in barbecue; and a gazebo, which forms the entrance to a manicured garden, until they arrive at what looks like a smaller version of the main house.

Once they're inside, the housekeeper enters a code into a panel on the wall. The door before them slides open. The housekeeper stands off to the side, giving Jasmyn space to enter.

"Welcome in," says a woman's voice. "I hope you don't mind us getting serviced while we chat."

The room is dim with candlelight. It takes Jasmyn's eyes a few seconds to adjust and for her to understand what "getting serviced" means. Angela and Benjamin Sayles are lying on massage tables. They are completely naked and their pale brown bodies glisten with oil. Benjamin Sayles is on his back. His penis is erect and straining toward the ceiling. His masseuse isn't currently massaging him *there*, but had she been? Angela Sayles is on her stomach. Her masseuse is placing small smooth black stones along the length of her spinal column.

Jasmyn spins away from them. "Jesus Christ. I'm sorry. I didn't know," she says. The apology is out of her mouth before she can think it through. Why should she be the one to say sorry? She hadn't intruded on their privacy. They'd invited her in.

Even though she has her back turned, Jasmyn still covers her eyes with her hand.

"Told you we'd embarrass her," Angela Sayles says to her husband. Her voice is mildly scolding but filled with humor.

Benjamin Sayles chuckles. "Why don't you take her to the salon? I'll join you after."

But Jasmyn has no interest in recruiting these people. "You know what? You're busy. I can come back another time."

"Nonsense," says Angela Sayles. "I'm so sorry to have embarrassed you. We sometimes forget that not everyone is as comfortable in their own skin as we are."

Where to even begin with these people? Are they saying she's not enlightened because she didn't want to see their pale, naked asses? Jasmyn opens her eyes and steps toward the exit. From behind her, there's movement and then a hand on her upper arm.

"I'm so sorry again," says Angela Sayles. "Come with me to the salon? I'd hate for you to leave without knowing why you came."

Jasmyn looks at her. At least she's wearing clothes now, a plush white robe with *Liberty Wellness Center* monogrammed on the lapel. Maybe she should go to the salon and say her piece, just to stay on good terms. Last thing she wants—and, she knows, the last thing King would want in this place that he loves—is to have any sour feelings with their neighbors.

Like the massage room, the salon requires an entrance code. Why do they have security codes on rooms inside their own house? She'd noticed security cameras on the house's exterior, but this took things to another level. Does paranoia come with the territory when you're this wealthy?

Angela Sayles pushes the door open with a flourish. "Et voilà," she says.

Jasmyn steps into a room that seems to be made of light and glass. She feels as if she's inside a gemstone, a watery blue topaz or aquamarine. The ceiling is covered with dangling crystal objects all refracting light. The smell of lavender is everywhere.

"Welcome to our sanctuary," says Angela Sayles.

Jasmyn turns in place taking it all in. On the opposite side of the room, there are two plush reclining chairs, the kind you see in high-end luxury spas. Rows of bright blue medicine dropper bottles sit on a shelf behind them. Across from the shelving, two large free-standing claw-foot bathtubs are filled with a milky white liquid.

Since the embarrassment of seeing her naked before, Jasmyn hasn't really looked at Angela, but she looks at her now. Angela Sayles is the kind of Black woman that white women say is beautiful. To be honest, Black women are guilty of it too. She has "good" 3A hair and the shade of her skin is lighter than a paper bag—she definitely passes the paper bag test. Her features—narrow nose, thin lips—are more stereotypically white than Black. Her eyes are a pale, glassy brown. Some enslaved ancestor of hers had probably been raped by her owner. Jasmyn wonders if Angela knows that America's history of slavery is written into her pale skin and her "good" hair.

"Do you mind turning around for just a moment?" Angela Sayles asks. She's standing next to one of the bathtubs.

Jasmyn turns away immediately. She has no desire to see this woman naked again.

A few seconds later, when Angela Sayles says she's ready, Jasmyn turns to find her almost completely submerged in the bath.

"Now," says Angela Sayles, "what is it you wanted to discuss?" She tilts her head back and closes her eyes.

Jasmyn can't remember the last time she'd met people this strange. In fact, she'd *never* met people this strange. Why hadn't Angela simply heard her out *before* getting into the tub? Now Jasmyn has to stand here making her pitch while pretending this scenario is totally normal, like the two of them share an intimacy that they do not.

Is Angela deliberately trying to make her uncomfortable, and if so, why? Jasmyn looks away from the tub and tells herself just to get it over with. The sooner she tells Angela what she came for, the sooner the other woman can turn her down, and the sooner Jasmyn can get the hell out of there and call Keisha so they can have a good long laugh.

Like she'd done with the Wrights two nights before, Jasmyn makes her case for a Liberty chapter of Black Lives Matter. Just as she expects her to, Angela Sayles turns her down, saying much the same thing the Wrights had said. *Life gets to be so full. Sometimes you need to let some things go.* Jasmyn doesn't press her, just thanks her for her time.

As she's leaving, she watches Angela Sayles sink farther down into the bath until all that remains to be seen is her pale brown face, slack with pleasure, floating in a sea of milk.

Later, when Jasmyn tells King and then Keisha about this visit, she'll leave this part out: how, as she'd stood there watching Angela Sayles marinate, she'd felt a sudden wrongness in the air, diffuse but unmistakable.

And because it didn't make any rational sense at all, she won't tell them how she'd felt, for the briefest of moments, afraid.

Excerpt from an interview with Angela and Benjamin Sayles in the "Power Couples" issue of *Mahogany Magazine*

INTERVIEWER: What do you say to those people who are critical of plastic surgery, who say it shouldn't matter what a person looks like on the outside?

AS: I'd say please join us adults in the real world.

BS: Please excuse Angela. She sometimes gets a little defensive. First off, I'd just mention that Angela and I do a good amount of pro bono work—reconstructive surgery for victims of traumatic accidents, burn injuries, car accidents, and the like. I don't think anyone would fault us for those kinds of surgeries. I suppose the issue is that a lot of people out there think only a shallow, self-involved person would choose to have one of our procedures. They think plastic surgery is only about getting a better nose, trimming off a little bit of that thigh fat, making yourself a little more buxom. But it's about so much more than that. It's about esteem. We help people to feel better about themselves. We give them outer beauty to match their inner beauty. We give them the tools they need to face a world that can be cruel. Yes, sometimes that means giving them a nicer nose, but where's the harm in that? Why not make the most of the gifts God gave you? We have the technology and tools to overcome most flaws, why not take advantage of them?

AS: What Benjamin means to say is that a well-wielded scalpel can change the world for the better.

10

Jasmyn talks King out of using the valet at the Downtown LA restaurant where they're going to meet friends. Why waste money when she has a perfectly good parking spot at the courthouse just six blocks away?

"You're not really worrying over twenty dollars," King says after he parks the car.

"What? That used to be a lot for us," Jasmyn says.

King throws her a knowing look but doesn't say anything until after he opens her door and helps her out. "I think I understand," he says, smiling like he has secret knowledge.

Jasmyn bumps his shoulder. "And what is it you think you understand, mister?"

He gives her hand a quick kiss. "Baby, it's OK that we have money now."

"Twenty dollars is still twenty dollars," she says. "Besides, between being in the office and the courthouse, I never get to walk around down here anymore. The fresh air will be nice."

King laughs. "If it's fresh air you want, we should go back to Liberty."

They take the elevator down and exit out onto the street. The evening air is warm, unusually humid, and definitely not fresh.

No doubt about it, Downtown LA smells worse than Liberty. But Jasmyn likes that about it. It smells like a real city, with exhaust and grime and urine and dead and dying things. She loves Liberty but doesn't want it to make her too soft, too comfortable. The higher up in a tree you go, the farther away you are from your roots.

They turn a corner and spot a small homeless encampment two blocks ahead.

"Jesus, that's new," Jasmyn says. She tightens her grip on King's arm. "It wasn't here just last week."

Mixed in with the tents, folding chairs, and sleeping bags, Jasmyn sees piles of garbage with everything from empty fast-food containers to tampons to liquor bottles.

"Come on, we should cross," King says.

Jasmyn glances over to the other side of the street. It's deserted except for a couple of homeless men sleeping in storefronts. Looking around some more, she realizes that no one else is walking out here. Maybe King was right. They should've valeted. Shame swamps her as soon as she thinks it. What she should be feeling now is compassion, not fear.

She shakes her head at King. "No, it's fine. Let's keep going."

King stops and turns to face her. He takes both her hands in his. "Baby, you don't have to prove anything—"

"Who says I'm trying to prove something?" she says, as irritated with King as she is with herself. "We need to be helping these people, not crossing the street pretending like they don't exist."

King looks at her like she's naive. "Some of these people are dangerous—"

"It will be fine," Jasmyn insists.

"All right," King says, capitulating. "Just stay next to me."

"OK," she says, and lets him pull her in close.

Half a block later, King guides her around a smattering of broken glass mingled with something foul-smelling that she can't identify.

"Jesus, why do we let this happen to people?" It never fails to wound her, the way she can't save everyone.

"I don't know, baby," King says. "I don't know."

The sidewalk grows filthier the closer they get to the encampment. Jasmyn studies the ground, picking out a narrow path between the tents and the street where they can walk. Glass crunches beneath her heels.

They're right on top of the encampment when a voice says, "Evening, folks."

Jasmyn tightens her grip on King's arm and tries not to betray how startled she is. Just ahead there's a man she hadn't noticed. He's sitting at the mouth of his tent watching their approach. He's Black but covered in so much grime he seems gray.

King throws his shoulders back and straightens himself up. He nods at the man. "Evening."

The man smiles and Jasmyn sees that even his teeth are gray.

"Nice night for a stroll," he says. His tone is light and easy, like they're all just being neighborly and enjoying a springtime evening together.

"It sure is," Jasmyn says, and then immediately feels ridiculous for saying it. She stops walking. "How are you, brother?" she asks.

The man looks at her with glassy eyes. "Can't complain, my sister," he says.

Next to her King tenses but doesn't try to move her along. She pulls a twenty-dollar bill from her wallet and hands it to the man.

"Thank you kindly," the man says and smiles his gray smile again. "I appreciate you."

Jasmyn is struck again by his easy peacefulness. "You're welcome," she says.

A half a block later King kisses her on the temple. "I'm glad we walked," he says. "You were right about the valet money."

When they get to the restaurant, their friends Tricia and Dwight are already there. Tricia barely waits for them to sit down before getting into it. "So, how's things in bougie-ass Liberty?" she asks.

Jasmyn and Tricia have been friends since college, so Jasmyn knows Tricia is only teasing but still, an embarrassed heat washes over her neck and face. She feels exposed, as if she's being accused of something.

"It's not all that bougie," she says.

Even if it *had* been an accusation, what is her crime exactly? That she lives someplace safe and beautiful and, yes, expensive? This is America. Safety and beauty cost money. Tricia knows that.

Jasmyn spends a good couple of minutes extolling the virtues of Liberty. She tells both Tricia and Dwight how nice it is to live surrounded by Black people. "Every single teacher, the baristas, the cops." She leans toward Tricia as if she's sharing a secret. "Listen, I can't tell you what a relief it is to be able to *relax*." As she's saying the words, she realizes how much she means them. "I was in our pharmacy the other day and the security guard didn't follow me around."

Tricia laughs and shakes her head. "I hate how they do that. Like, what? I'm going to shoplift some cough syrup or some crappy lipstick?"

"Right? It's ridiculous," says Jasmyn. "Know what else? I haven't been mistaken for an employee in any place there yet, either."

Tricia slaps the table. "Listen. That. Shit. Is. Not. Funny," she says, punctuating each word with a clap. "I could be wearing a damn wedding dress and some somebody is going to come up to me and ask what aisle they can find the tampons in."

Jasmyn laughs so hard her face hurts. It's all so absurd. What else is there to do but laugh? There's more she could say to Tricia about the benefits of Liberty, too. At the high-end boutiques, no one assumes she can't afford the items on offer. On the streets, no one clutches their purse just a little tighter when she or Kamau or King walk by. No one locks their car door, either.

Of course, not everything there is perfect. But maybe because she's still feeling defensive that Tricia had called Liberty bougie, she doesn't tell her about the imperfections. Jasmyn doesn't tell her that, after living for six weeks in a town filled with Black people, she's found only one so far who she actually likes. She doesn't reveal that neither she nor Keisha had been able to sign a single person up for their Black Lives Matter chapter yet. Keisha had told her she'd asked almost every preschool parent she talked to all week. They all said the same thing: too busy. Even now, Jasmyn wants to shake them, tell them that being busy is no excuse for not getting involved. Not to mention how annoyed she is that they all seemed to find enough time to go to the Wellness Center and do all their self-care nonsense. The image of Angela Sayles sinking into her bathtub flashes in her mind but she quickly dismisses it. For the life of her, Jasmyn can't imagine why the sight of it had seemed so ominous before. Angela Sayles was just a frivolous rich woman with too much time on her hands.

"I'm just messing with you about it being bougie," Tricia says. "That all sounds nice."

Jasmyn hears the little bit of envy in Tricia's voice and feels guilty for causing it.

"What about you, King? Anything you miss about the city?" Dwight asks.

King sips his beer before answering. Jasmyn has the sense he's testing out his words, the way you test fruit for ripeness in the supermarket. "Man, it's not like we on another planet. We still come to the city for work every damn day."

The way he says it makes Jasmyn wonder if he'd change even that if he could.

The food arrives and she changes the subject. "You see that video of the white woman in the park?" she asks.

Tricia slaps the table and laughs. "Homegirl didn't even care she was being filmed."

"Bet she cares now," Dwight says and laughs too.

They move on from that racist video to two even more racist ones, and then to what the racist president said most recently, and back to another video King had never even heard of. Eventually they come to the Tyrese and Mercy Simpson case.

"They put a bullet in that baby girl's lung," Jasmyn says. She still can't believe the words even as she's saying them. Again, she flashes to the traffic stop from last spring. What if that had happened to Kamau? She could never survive a thing like that.

"The things they do to us," Tricia says. Her eyes fill with tears. Jasmyn reaches across the table and squeezes her hand.

"I read today that she's out of the ICU," says King. "Looks like she's going to survive it."

"Small mercies," says Tricia. Dwight leans over and kisses her on the forehead.

"You know what else I can't get over?" Jasmyn asks. "All the news ever talks about is the protests and the 'looting.' Swear to God, they care more about property than they care about actual human beings."

"That's the truth," says Tricia.

There's not much to say after that and they sit in silence until the waitress arrives to take their dessert order.

Jasmyn and Tricia decide to share a slice of chocolate cake. Dwight is too full to eat anything else.

King orders a single glass of port that costs three figures.

Jasmyn pretends not to see the price and then pretends not to see the look Tricia and Dwight share over it. If Tricia didn't think she was bougie before, she surely does now.

When the bill comes, King insists on paying. Tricia and Dwight don't protest.

They leave the restaurant and walk two blocks to a hotel bar Dwight had heard about. Except for their waitress, they're the only Black people there.

As he's pulling out her chair, King whispers into her ear. "Not like this where we're from," he says, proud.

It takes Jasmyn a second to realize he means Liberty. Liberty is where they're from now.

Drinks start off well. Tricia orders a club soda instead of her usual cosmo and it occurs to Jasmyn that Tricia hasn't had any alcohol so far.

As per their usual, King and Dwight dive right into sports talk, this time about basketball.

Jasmyn takes the opportunity to shift her chair closer to Tricia. "How are things at work?" she asks. Tricia is a trauma nurse in the ER of a mid-size, underfunded, and understaffed hospital in the mid-city area. Most of the patients are either Black or Mexican, and poor.

Tricia pushes out a heavy sigh. "Last week was rough. Family of four got T-boned by a semi. The mom died before we could even get her prepped for surgery. The dad and one of the kids died two days later."

"Jesus, Trish, I'm sorry," Jasmyn says. She reaches over and takes Tricia's hand in her own.

Tricia shakes her head and looks down at the table. "All these years and it still hasn't gotten any easier," she says, voice low. "My charge nurse found me crying in the bathroom after the mom passed. For years she's been telling me that I need to get tougher and build up a hard shell. She says I can't fall apart after every bullet wound or car crash, but I don't know how to do that." She looks up at Jasmyn. "How can I do the job if I don't care?"

Jasmyn understands exactly how Tricia feels, of course. She knows how the work—lifesaving, life-changing, important work—burrows itself deep into your being. There is no not caring. Every case she loses, every *person* she loses to the system, wounds her. Every loss alters something inside her.

She squeezes Tricia's hand. "You doing OK?"

"I'm all right. I've had a few days to live with it," she says. "Now, how about you? How's lady justice treating you?"

Jasmyn releases Tricia's hand and sits back. "Lady justice is biased as hell, but I got her number the last few days. Won all my cases this week."

Tricia holds up her club soda for a toast. "That I like to hear."

Jasmyn takes a sip of water before leaning back in. "You know, you weren't wrong before. Liberty is a little bougie."

"I knew what I said was gonna bother you," Tricia says, smiling. "I didn't mean anything by it. Listen, if I had all that money? I might get a little bougie too."

"Maybe *bougie* isn't the right word," Jasmyn says. "What I'm trying to say is that the people are not like I expected them to be."

"How do you mean?"

Jasmyn frowns, not quite sure how to describe them. "You know how your charge nurse told you that you need to build up a tough shell? Well, it's like these people have impenetrable shells when it comes to our issues."

Tricia raises her eyebrows. "Don't like the sound of that."

"Right?" says Jasmyn. "And the truth is, so far I've made only one friend. You'd like her, actually. Her name is Keisha. Maybe the three of us could go out." She sighs. "I don't know. I thought I'd have a whole community of people by now."

"You haven't been there *that* long," Tricia says.

"Yeah, you're right," Jasmyn says. "But it's more than that, too." She leans in, about to tell the story of trying to recruit the Sayles when Dwight clinks his glass with a fork.

"Time for a little personal news," he says.

Tricia gives him a smile so wide, it makes Jasmyn smile too.

"We're pregnant!" Tricia announces.

"It's a girl," says Dwight. "Lord, help me!"

Jasmyn lets out a whoop and gets up to hug Tricia. "I knew there was a reason you were drinking all them club sodas."

Tricia laughs and rests her hand on Jasmyn's stomach. "Pretty soon, I'll start showing too."

"You should move to Liberty," Jasmyn says as she sits back down. "What do you think, King? How perfect would that be? Our kids can grow up together."

King shakes his head and smiles. "Let's not plan out their whole lives for them," he says.

Jasmyn studies him for a second. Why isn't he enthusiastic about this idea? It's another second before she realizes. Tricia and Dwight could never afford to live in Liberty.

Jasmyn can feel Tricia looking back and forth between them.

"We're fine where we are," Tricia says. "We got roots there."

"So, tell me all about how you found out and everything," Jasmyn says, and not just to move them past the small awkwardness. She loves hearing stories of the big events in people's lives, the things that shift them from living one kind of life to another. In her job she sees a lot of big events, but the change they usher in is almost never good.

Tricia rubs her hands together and smiles. "So y'all know we'd been trying to get this baby thing happening for a minute. Well, we're out at a party and Dwight brings me a drink." She laughs. "Before you say anything, I know you're not supposed to drink when you're trying, but like I said, it'd been a minute. So Dwight hands me a cosmo, my usual. I took one sip and wanted to spit it right back out. As soon as that happened, I knew I was pregnant."

King laughs. "There it is right there. That baby already showing you who the boss is."

"Lord, help me," Dwight says again.

"Anyway, I sent Dwight out to the drugstore to get me a test," says Tricia.

Dwight jumps in. "I roll up to the pharmacy down the block and I see they have a whole shelf full of nothing but tests."

"Would you believe he brought me back five tests?" Tricia says, laughing. "I was like, how much pee does this man think I have?"

Dwight shrugs. "I wanted to be sure, sure, sure."

"Long story short," says Tricia. "I went into the bathroom and did my business and it was positive." She does a happy dance in her chair.

"When we got home she drank maybe a hundred glasses of water and peed on the rest of the sticks," says Dwight.

"Like you said, I wanted to be sure, sure, sure," Tricia says.

From there Tricia moves on to when they found out the baby's sex and the moment they heard the heartbeat for the first time. "It was so loud. At first I thought it was mine," she says.

Jasmyn interrupts her. "Just tell me your OB is a Black woman."

Tricia shakes her head.

"You need to get yourself one," says Jasmyn. "You know the mortality rate for Black women during childbirth is three times what it is for white women?"

"Really? That high?" Tricia says. She touches her stomach.

"It's criminal," Jasmyn says.

"I've been with my gyn—"

But Jasmyn interrupts her again. "You planning on an epidural or doing it natural?"

"Oh, please," Tricia says. "Natural? Couldn't be me. They're going to have to give me all the drugs."

"This woman cries over paper cuts," Dwight says.

Jasmyn barely smiles. "That right there is another reason to get a Black doctor. You know white doctors prescribe less pain medicine for Black patients than for white ones?"

"I'd heard something like that," Tricia says.

"These people, I tell you." Jasmyn shakes her head. "Remember the Tuskegee syphilis thing? They let those poor men suffer—"

"Ease up, baby," King says, finally. "We celebrating right now."

Jasmyn looks at Tricia and Dwight and realizes they're frowning down into their drinks. "Shit, my bad," she says. "I'm sorry. I got carried away. Sometimes the world gets to be a lot. There's just so much injustice, you know?"

King leans in and kisses her temple. "Let it go for this evening," he whispers in her ear.

She nods at him. Of course, he's right. There's a time and a place.

"Lighter subject," Jasmyn says, clapping her hands together. "I need you to know that you have to get all the sex you can in now. After that little girl gets here, it's over for you," she says.

Dwight groans while Tricia laughs. "That's what I've been reading," she says.

They talk about the first-year milestones, rolling over and crawling and walking. They talk about breastfeeding and first foods and first words and all the things you talk about with expectant parents.

At some point, when King is telling a story about getting peed on by Kamau while changing his diaper, Jasmyn reaches across the table and squeezes Tricia's hand.

"I'm sorry about before," she whispers.

Tricia shakes her head and whispers back. "It's all good." She points at her stomach. "Can you believe I got a baby in here?" Her smile is radiant.

For the rest of the evening, Jasmyn makes sure to stay clear of anything to do with race or racism as it relates to pregnancy. She feels guilty for bringing it up in the first place. She should've let Tricia and Dwight enjoy their moment. All the same, she makes a mental note to check in with Tricia in a week or so and recommend some Black obstetricians. The four of them might be forgetting about racism for the night, but racism isn't forgetting about them.

≈

The first thing King says to her the next morning is that she should join the Wellness Center. They're still in bed, but he's propped up against the headboard. He holds a hand up before she can tell him all the reasons she isn't interested in going. "Tomorrow night they're giving a big tour for nonmembers. Free classes and all that," he says.

Jasmyn knows he's mentioning it because of last night, because of how she'd been the rain on Tricia's baby announcement parade. It makes her defensive. "You don't think you spend enough time up there for both of us?" she snaps.

Surprise and then hurt flashes across King's face before he looks away from her. He takes off his glasses and cleans them with the hem of his shirt. It's the kind of thing he does when he's upset but is doing his best to keep calm.

"I spend time up there because I need the stress relief," he says, voice low and tight. "Because I work all the damn time." He looks back at her. "Or didn't you notice that part?"

Guilt floods her. She knows she's not being fair. She pushes herself up to seated and scoots closer to him. "I'm sorry," she says. "I know how hard you're working. How hard you're working for us."

She nudges his shoulder with her own but he doesn't respond. Instead, he tips his head back against the headboard and closes his eyes.

"I'm sorry," she says again. "I didn't even mean it."

"You sure about that?" King asks, skeptical.

"Yes," she insists, nudging him again. She waits a few seconds before adding, "Don't get me wrong, I still want you to get back to Mentor LA."

He lifts his head and looks at her. "My God, woman," he says, chuckling low. "Anyone ever tell you how relentless you are?"

Jasmyn smiles at him, relieved to be past the argument. She rests her head on his shoulder. "What they got you working so hard on, anyhow? Still that fancy-water-energy-drink thing, Awake?"

He nods. "I need to do right by it. It's a huge investment for us. You wouldn't believe the ungodly amount of money we spent on branding and packaging to make it seem like it's more than water with caffeine and food coloring."

She laughs, bemused. "When you going to bring some home for me to try?"

"After the baby comes," he says. "Way too much caffeine in it for you." He shifts himself into a more upright position. "Anyway, quit trying to change the subject from what we're talking about." He squeezes her hand. "Will you go up to the spa tomorrow?"

She sighs. "You're not gonna let this go, are you?" His insistence on her going is exasperating. "Why you want me to join so bad?"

"Baby, last night was—" He stops himself and rubs at his glasses again. "Baby, you need to relax. *I* need you to relax."

She presses her lips together and resists telling him no. As bad as she feels about being such a downer last night, she doesn't need relaxation "therapy" or whatever people are calling it these days. Still, King doesn't ask for very much. And what he's asking for isn't a lot, is it? She can go to a tour. She doesn't need to become a member.

She lets her exasperation go. "All right," she says. "I'll do it."

Jasmyn eyes the gated security checkpoint ahead of her and wonders if she inadvertently missed a turn somewhere. Her GPS says she didn't. She looks back up. There are guard booths on either side of the road and the gate seems heavy enough to stop a tank. Why on earth does the Wellness Center need all this? It's a spa, not a prison.

A guard steps out of the booth on the right and signals for her to roll her window down. Jasmyn notices that he's armed. It shouldn't surprise her, she supposes. Even mall guards are armed these days.

There are more security protocols here than most courthouses she's been in.

Jasmyn would laugh at how extreme it all is if she wasn't vaguely unnerved. On top of that, she's annoyed. She'd had to leave work before she could finish her notes on a tricky case. There's at least an hour, maybe two hours, of work waiting for her when she gets home.

Still, she has to tread carefully here. She rolls the window down.

"Good evening," says the man. "Welcome to the Liberty Wellness

Center. Can I see some identification, please?" He's dark-skinned, slim, and tall, with the kind of face you forget as soon as you look away from it. His uniform is a generic gray and he's wearing what looks like a sheriff's badge, except it's inscribed with the letters LWC.

She hands her ID over to the guard, making sure to make eye contact. People are less likely to give you a hard time if you personalize your interaction with them. "My appointment is at six p.m.," she says. Her voice is confident and firm, leaving no room for him to doubt her.

While the first guard checks her ID, a second one emerges from the booth on the left. He's not as tall or as thin, but he's just as forgettable as his compatriot. He gives her a brief nod. Jasmyn nods back and rests her hands on the steering wheel. She can't explain it, but she feels better knowing she can put the car into reverse and get out of there quickly if she needs to.

The first guard returns to her window. "You're good to go, Mrs. Williams."

"Thanks," Jasmyn says, taking her ID. On impulse, she decides to dig a little. "Why do they need two of you working this gate?" she asks, making sure to smile as she asks it.

The guard returns her smile. "Safety first" is all he says. He straightens and raps on the roof of the car. Up ahead the heavy gate slides open.

Jasmyn rolls up her window and pushes out an audible breath, relieved to be rid of them. She pulls forward but watches the men in her rearview mirror. They don't talk to each other, just go back to their respective booths. She sighs again. That was all a bit excessive. But, she supposes, a lot of things about Liberty are excessive.

The rest of the drive is uphill along a winding, palm-tree-lined path.

On a parallel service road, she spots white delivery vans with LIBERTY WELLNESS CENTER stenciled on the side. A few minutes later she finds herself at yet another checkpoint. The guards, both women this time, are also armed. They nod, but don't speak to her directly. One of them gets on the radio, no doubt verifying Jasmyn's right to be there. A few seconds later, they open the gate and wave her through.

This security song and dance can't all just be for safety, can it? What are they guarding so closely? Fancy equipment? High-end serums? Jasmyn chuckles to herself. *Gold bath bombs?*

Beyond the checkpoint, the road changes from paved to gravel, and Jasmyn spends the next ten minutes driving slowly so as not to kick up rocks and damage her car. Finally she crests the hill to a large circular roundabout.

The valet who opens her door welcomes her by name. "Welcome in, Mrs. Williams." He extends his hand to help from the car. His smile is wide and deferential.

She gathers her things, suit jacket, purse, and laptop bag before stepping out. "Thank you. The keys are inside," she says.

"Wonderful, Mrs. Williams. Enjoy your visit," he says with another wide smile.

Now *this* is what she'd been expecting from a place like this. Friendly, efficient service.

Instead of going inside right away, she stops to take in the view. The sun has just set, and the sky is postcard perfect. She snaps a photo with her phone and texts it to King. From this height, Liberty looks like any other suburb. From here, you can't tell that it's a place with a beautiful dream, a place built to be a safe haven. She takes a smiling selfie and sends that one to King, too.

The short walkway to the front door is lit with small path lights and paved with flat white rocks designed to look like stones. Above the sliding glass doors, a sign simply says WELLNESS. Jasmyn snorts. This is just a glorified spa after all. She looks back over her shoulder and wonders how upset King would be with her if she turns around and leaves. But no. She'd promised him she'd relax and keep an open mind, and she's going to do just that. She tilts her head from side to side, stretching the muscles in her neck. They *are* a little sore. A massage might be nice. Also, she admits to herself, she's curious about this place. What is it about this spa that keeps King and the others coming back so often? She shifts her suit jacket from one arm to the other and holds tight to her laptop. She steps forward and the door glides open for her.

Immediately, she's flanked by two smiling Black women. Jasmyn thinks maybe they're twins. Both are in their early twenties and both have pale brown skin and pale brown eyes and straight hair cascading down the middle of their backs. When she looks closer, though, she sees they're similar, but not the same.

"Welcome," says one of the women, the one on her left. She takes Jasmyn's purse and jacket and laptop.

"Careful with that," Jasmyn says, meaning her computer.

"Of course. We'll take the utmost care," the woman says.

The woman on the right hands Jasmyn a delicate white-and-gold porcelain teacup. "Silver needle tea for cellular health," she says.

"Thank you," Jasmyn says, but doesn't sip it. She's never heard of this kind of tea. Who even knows what's in it? If she weren't pregnant maybe she'd give it a try, but for now she decides to skip it.

The reception area is exactly what she expected—white walls, low lighting, and rows of shelves stocked with beautiful bottles. Some kind of spa soundtrack plays in the background, running water interrupted with the occasional muted wind chime.

The not-twins usher her over to the guest concierge services desk. A man named Desmond, according to the golden name tag pinned to the lapel of his white suit, greets her. He's definitely mixed, Jasmyn thinks. His skin is medium brown and his short black hair is loosely curled.

"Welcome, Mrs. Williams. We're so grateful to have you. I won't take too much of your time. I'm here to facilitate your first experience with us."

First and *only* experience, Jasmyn thinks, but doesn't say. She places her tea on his desk and waits.

"We generally begin with a series of intake questions in order to customize your session for a maximally beneficial outcome. Are you amenable to that?"

Maximally beneficial? Who talks like that? And these people certainly have a high opinion of what a nice massage can do for a person.

"Go ahead," she says, careful to keep her tone polite and her face neutral so he doesn't guess how silly she thinks this all is.

"When did you last go to a spa?" he asks.

It was for a bachelorette party at a place far less luxurious than this one. It hadn't been fun. She'd felt bad for the woman giving her the foot massage and pedicure. Jasmyn had wondered if she found it humiliating to touch other people's feet. During her massage all she thought about was how much the masseuse's own muscles must suffer from taking away everyone else's hurt all day.

Jasmyn doesn't say any of this to Guest Concierge Desmond. Just says that it was too long ago to remember.

He asks her what she hopes to extract from her wellness journey. To placate her husband, she thinks but, again, doesn't say.

The last question he asks is if she's ever had a profoundly transformative experience. She touches her stomach and is transported back to hearing Kamau's first wail in the hospital. Everyone had told her how instant her love would be. But she didn't understand, not really, until she held him. It was like being flooded.

"Yes," she says. She doesn't elaborate, and he doesn't seem to need her to.

He smiles then and stands. "Thank you for your time, Mrs. Williams." He gestures to the not-twins. "They'll escort you to the changing rooms."

"And along the way, we can share some of our newest environments with you," one of the women says. She places a guiding hand on the small of Jasmyn's back.

Jasmyn yelps and jolts away before she can stop herself. She covers her mouth with her hand, feeling somewhere between annoyed at the unexpected touch and embarrassed at her outsized reaction.

"Sorry," she says. "I wasn't expecting that."

The woman's eyes widen. "Would you prefer that we don't touch you, Mrs. Williams?"

How is she supposed to answer that question without offending this poor lady who is just doing her job? No doubt her superiors trained her to touch the clientele as a way to forge some kind of intimacy. But not offending the woman is no reason for Jasmyn herself to be uncomfortable. Still, why make a fuss?

She waves away the woman's question. "It's fine. You surprised me is all."

The woman nods but as they begin walking Jasmyn notes, gratefully, that she keeps her hand to herself.

The first "environment" is an enormous room called Falling Water, intended for "tranquility and reflection." The walls are made from huge slabs of black mineral rocks that shimmer beneath a gentle cascade of water. Jasmyn can't help feeling slightly awestruck at the scale and beauty of it. She drags her fingers over the cool, wet surface and cranes her neck trying to find the water's source, but it's hidden from view.

Another room, this one called Earth and intended for "attachment and grounding," has no furniture, just sand-colored throw pillows of varying sizes arranged artfully on lush white carpeting. A warm breeze, blown by some invisible machine, washes over her skin.

"This place is wild," Jasmyn says. Both women beam at her, as if she meant it as a compliment. Jasmyn's not sure whether she did.

The rest of the spa is a revelation, populated with sights and scents and sounds Jasmyn has never experienced before. She has a feeling that this place, and others like it, are a secret that has been kept from her. A secret that's been kept from most of the world. If regular working-class people knew that places like this exist—places built only for indulgent pleasure, places that turn their face away from the world and its discontents—they would riot.

They walk down a long hallway past a series of private changing rooms until they arrive at one with a small hanging wooden plaque: WELCOME JASMYN. The words are etched into the wood as if her eventual membership is a foregone conclusion.

One of the not-twins, the paler one, hands Jasmyn another one of those teal boxes tied in gold ribbon. "A gift," she says.

Inside the room, Jasmyn opens the box to find a black silk robe. She undresses and slips into the smoothest, most supple fabric she's ever worn. Back outside, she finds a pair of sheepskin slippers in just her size. Her name is stitched into the insoles.

The not-twins escort her down a series of curved hallways lined on either side by closed, cream-colored doors that she assumes lead to the various treatment rooms. The air in this section of the spa smells scrubbed clean, the way it does after a heavy rain. One of the doors, a large blond-wood one with no descriptive plaque, has a security panel on the wall next to it. Jasmyn frowns at it. "What's that all about?" she asks.

The not-twin on her left falters, but only for a second. "Those are our private treatment rooms, Mrs. Williams. For our more experienced clients."

The other not-twin claps her hands together. "Not to worry, though, I'm sure we'll get to know your specific needs soon enough."

Jasmyn laughs. Now she understands why the woman faltered before. She doesn't want Jasmyn to feel as if she's being excluded from some "experience." Jasmyn almost wants to allay her concerns by telling her that she has no intention of joining the Wellness Center, let alone ascending any sort of ridiculous and, frankly, cultish-sounding hierarchy.

After a while they arrive at an empty waiting room decorated with cream sofas and recliners topped with plush pillows and throws.

"Slow night?" Jasmyn asks one of the not-twins, taking note of the fact that she's alone.

The woman only smiles and hands her a slim gray leather folder embossed with WELLNESS MENU in gold foil. The menu itself is made from heavy cream paper, the kind you'd use for wedding invitations or funerals.

Jesus. The amount of money they're spending on this place. Jasmyn knows it won't do her any good to dwell on the number of homeless Black kids they could house here. Or the treatment rooms that could become dormitories. Or how there'd be plenty of space for community gatherings. Not to mention the job training programs they could sponsor with the money they rake in. The rehab and gang intervention programs and the—

She stops and forces herself to relax and focus on the menu. It's divided into three sections: Mind, Body, and Spirit. The difference between Mind and Spirit has never been clear to Jasmyn. The whole menu reeks of cultural appropriation and reads like a foreign language. *Cranial sacral reiki healing attunement acroyoga vata kapha pitta ayurvedic doshas.* How can she choose when she has no idea what they're even talking about? Should she choose Binaural Beats Therapy to balance her energy fields? What about a Chakra Sound Chamber or some Singing Bowl Therapy or an Interactive Aura Reading or Aural Photography or a Full Moon Bathing Ritual? Most of the therapies focus on "healing for the whole body" or the "releasing of toxic energies."

Jasmyn sets the menu down and flicks it away from her with the tips of her nails. They can't be serious, these people. She can't believe that this is what King has been wasting his time with. He'd never been interested in spas before.

In a peripheral way, Jasmyn has always suspected that the self-care industry was a scam gone too far. Now, she's sure of it. The world would be a better place if people spent more time taking care of one another instead of just taking care of themselves.

Still, she has to choose something. She sighs, picks the menu up, and continues from where she left off. Her eyes snag on *Past-Life Regression.* Even if that was a thing that was possible, what Black person in America would choose to do that? So they could regress to being enslaved? Or to being in the Jim Crow south? Or to the end of Reconstruction?

Black people certainly could not afford to be nostalgic in this country.

In the end, she decides on a manicure and a pregnancy massage.

"Excellent selection, Mrs. Williams," says the shorter of the not-twins. She leads Jasmyn back through the labyrinth of treatment rooms. They pass the locked room, the one with the security panel again. Jasmyn looks at the door, curious to catch a glimpse of the sort of person who has climbed far enough up the hierarchy to be allowed back there. A red light on the panel blinks once. Jasmyn stares at it, waiting for it to blink again.

Leave, thinks Jasmyn.

The thought is sudden and insistent and inexplicable.

Leave.

Jasmyn shakes her head, trying to clear it.

Leave.

The red light blinks again, and the thought vanishes as suddenly as it came.

"Are you OK? Mrs. Williams?" one of the women asks. Her concern is evident.

Jasmyn looks around, confused by her own reaction. She presses a hand to her thrashing heart. "I—yes," she stammers out. "I'm fine. I don't know what came over me." She looks past the women and down the long hallway. The exit is back there somewhere. Maybe she *should* leave.

But why? There's no danger here. She rolls her neck and shoulders, willing herself to calm down. King really is right about her needing to relax.

"I'm fine," she says again to the women. "Lead the way."

12

The treatments are wonderful. The massage table has an opening for her belly that offers support without discomfort. The room smells of plumeria and her therapist's hands find knots in muscles she didn't know she had. When was the last time she'd been pain-free in her neck and shoulders? She leaves the room feeling boneless.

Her manicure is overly elaborate but, again, wonderful. The woman massages Jasmyn's hands and soaks them in a series of "infusion serums" that leave them feeling miraculously soft, as if they'd never known a day's hard work.

The not-twins are waiting for her outside the nail salon. "I trust everything was to your satisfaction, Mrs. Williams," says one of them.

"It was," says Jasmyn, surprised at how much she enjoyed herself.

"Excellent," says the other not-twin.

Again, Jasmyn follows as they lead her through more doors and around another series of hallways.

"How do you all not get lost in here?" Jasmyn jokes. "I'd never find my way without—"

Before she can finish her sentence, someone wails. A woman. It's a keening sound, high and hollow. The sudden, treacherous violence of fresh grief.

Jasmyn freezes. She can feel her heartbeat in the soft palate of her throat.

Up ahead, the door with the security panel is slightly ajar. The scream came from in there, she's sure of it.

Quickly now, she heads for the door. It slams shut just as she reaches it.

She spins to face the not-twins. "What was that?" she asks. The baby kicks. Jasmyn cradles her stomach with her hands. "What the hell kind of treatments are you doing back there?"

Alarm flashes across the face of the taller not-twin. But then, she smooths it to the pleasant-enough, transactional smile of customer service. "That was nothing to worry about, Mrs. Williams," she says.

Jasmyn is more than worried. She's afraid. "Someone was screaming for their life," she whispers, hand at her throat.

"Mrs. Williams, I assure you that all of our treatments are patient directed and safe," says the shorter one. She reaches out, gesturing for Jasmyn to continue on, but Jasmyn backs away.

"You expect me to believe that someone asked for whatever made them scream like that?"

"Sometimes the muscles in my neck get so tight, it hurts to get a massage," says the shorter not-twin.

The taller one nods her agreement. "That's certainly happened to me as well," she says.

"Sometimes even an exfoliation can do it," says the first.

"Especially if you have a lot of blackheads that are rooted deeply," explains the second.

Both women are speaking in the soothing, singsong voice you'd use on a child who's spooked from a bad dream or a sinister-looking shadow.

But she's not a child and this is not a dream. She knows what she heard.

Again, she thinks of the armed security guards and heavy gates at the entrance. She remembers the Sayles and how they'd secured the door to the spa inside their own home. Jasmyn stares at the blond-wood door as if somehow its blank face can tell her what she doesn't know.

"Mrs. Williams, shall we continue on to the salon?" the shorter not-twin asks. "Mr. Williams and the others are waiting for you there."

"King's here?" Jasmyn says. Relief floods her. She straightens, feeling suddenly silly. King comes here all the time and he's never once said he found it strange or unsettling. She forces herself to take a deep breath, and then another. Of course it's just some treatment. What else could it be? This kind of stress is not good for the baby. "Yes, let's go," she says.

Both women smile. "Wonderful."

Finally, they arrive at a set of enormous gray double doors.

"Is there anything else we can do for you, Mrs. Williams?" one of them asks.

"No," Jasmyn says, already pushing through the door, eager to see King. "Thanks for your help."

But the room—the salon—is empty when she walks inside. It's a large, circular space with shimmering white walls and cathedral ceilings. Like the "environment" she'd seen before, thin sheets of water cascade down the walls, this time tipping over kinetic bamboo obstacles. The air smells perfumed and expensive.

It also looks set up for a party. Fresh fruit and cheese plates sit atop fluted white-and-gold cocktail tables. Against the back wall, white velvet booths surround marble tables.

Clear blue glass bottles of Awake water are everywhere. Jasmyn smiles and makes a note to tell King how good they look.

Only then does she remember that the not-twins had said, "King *and the others.*" Is she about to get a hard sell to join? It's true she'd had a good massage, but hearing that scream destroyed any feeling of relaxation she'd had. This whole operation with its woo-woo therapies is just too out there for her taste.

Across the room, a door she hadn't noticed opens.

It's King.

She practically runs into his arms. "Why didn't you tell me you were going to be here?"

"Thought I'd surprise you," he says.

"You called Tania?" she asks. Tania, a college junior, was an old neighbor of theirs. She'd been babysitting Kamau since he was four.

King shakes his head like she's crazy for even asking. "Nah, I left him alone," he jokes.

"Dumb question," she says.

He smiles wide at her and his eyes crinkle.

Something inside Jasmyn trips. His smile—the easy joy of it—takes her back to the day they met. She'd been at a bar waiting for her girlfriends to show up. He had come up to her and said they were destined to meet. It was corny, but it worked on her. He'd been so beautiful—rich dark skin, bright black eyes, and full lips. It wasn't just his looks she fell for, though. It was his attentiveness, too. He listened to her like no one else, remembered all her little likes and dislikes, every word of their conversations.

Now something about seeing him in a foreign space reminds her of just how physically attractive he is. And, even after all their years together, he's always tuning in to her needs.

Still, if she's being honest with herself, there's a kind of weary exhaustion to him lately. His long hours are piling up. And, of course, because he's Black and this is America, he has to work twice as hard to get half as far. On top of that, she's insisting he go back to volunteering with the Mentor LA program.

Is it her fault he looks so tired these days? Is her insatiable drive to make the world better part of the reason he spends so much time in this place?

He tilts her head up and kisses her on the lips. "What treatments did you get?" he asks.

Before she can answer, the door he'd come in through opens again. Ten or so people walk in. Jasmyn recognizes a few of them. Catherine

Vail, who'd gossiped to Keisha and others at school about Jasmyn being "such a mess" after the news broke about Tyrese and Mercy Simpson. She sees the Wrights, the ones whose foyer smelled like a lavender factory. Behind them are Angela and Benjamin Sayles. This time, Jasmyn is relieved to see, they're not naked. Like King—and everyone else except for Jasmyn—they're wearing white silk robes. She fingers the belt of her own robe. Black for nonmembers, she guesses. That certainly makes it easy to identify who belongs and who doesn't.

Instead of heading to a table or mingling with one another, they form a circle in the room's center.

"Gimme one second, baby," King says. He walks over to the group and enters the circle between Angela Sayles and someone that Jasmyn doesn't know.

They all join hands and close their eyes.

The image of the laughing yoga people in the park flashes through Jasmyn's mind.

"This is a sacred space," says Catherine Vail. Her voice is low and hoarse.

"This is a sacred space," the others repeat in unison.

"This is a healing space," says Angela Sayles.

As before, the others repeat it.

"This is our space," says Benjamin Sayles.

"This is our space," they all repeat.

Benjamin Sayles again: "Eyes on the prize."

"Eyes on the prize." This last response is louder. It has the quality of an amen at the end of a sermon. They release one another's hands and open their eyes.

Jasmyn covers her mouth. She's not sure if she finds this bizarre spectacle hilarious or horrifying.

Back at her side, King takes her hand and whispers into her ear. "Before you say anything, I know it's kind of out there. It's just this little ritual they do."

Jasmyn looks up at him. "Baby, it's more than *out there*. It's like you're all in a cult."

He lets go of her hand and gives her that look—the weary-down-to-the-bones one.

"I'm sorry," she says, feeling guilty. "I don't mean to make fun. I know you like this place."

"Just give them a chance. For me," he says.

She hears the plea in his voice. "OK, baby."

His easy smile is back, and she's glad she apologized. This place is ludicrous but ultimately harmless. The scream from earlier rises in her mind again. Maybe not *harmless* exactly, but she's sure those "experienced" clients know exactly the harm they're signing up for.

King throws his arm around her shoulders. "Now, let me introduce you to some people."

She presses in close to him. "Can't we just go home?"

"Not yet. This reception is for *you*. They do it for all potential members." He squeezes her shoulder. "Folks here just want to get to know you."

She's being interviewed? For something she doesn't even want? And why hadn't King warned her about this before?

Jasmyn grabs his hand and tugs him off to the side. "I don't care what they want," she says. "Why would you blindside me like this?"

King palms the back of his neck, immediately contrite. "You're right. I'm sorry. I should've checked with you."

She folds her arms across her chest. "Damn right you should've."

King nods. "Let me just go tell them we're not up for it tonight."

She sighs, puts a hand on his shoulder to stop him. "No, wait. It's all right." She doesn't want to stay and mingle, but she doesn't want to cause any kind of scene or set any tongues wagging, either. "I'll do it. But you're going to have to make it up to me."

"Root beer floats forever," he says.

"That was already in the marriage contract," she jokes. "You gotta come up with something else."

He smiles and kisses her forehead. "I'll think of something."

She sighs. "Let's just get this over with."

One by one, people drift over. First are the Sayles. Jasmyn squeezes

King's hand and he squeezes back. They'd laughed together for a full twenty minutes when she told him about their naked massages. "You just never know what people are really like behind closed doors," King had said.

Now Benjamin Sayles shakes King's hand. Angela Sayles leans in for air kisses. This close, she's even more flawless than Jasmyn remembers. Benjamin, too. They're like walking advertisements for the benefits of plastic surgery. *How much of their faces are real?* she wonders. Maybe they practice their plastic surgery skills on each other.

Next is Catherine Vail, her hair wrapped up in a white microfiber towel. On her tall, slim body, the robe seems like evening wear.

"Nice to see you again," she says. Jasmyn just shakes her hand.

Another woman who Jasmyn swears she knows from somewhere is next. Before the woman can introduce herself, the door opens again.

Jasmyn feels King's shock. He pulls his arm from her shoulders, claps his hands together, and shouts his excitement across the room. "Carlton, man, I didn't think you were going to make it."

The atmosphere in the room shifts to a kind of hushed excitement, as if a celebrity has entered the room, but they've all agreed not to gush. He *is* a kind of celebrity, she supposes, since he founded Liberty in the first place.

Carlton Way looks the same as he did the last, and only, time she met him, three years ago. He's well over six feet tall and everything about him is broad and solid. From looking at him, you'd guess linebacker, not finance guru. His head is bald, purposely shaved, and he has no facial hair.

His walk, as he heads over to them, is equal parts swagger and authority. Jasmyn remembers this about him, his expectation to be noticed and deferred to. Like the first time she met him, she finds his attitude fascinating and irritating.

She puts a smile on her face, ready to be re-introduced, but Carlton doesn't look at her once. He and King dap and back-slap each other as they hug. She watches the genuine happiness on King's face. Usually he talks about Carlton like he's his boss and mentor but watching them now, it's clear they're closer. They seem almost familial. Carlton could be an older brother.

"Was hoping you would make it," King says.

"Wouldn't miss it. Just had to rearrange some things so I could be here." Carlton has the smooth, reassuring voice of a pilot.

His words make King smile even wider. He's the kid at Christmas who's gotten everything on his list. "I appreciate that," King says. He turns to Jasmyn. "Baby, you remember Carlton Way."

"Of course," she says.

Carlton leans in and kisses both her cheeks. Jasmyn won't swear to it in a court of law, but she's almost certain he sniffs her.

"And how is the war against racism going?" he asks.

Jasmyn is momentarily too surprised to speak. Of all the things he could ask her about first—being a mother or being pregnant or being a public defender—he chooses to ask her about racism? Is that what he thinks the most important thing about her is, her fight against racism? She doesn't even remember talking much about it at that first dinner.

"I heard you were upset earlier," he says, changing the subject.

King squeezes her shoulder, concerned. "Did something happen?"

Carlton chuckles and responds before Jasmyn has a chance to. "It's nothing," he says to King. "She heard one of our advanced clients releasing, is all."

Releasing? *That's* what he's calling it? And why would the not-twins bother to tell him about the incident at all?

"That woman was *screaming*," Jasmyn says.

"The process of releasing painful things is often painful," Carlton says. He gives her a look somewhere between amused and patronizing.

If he weren't King's boss, she'd tell him what she really thought of this place.

Carlton laughs. "I see Liberty hasn't quite rubbed off on you yet."

And now what does that mean? She turns to King, expecting to share a confused look with him, but he doesn't seem to notice anything is off. They'll have words about it later. She knows he's grateful to Carlton for everything he's done to change their lives, but that doesn't mean he needs to put blinders on where the man is concerned.

"All right, all right, stop hogging time with the new girl," says the older woman that Carlton had forestalled before.

Jasmyn turns toward her, never more grateful to be interrupted by a stranger. The other woman is short and round with skin as dark as Jasmyn's. She looks to be in her midsixties. And, thank God, she wears her graying hair natural, in a short, tightly coiled Afro.

She has one of those friendly, quick-to-laugh faces. Again, Jasmyn feels as if she's met her before, but can't quite place her.

Instead of giving her a double-cheek kiss, the woman holds out her hand for a shake. "I'm Nina. Nice to meet you, Jasmyn."

"Likewise."

"How are you finding your wellness experience?" Nina asks.

Jasmyn starts to answer but Nina interrupts. "Wait, let me guess. You liked the pregnancy massage and the manicure, but you can't figure out why anyone would do any of the other ridiculous therapies on the menu." She laughs, a high, merry, contagious sound. "Am I right?"

Jasmyn smiles a genuine smile at the woman. "How'd you guess?"

"I'm a psychiatrist. Hazards of the trade."

Now Jasmyn understands why she's so familiar. Her full name is Nina Marks. She used to be a brain surgeon but is now a psychiatrist. She has a popular relationship therapy podcast, and sometimes she's on TV as an expert on trauma, too. She's one of those impossibly smart people.

"How are you adjusting to life in Liberty?" Nina asks.

"I'm adjusting fine," Jasmyn says.

Nina laughs her high laugh again. She leans in and stage-whispers, "Don't worry. When we first moved here, my husband hated it, too."

"She doesn't hate it," King says.

Jasmyn looks at him. "Baby, I can speak for myself," she says.

Next to King, Carlton grins like he's enjoying himself immensely. How upset would King be, she wonders, if she asked Carlton what his damn problem is. Probably very.

She turns back to Nina. "Like King said, I don't hate it at all." She's not sure why Nina jumped to that conclusion. "Like *I* said, I'm still adjusting, getting my bearings."

King nods his agreement.

Nina laughs some more. "Kingston and Carlton, be dears and let us women alone, would you, please?"

King looks between them and smiles. "All right, all right, I see how it is. This is a man-free zone." He kisses Jasmyn's forehead. He and Carlton cross the room together.

Nina touches her arm. "Come on, let's go and spill all the tea, shall we?"

≈

"First things first," Nina Marks says as soon as they're sitting in one of the booths. "Did you really enjoy your therapies?"

Jasmyn rolls her shoulders before answering. "Probably the best massage I've ever had," she says, truthfully.

"We're glad to hear it," Nina says. "And I hope you weren't too bothered by Catherine's . . . theatrics." Here Nina pauses to smile and wink before finishing her sentence. "She can be quite dramatic."

Jasmyn hides her surprise by picking up and examining one of the Awake bottles. King was right about the caffeine content being high.

Was it really Catherine Vail who'd screamed? The woman seemed too unfeeling for all that.

And why is Nina Marks bringing this up again? The charitable part of Jasmyn thinks Nina is simply checking in, making sure she had an enjoyable experience. The less charitable part of her thinks both she and Carlton want to ensure she doesn't gossip and sully the spa's reputation.

Jasmyn decides to go with the more charitable explanation. "I didn't expect it and overreacted a bit. I'm fine now."

Nina seems relieved. "Glad to hear it," she says. "Why don't we eat and get to know each other?"

As soon as Nina suggests it, Jasmyn realizes how hungry she is. She picks up her fruit and cheese plate and eats while Nina Marks fills her in on her own journey to Liberty.

"I'd known Carlton for some time, but it wasn't until after the Phillip Jackson murder that he approached me with the idea for Liberty."

Jasmyn nods. That murder had galvanized all types of people. The protests she'd gone to were at least 20 to 30 percent non-Black. She remembers reading article after article speculating about why this murder—among the myriad murders—seemed to hit a nerve. Most opinions coalesced around the fact that in the recording you could hear him pleading for his life. "Please," he'd begged. "It's not me. It's not me." Jasmyn remembers vomiting in a bathroom stall at her work the first time she heard it. In the days after the murder, the media followed its standard operating procedure and went digging into the victim's background, trying to find something criminal in his past to justify his murder. They found nothing. He was a college student with no record of any kind. He was on his way home from a study group.

Even now, all these years later, nausea rolls through Jasmyn just thinking about it. She puts down her plate.

Nina reaches out and takes her hand. "I feel it, too."

Jasmyn looks up to find her own pain mirrored in the other woman's face. Something tight and wary inside Jasmyn loosens. Nina Marks *understands*. She squeezes Nina's hand. "Thanks for that," she says.

"Of course," says Nina.

From there they move on to talking about Nina's old neighborhood, Beverly Hills.

"What was that like?"

Nina shakes her head. "I never met a more uptight, entitled, and fragile group of people."

Jasmyn laughs. "I know that's right," she says.

Nina continues on. She and her husband have two boys, fifteen and seventeen, and she wants them to spend time in a place where they don't have to worry about their safety.

Jasmyn wants to ask Nina when she'd given her boys the Talk, but she already likes the woman and doesn't want to confess to her that King hadn't yet sat Kamau down for it. She doesn't want Nina to think she's being neglectful or, worse, derelict in her duty to her son.

Talking to Nina Marks is easy. It occurs to Jasmyn that it's probably because the woman is good at drawing people out. She's a psychiatrist, after all. Still, she finds herself relaxing. She doesn't feel the need to be watchful or cautious with her words. She feels as if she's in the company of good friends in a place she belongs. Maybe Nina Marks can give her the real inside scoop on Liberty.

Jasmyn leans forward as far as her belly will allow. "So you said your husband hated it when you first moved here. What did he hate exactly?"

Nina laughs and nods like she's been waiting for this question. "He felt exactly the way that I'm sure you feel. He loved the sense of security and peace and Black excellence that Liberty has to offer. But he also worried that by living here he was abandoning his roots and his people. He felt like he was betraying the community by becoming wealthy and living far away from where he came up."

Jasmyn is surprised by just how well Nina Marks understands her misgivings. "How did he get over those feelings?"

"He made a new community *here* with like-minded people," she says. "And of course, he still works hard to help his old one."

Jasmyn leans back. "To be honest with you, I've been trying to find community, but so far I'm coming up short."

"Well, you and I only just met, right? We're like-minded," Nina says with a smile. "These things take time. You'll find what you need. I'm sure of it."

Jasmyn nods and leans forward to spear a last bite of cheese. Nina Marks is right. It's been only a few weeks. So what if she hasn't found and settled in with a full community of her kind of people yet? It's only a matter of time until she does. She's being impatient.

For the next forty or so minutes they talk about where they went to school and where they met their husbands. They talk about the struggle to balance motherhood with a meaningful career. They talk about how hard it is to be a successful Black woman.

"What's the most difficult part of your job?" Nina asks.

"All the racism," Jasmyn says. She laughs even though she's not joking. Nina seems to know that and waits for her to continue.

Jasmyn tells her about the prejudice inherent in the legal system. She talks about the gangs and the drugs and how hard it is to get kids out of that life.

"And then once they're in the system, that's it. It's like a hungry beast. Sometimes I feel like our kids exist only to feed it. Sometimes I feel like the beast might eat me, too."

Nina Marks looks at her.

There's a clanging part of Jasmyn that realizes she's revealed more than she normally would. She has the sensation that everyone is watching her, but when she glances around the room no one is.

"I understand how you feel," Nina says. "I understand just how hard the work can be." During the course of their conversation, Jasmyn learns that, along with relationship counseling, Nina works with veterans and anyone else dealing with trauma. She even does pro bono work for community clinics that help deprogram former gang bangers. "Trauma is a tricky thing," says Nina. "We're only now realizing just how deeply it affects all parts of the body—our brains of course, but also our nervous system, and even our hormones. It's a fascinating area of study. Once you can locate trauma in the body, you can really begin to treat it."

Jasmyn nods along, fascinated and impressed by Nina's obvious passion. "Do you ever get overwhelmed by all the trauma you see?"

Nina shakes her head. "At heart, I'm a physician. Every case presents an opportunity for me to cure, to make someone's life better."

"Incredible," Jasmyn says. "As a Black woman and a mother and a public defender, I want to say how much I appreciate you and the work you do. Especially with the ex–gang bangers and what have you. So many of our boys get written off," she says.

"It's a terrible shame," says Nina.

One of those small moments of quiet descends on the room. It lasts for only a moment before the din rises again.

"Do you remember the first time you realized you were Black?" Nina asks.

They're firmly out of small talk territory now but, again, Jasmyn finds she doesn't mind. Maybe this is the way of things when you're talking to a psychiatrist. If Jasmyn's job makes her inherently suspicious, maybe Nina's job makes her inherently ask probing, personal questions.

"I've always been Black," Jasmyn says. "No realization to be had."

"No, you've always had brown skin," Nina says, and rubs a finger over her own forearm. "You haven't always been Black." She put air quotes around Black.

Now Jasmyn understands and she's a little disappointed to be honest. Nina is too smart for the academic argument she's no doubt going to make. Her next sentence will be about race being a construct or something else not remotely useful. It isn't even that Jasmyn disagrees, but, in the end, who cares if race is a construct? The barriers it erects are real enough.

Jasmyn shakes her head and reiterates. "I've been Black as long as I can remember," she says.

Nina Marks leans in. "And when did you first realize what a huge problem that was?"

The question chases away the fog of good feeling that had cocooned her. Again, she feels the sensation that she's being watched. Again, when she checks, no one is.

"My Blackness is not a problem. *Racism* is the problem." She doesn't mean for it to sound as angry as it does, but her anger doesn't seem to faze the other woman. It seems to Jasmyn that Nina Marks had been expecting it. It seems to Jasmyn that Nina Marks may even have provoked it.

Jasmyn looks for King and finds him already walking toward her. She scoots to the edge of her seat and prepares to heave herself to standing. "Well, it's time to get this one home to bed," she says, nodding down at her stomach.

"Of course," says Nina. She seems amused.

"Is something funny?" Jasmyn asks.

Nina Marks's eyes grow merrier still. "Yes," she says.

Finally King is at Jasmyn's side. He puts his hand on her lower back. "Ready?"

She nods. More than ready.

Nina Marks extends her hand. "It was a real treat getting to know you," she says.

A few minutes ago Jasmyn would've felt the same. A few minutes ago she was ready to text Keisha that she'd found another of their kind. Now she just feels let down. Does Nina Marks really think being Black is a *problem*?

"Nice meeting you too," Jasmyn says.

"We'll see each other again," says Nina Marks. "I'm sure of it."

Jasmyn slips her arm around King's waist, presses herself close. After he says his goodbyes, he steers them through the labyrinth of treatment rooms, and she tries not to resent how well he knows his way around the place.

When they get home, Tania tells them Kamau isn't feeling very well. She'd tried calling to tell them, but both their cellphones went straight to voicemail. Jasmyn finds him burning up under his covers. Here is where she should've been tonight, at home with her baby boy instead of indulging in self-care nonsense. She wakes Kamau up just enough to give him some medicine and changes him out of his damp pajamas into nice clean, dry ones. She climbs into bed with him and nuzzles his impossibly soft cheek. His eyes open briefly. "Love you, Moms," he says, and snuggles deep into her arms.

"I love you, too, baby boy." She stays with him, checking his temperature every few minutes until, finally, his fever drops.

By the time Jasmyn climbs into bed with King, she's exhausted. Still, she doesn't want to end the night without letting him know how she feels about the Wellness Center. "Baby, you don't think it's strange there?" she asks. "The people seem kind of off to me."

He sighs and props himself up on an elbow to look at her. "I told you it was just a dumb ritual," he says.

But it's not just them holding hands and chanting that's bothering her. It's Catherine Vail screaming, and the fact that Carlton Way made light of Jasmyn's reaction to the screaming, and the way Nina Marks said Blackness was a problem.

She doesn't bother to say any of that to him. He's defensive about the place and she's too tired to argue.

It occurs to her then that no one had actually extended an invitation to join the spa and, after all, hadn't that been the purpose of her visit in the first place? She says as much to King.

"But baby, you didn't like it," he says. "You didn't want to join in the first place, right?"

"Yeah, but they don't know that," she says.

King shifts to lie on his back. He throws a hand over his eyes. "Who knows, maybe they'll still ask," he says.

"They can ask all they want, I won't be joining," Jasmyn says.

King half laughs, half sighs. "You know you not making any sense right now, right?"

She knows, but still she doesn't like that they didn't ask her.

Her dreams that night are terrifying and obvious. She's trapped inside the Wellness Center, lost in the maze of hallways and treatment rooms. From somewhere close, King and Kamau are yelling for her. "Help us," they beg. "Please help us."

She stumbles down hallway after hallway, her hugely pregnant stomach shifting painfully with each step.

"Where are you?" she yells. "I don't know where you are."

But no matter how much she searches, she can't find them. No matter how much she screams for them, they're always just beyond her reach.

Delineating the Impact of Racial Trauma on Black Americans and the Black Diaspora

Nina Marks, PsyD, PhD, MD

ABSTRACT

Since the dawn of slavery, Black Americans and members of the Black diaspora residing in the United States have experienced and been negatively impacted by structural racism. In slavery's long shadow, these groups still suffer health inequities and socio-economic disadvantages.

In this study, the author presents a comprehensive review of the growing body of research literature detailing these findings.

The author ends the review by proposing a method for measuring the physiological effects of racial trauma on the Black body and psyche.

Keywords: race, racism, racial trauma, PTSD

13

The following week doesn't improve much. The harrowing feeling from Jasmyn's dream lingers, leaving a pall over the days. Kamau is too sick for school and stays home for most of the week. Jasmyn loses a case that she thought she had a good chance of winning. And, on top of all that, she and King get into it about him finding another young man to mentor through Mentor LA. He says he will, but what Jasmyn wants to know is *when*. After the argument, she feels guilty for pressuring him while he's working so diligently, but she also doesn't want him to forget that their first duty is to their community.

By the time Keisha texts on Wednesday, Jasmyn is ready for something to go right.

Keisha: I found someone
Keisha: Blackity black black black
Keisha: Blaaaaaaaacccccccckkkkk

Jasmyn stops climbing the courthouse steps to laugh. She texts back.

Jasmyn: You sure?
Jasmyn: Can't take any more of these post-racial blacks
Keisha: Yaaasss I'm sure
Keisha: His name is Charles
Keisha: He's an architect if you can believe that
Keisha: I checked for his black card and everything
Keisha: He's legit
Keisha: Wants to meet for drinks later
Keisha: You in?

But Kamau is still sick and she needs to get home and relieve King, who'd taken the day off to be with him. They decide to meet on Friday.

By the time she gets home, Kamau's fever has broken. King apologizes for their fight and promises he's just a couple of weeks away from rejoining Mentor LA. Right before bed, she checks in on the Mercy Simpson case. Grand jury proceedings were set to start in a couple of weeks. She hopes for all their sakes that the jurors make the right decision.

"God knows," she says to King, "this city will burn if they don't indict that cop."

Jasmyn can picture the protests even now. Who, she wonders, from Liberty will join her if and when the time comes?

14

"The only way to make this country not racist is for all the white people to die off," says Charles.

Keisha guffaws and takes another big sip of bourbon.

Jasmyn laughs, too, but looking at him, she isn't sure Charles is joking.

He waits for them to stop laughing. "Hear me out. It's been one hundred and fifty-seven years since the end of slavery. The Civil Rights Act passed in 1964 and the Voting Rights Act passed in '65 and we still dealing with racist bullshit. To paraphrase James Baldwin, all this mess has taken our grandfather's time, and our father's time, and how long are we supposed to wait for their progress?" He sips his wine. "Seal them in a barrel and send them out to sea is what I say."

Jasmyn laughs again and reads the *told you so* look on Keisha's face. She'd been right about Charles being a real one. Still, even though she understands where he's coming from—how tired he is of waiting for progress—wanting to seal white people in a barrel is beyond extreme.

The three of them are sitting on an outdoor couch in Charles's sprawling, flower-filled backyard garden. It's one of those gardens designed to seem wild and overgrown, but it's actually meticulously planned. Jasmyn is sure the landscaping bill is hefty. It's beautiful though, filled with lavender, jasmine, and rosemary plus other plants and flowers she doesn't know the names of. There's a large avocado tree toward the back and smaller lemon and lime trees on the side.

They'd planned on going out to a bar, but Charles changed things at the last minute. His wife was supposed to stay home to take delivery of a piece of art he'd commissioned, but something had come up at her job. The delivery needed someone to sign for it, and so he'd invited them to his house instead.

Jasmyn's not sure who she expected when Keisha said she'd found a "Blackity black black black" architect, but the man in front of her isn't it. He's well over six feet tall and rail thin with long, skinny locs that hang to the middle of his back. His complexion is on the darker side of brown and Jasmyn has never seen cheekbones so high on a man. In another life he could be a model. His charcoal suit is perfectly fitted.

Jasmyn pours herself a glass of lemonade from the pitcher Charles had set out. She leans back against the couch cushions. Nina Simone is playing softly on hidden speakers. The sun has just set and the evening air is cool.

"So, how long have you lived here?" Jasmyn asks. She sips her lemonade. It's just barely sweet, the way she likes it.

"Five months, twenty-two days, and eighteen hours too long," Charles says, and laughs one of those loud, contagious laughs that makes you want to laugh with him.

"Lord, that's about a month longer than me," Keisha says.

"But why don't you like it?" Jasmyn asks, intrigued. Yes, she has her own misgivings but ultimately she knows the good of Liberty far outweighs the bad of a handful of careless, self-involved people.

Charles grips his wineglass by the stem and spreads his arms out over the top of the couch. "What's to like?" he asks. "Asha, my wife, is the one who wanted to move here. I mean I didn't object too much to the move. I liked the *idea* of it."

"I felt the exact same way," Keisha says, nodding.

Charles drains the last of his wine. "This place is supposed to be some kind of utopia, right? But it doesn't feel utopian to me. The people here are . . . different."

"Too rich?" Jasmyn asks.

"Nah, not that. It's like their Blackness is a coat they're wearing, one they can just shrug off any old time, you know what I'm saying?"

Jasmyn nods. Yes, *this* is what she'd been feeling with the Sayles and the Wrights and Catherine Vail and even Nina Marks. Like their Blackness is only skin deep.

Charles pours himself another glass. "And don't get me started on that Wellness Center they got going on. Asha might as well take out a mortgage on that place for all the time she spends up in there getting healing salts rubbed all over her body or whatever."

"I was just there a few nights ago," Jasmyn confesses.

Charles gives Keisha a look that's not hard to read: *You sure about her?*

Jasmyn rushes to explain herself. "My husband's been on me to try it out."

Charles nods, but the skepticism is still on his face. "So, what, you a convert now?" he asks.

"Who you kidding?" Jasmyn puts her glass down louder than she means to. "It's ridiculous up there. Bunch of bougie Black folks talking 'bout self-care all day. Couldn't be me."

"You never did tell me how it was," Keisha says.

Jasmyn means to say that it was fine, that the massage was good, etc. But what she says instead is: "Someone was screaming." Her heart kicks at the memory of it. The sound had been so beyond hope. All at once, she can't quite catch her breath.

"Hey now, you doing OK?" Keisha asks, grabbing her hand. "You're not about to give birth, are you?"

"Jesus God, no," Charles says.

Jasmyn takes a deep breath, surprised by her own reaction. "I'm fine," she says.

Keisha lets go of her hand and leans back. "You better be fine. I'm not out here trying to deliver any babies."

Jasmyn sips her lemonade and wills herself to relax.

"Let me get this straight. You heard someone screaming and you didn't get the hell out of there?" Charles says. "You sure you're Black?"

Jasmyn sees on his face that he's only half joking, that he's still wondering whose side she's on. He'd figure it out soon enough, she thinks. That thought pulls her up short. It's strange that here, in Liberty, she should have to prove which side she is on. Shouldn't there be only one side?

"The staff explained what was going on to me," Jasmyn says.

"But it's not sitting right with you," says Keisha.

Jasmyn nods. She still can't quite put her finger on what's bothering her, but she can't deny anymore that something *is* bothering her. The same part of her that knows when a cop or a defendant is lying is clanging for her attention.

"Let me ask you something," Keisha says. "They do that chanting thing?"

"Eyes on the prize," Jasmyn whispers.

"Eyes on the fucking prize," Keisha whispers back.

"This is a goddamn cult y'all are talking about," Charles says.

Keisha turns to Charles. "You been up there?"

"Asha's been on me about it for months, but I keep dodging her." He shakes his head. "Probably just a matter of time before I have to give in. In the interest of marital harmony," he says.

"Well, maybe they'll invite *you* to join," says Jasmyn.

Keisha whips her head around. "They didn't invite you, either?"

Jasmyn shakes her head. "King says he hasn't heard anything from them about it."

"Guess we don't seem like the type to drink the Kool-Aid," Keisha says.

Jasmyn laughs, then turns serious. "But I wanted to ask you: You meet a woman named Nina Marks when you were up there?"

"Sure did," Keisha says. "I don't think she liked me very much. Talking to her felt more like a psych evaluation than a conversation." She purses her lips, considering. "She's not all bad, though. Got me documenting all the racist things that I can remember for some big-deal research grant she got."

Jasmyn raises her eyebrows. "She didn't ask me to do anything like that."

"I'm sure it's just a matter of time," Keisha says with a shrug.

"Definitely a cult," Charles says. He laughs freely and Jasmyn can tell he's not feeling skeptical about her loyalties anymore. "You know that place was always meant to be the centerpiece of Liberty?"

"What's that mean?" Keisha asks.

"I thought maybe it was something that got added after Liberty was founded, but it wasn't. I looked into the city planning and zoning docs and all that after we moved here. Should've looked into them *before* we moved." He sips a fresh glass of wine. "Anyway, they *always* planned for the Wellness Center to be up on that hill looking down on everything. You believe that?" He takes another sip. "A different kind of place would put a church up on that hill, you know what I'm saying?"

Jasmyn's heart rate kicks up at this information. Is *that* what's bothering her? The way it seems like the people of Liberty worship a different God than the one she knows?

Charles leans forward and refills her lemonade. "Anyway, enough about all that. Keisha tells me you're a public defender? Don't mind me, but most of the PDs I know can't afford to live—"

Before he can finish, the doorbell chimes. "That's my delivery," he says, springing to his feet. "Come on," he says. "You ladies are going to want to see this."

≈

The delivery men unload a large, flat, rectangular crate from their truck. Charles instructs them to follow him to the "museum wing."

Jasmyn thinks maybe he's exaggerating when he says "museum

wing." She pictures a medium-sized room with a few paintings hanging on the wall. But he isn't exaggerating. It really is a wing, three large interconnected rooms at the end of a long hallway.

The first room they enter contains what Jasmyn thinks of as African art, with hand-carved tribal masks and life-sized sculptures. The second room is dedicated to photographs, most of them in black and white. There's an enormous picture of a Black woman in her Sunday best. She's with her daughter standing under the COLORED ENTRANCE sign in front of a restaurant. Another photo is of police hosing down Black protestors in Alabama. Another is of Ku Klux Klan members at a rally. Jasmyn and Keisha tour the room and study the photos in silence. The third and final room is empty save for a single spotlight directed at a blank white wall with bracket mounts.

It takes the delivery men just a few minutes to open the crate. Charles stops them as they're about to unearth a painting.

"Ladies, do me a favor and close your eyes until they got it mounted on the wall. I want you to experience the whole thing in its full glory."

Jasmyn looks at Keisha to see if she's OK with it. Keisha grins and closes her eyes, up for anything like always.

Jasmyn closes her eyes, too. Of all the things she expected to be doing tonight, standing with her eyes closed in a private museum in the home of a rich Black man she's just met wasn't one of them.

The mounting only takes a few minutes. The sound of the delivery men's labored breathing and the creak of their stepladders lets Jasmyn know they're working. Charles instructs them how he wants it positioned until he's satisfied.

"I'll walk them out," Charles says. "You ladies can take a look now."

Jasmyn opens her eyes and gasps.

The painting is of a lynching.

No.

The aftermath of a lynching. The moment after they cut the body down, but before the congregation of white people desecrate it further. Before they cut off body parts to save as souvenirs. Before they take pictures and turn those pictures into postcards to be sent via mail to faraway family and friends. *Wish you were here.*

The victim's body lies on gray asphalt, his brown skin lurid with bruises, wounds spilling vivid reds and yellows and blues. But it's the white people in the audience that hold Jasmyn's attention. The artist has captured the wild, rabid joy of their hatred. Here, preserved, is their glee and their menace. Their hate is a sumptuous and extravagant thing.

Charles walks back into the room. "It's called *Aftermath*," he says.

Next to her, Keisha keens. Jasmyn takes her hand and squeezes.

"When is enough *enough*?" Keisha asks.

Charles is the one to answer. "It's never enough for them."

Sometimes Jasmyn will meet a defendant who has a soft helplessness that reminds her of Kamau. It's something in the bright blackness of his eyes. Or something in the way his hand clenches and opens and then clenches again. In those moments Jasmyn knows, given a chance, she would forfeit her present for a chance to remake the past. She would hide her continent from the relentless grasp of "explorers." She would dismantle the hulls of slave ships, board by board, with her bare hands. She would render stillborn the very idea of America.

But she can't remake the past, and there's no use wishing that she could. Jasmyn stares at the world that had once existed, a world that—if not for the constant vigilance of people like her and King and Keisha and Charles—could surely come again.

She steps closer to the painting, her movement almost involuntary. The paint is so thick in places it seems to her as if it might bleed into real life. As if it were simply waiting on permission or for the right moment to come alive. Inside her chest, her heart beats a familiar rhythm. Fear and anger. Anger and fear. She closes her eyes and wishes, just for a moment, she could teach her heart a different song and, too, some other history.

15

A week later, Jasmyn is making breakfast when King walks into the kitchen. He sniffs at the air. "You making ackee and saltfish?"

Jasmyn nods and gives the browning onions, tomato, and fish a stir. "Went back to our old hood to get it," she says.

King looks at her. "Why didn't you go to the Caribbean market here?"

Jasmyn shrugs. "Felt like checking in on Miss Maggie, see how she's doing." She doesn't add that she was feeling nostalgic for their old neighborhood.

"She still pinch your cheeks like you're not grown?" King asks.

Jasmyn laughs. Miss Maggie *had* pinched her cheeks and hugged her too long and too tight. But Jasmyn found that she didn't mind it.

"But I don't see you 'round here this long time," Miss Maggie said in her thick Jamaican accent.

Jasmyn reminded her that they'd moved. She was at the stage of old age where you had to tell her things multiple times before they stuck.

"Not to one of those white neighborhoods, I hope," Miss Maggie said.

"No, not one of the white ones," Jasmyn said and laughed.

Miss Maggie wanted to know more, but Jasmyn didn't want to talk about Liberty. She wanted to pretend that she was still from this neighborhood where everything was familiar.

Jasmyn shifted the conversation, asked after Miss Maggie's kids and grandkids. They were all doing fine. Business at the store was so-so. The neighborhood was doing all right, too. "It's too bad all you kids leave once you get a little success, though," she said.

She knew Miss Maggie didn't mean any offense, but Jasmyn felt a twinge of guilt for leaving like everyone else did.

They'd talked a while longer before Jasmyn left to spend some time checking out the rest of the neighborhood.

First, she'd walked to her and King's old apartment building. It had a new coat of paint that couldn't hide how shabby the building was. Still she'd gone into the little vestibule with the mailboxes and filled her lungs with familiar smells: floor polish, weed, and spicy foods. It was funny because when she lived there, she'd hated the odors, the way they seemed to seep into everything, her apartment, her clothes, her skin. In that moment, though, she'd found them oddly comforting, proof that she was once from someplace real. She picked at that thought. What did she mean by *real* exactly? That it is poor and, sometimes, not that safe? Did that make it more real than Liberty?

She left the building, walked down the main drag, and poked her head into the one Chinese restaurant. The man behind the bulletproof glass barely looked up at her. She walked by two wig shops and a barbershop. From the bakery on the corner, she bought herself a Jamaican beef patty. She didn't recognize any of the people working there. On the one hand, she was relieved that she knew no one. She hadn't wanted to make small talk and explain where she'd been all this time. On the other hand, though, not knowing anyone made her feel as if she were a balloon, untethered and drifting.

No one paid attention to her as she wandered the streets. Or, if they did, they didn't show it and she was grateful for that. She'd been afraid that people would look at her like she didn't belong, that somehow they'd know, from her clothes or her attitude or some indelible *something*, that she wasn't from around there, not anymore.

Beef patty in hand, she'd walked to her old bus stop, sat and ate and people-watched. She saw groups of laughing kids just out of school for the day. Probably some of them went to the school where King used to teach. She saw shift workers—nurses, security guards, and janitors—in uniform, all on their way to a long night of work.

What would they make of a place like Liberty? she wondered. What would they make of the Wellness Center? Of course they'd like it. Any one of those people would relish a giant house and disposable income. They'd relish a massage and a bit of pampering.

She'd stood then, a vague shame settling over her. What was she doing, coming back here, acting like a tourist? Compared with how hard life could be, what did she have to worry about?

Now, though, she doesn't say any of this to King. How to explain to him that she'd felt more herself, which is to say Blacker, in their old neighborhood than she did here? How to explain that she felt inexplicably safer, when she couldn't explain it to herself?

King leans in and kisses her forehead. "Smells good." He steals a fried dumpling from the plate of them she made earlier.

Jasmyn shoos him away, laughing. "Wait for breakfast."

He drops a kiss on her lips and sneaks another one.

Jasmyn adds the ackee into the mixture and stirs. The house will smell of fried fish and onions for days, but she doesn't mind. This dish was the first thing King ever made for her back when they were still new to each other. He used to make it for her every other Sunday when they first started living together. This was before Kamau. And before money.

The dish is King's favorite. His grandmother used to make it all the time for him and his brother when they were kids. Jasmyn knows some of King's favorite memories of Tommy are of them eating together in their grandmother's small kitchen. The first time King made it, he'd told her about the funny way Tommy had of eating his dumplings. First, he'd break them in half and remove the soft, doughy center. Then, he'd pack a spoonful of ackee into the small crater and pop the whole thing into his mouth. King eats his that way to this day.

Every time Jasmyn watches him do it, she laments Tommy's loss even though she never knew him. He would've been a brother-in-law to her, an uncle to Kamau, a protective brother to King.

She pictures an alternate future so clearly: Tommy in their house, sitting at their breakfast table and demonstrating for King and Kamau the proper dumpling-eating technique, the three of them making memories and rituals to pass on for generations.

"You making something else for Kamau?" King asks.

Jasmyn glances to where Kamau is sitting up on a stool at the breakfast bar playing some game on his tablet. He doesn't like ackee, but she is determined that one day he will. "Nah, he'll eat what I give him." She stirs the pot again. "Good for him to know where he comes from."

In the end Kamau eats two bites of ackee and half a dumpling. Jasmyn warns him that he'll be hungry and that she's not giving him another meal before lunch, but he just shrugs and says he can wait.

After breakfast they move to the family room. Kamau sits down to build Legos in his little play area.

Jasmyn watches him sort through his bricks and smiles. They'd given him his first Lego set when he was just three. He took to it immediately.

"Kamau, you think your baby brother will like playing with those too?"

He gives her a worried little frown and looks down at her stomach. "He probably won't know how to use them," he says.

"As a big brother, it'll be your job to teach him," she says.

He shrugs and keeps building.

Jasmyn suspects he's jealous, worried that his baby brother will take his place. She makes a mental note to talk to him about how mommies and daddies have hearts big enough for all their babies.

She sits down next to King on the couch. "We're going to have to expand this little play area for the baby," she says to him.

"Can you imagine?" King says, glancing over to Kamau. "The two of them sitting there and playing with each together, not a care in the world." He smiles but there's a kind of wistful regret in it.

Jasmyn knows he's thinking about losing Tommy. She slides closer to him and rests her head on his shoulder. "Nothing will ever happen to our babies," she says quietly.

For a few seconds, King doesn't say anything at all. And then: "I know it won't," he says. "I know." He pats her knee and kisses her forehead. "Watch last night's game with me?" he asks. His voice is overly bright in a way that lets Jasmyn know he's ready to move on from this conversation. He leans back and puts the game on.

Jasmyn watches for a few minutes before her mind wanders. Ever since Charles mentioned his research into Liberty's history, she's been wanting to do some investigating herself. She grabs her laptop from the coffee table and begins her search at the Liberty website. She spends a good ten minutes admiring the curated photographs of vibrant green spaces and gorgeous million-dollar homes and the lively main street populated entirely by prosperous Black people. Black people drinking wine at outdoor cafés. Black families picnicking in parks. Black couples in black-tie running into the theater. Jasmyn zooms in on the faces and realizes she doesn't recognize anyone. Probably they are professional actors hired to showcase all Liberty has to offer.

She clicks over to the History section and studies the photos there. There is Carlton Way at the Wellness Center groundbreaking ceremony. The Sayles are with him. Nina Marks, too. They're all together again at the ribbon-cutting ceremony from two years ago. Charles was right that the Wellness Center had always been a part of the plan for Liberty. They built it at the same time they were building the first homes. She clicks over to old photos of Main Street. It looks pretty much the same, except that, instead of the Liberty Theater, there's one of those generic office buildings that house multiple businesses. She searches the address to find out what kind of businesses were there before.

King cheers at something in the game and nudges her shoulder. "Baby, you missing it," he says.

She glances up at the screen and smiles. "This is last night's game. You already know who won."

"Still have to experience it."

"Just give me a sec," she says. A few more minutes of searching leads her down a rabbit hole that ends on a social media message board.

"Hold up, hold up. Hold. Up," she says. "King, pause that."

He glances between her and the laptop before pausing the game. "Something happen with the Mercy Simpson case?"

"You know there used to be a Black Lives Matter chapter right here in Liberty?" she says, slapping her thigh. Even as she says it, she doesn't quite believe it.

King's face is blank for a second before switching to a mild surprise. "What happened to it?"

She peers back at the screen and points to the photo of Main Street. "I don't know," she says. "There used to be an office building here and it looks like the meetings took place in one of the offices."

Jasmyn clicks back to the message board and keeps searching. She feels the way she does at the discovery stage of every new case. There's an official story—the one in police reports and court filings—and then there's the truth, and those are seldom the same.

It's only a few more minutes before she finds a defunct thread on another message board that leads her to the group's official page on a social media site. The page is private, but the list of members isn't. Jasmyn scans the list of seven names and recognizes two of them.

Angela and Benjamin Sayles.

"What the fuck?" she says.

Kamau whips his head around. "Mommy, you said the f-word," he says, eyes wide.

"Sorry, baby," she says. "Mommy just got surprised."

King pauses the game again. "Now what?"

"That old Black Lives Matter chapter I told you about? Angela and Benjamin Sayles were in it."

"So?" asks King.

"You don't remember I was over at their house asking about this very thing? You don't think it's weird they didn't tell me there had been one?"

King flips the remote in his hand and sighs. "I don't know, baby. Maybe they didn't want to bring it up because they don't want to join another one."

"I guess." She zooms in on the member list. "It was founded by a couple: Clive and Tanya Johnson. You know them?"

"No."

Jasmyn shows him the list. "What about the rest of these people?"

King scans the names and shakes his head.

She turns the screen back to herself. Since the group is private, she can't find out any more information. The most she can tell is that the last group activity, at least on this site, was from just over a year ago. Why did they disband?

"Baby, come on off the computer," King says. "Didn't we talk about relaxing more?" He puts his arm around her shoulder and squeezes.

She starts to tell him she'll be a few more minutes, but the look on his face is too pleading to ignore. Thinking about Tommy always sends him into a kind of tailspin. He needs her to be with him and she can understand that.

"OK, baby, just give me one sec," she says. She takes a screenshot of the founders' names and texts it to Keisha.

Jasmyn: There was a BLM chapter here before
Jasmyn: Guess who was in it?
Keisha: Tell me
Jasmyn: Angela and Benjamin Sayles
Keisha: !!!!!!!!!
Keisha: What the fuck?
Keisha: But that don't make no sense
Jasmyn: I don't understand it either
Keisha: Why wouldn't they mention that shit?
Jasmyn: I don't know
Jasmyn: Anyway

Jasmyn: Look at the picture I sent you

Jasmyn: There used to be other people in the chapter

Jasmyn: We should reach out to the couple who founded it. Clive and Tanya Johnson

Keisha: We should reach out to all of them and find out what happened

Jasmyn: All right sounds good

Jasmyn closes the laptop and moves closer to King.

"You good?" he asks.

Despite how weird it is that the Sayles didn't tell her about it, she's happy to know there once was a Black Lives Matter chapter in Liberty. It means there are more people like her here than she realizes. She, Keisha, and maybe even Charles would figure out what happened with the old group and how they could start a new one up.

She leans over and kisses King on the cheek. "I'm good now," she says.

16

"Don't think it couldn't happen again," Jasmyn says to everyone at the dinner table. "The way this country is going?"

The *it* she's talking about is slavery. The four of them—Jasmyn, King, Keisha, and her wife Darlene—have just seen a movie, *A Slave Story*. One review Jasmyn read called it "powerful, raw, and important" and she couldn't agree more.

"Don't forget, slavery was *the* economic engine of this country," Jasmyn says. "Made it into a powerful force—"

Darlene interrupts her. "But can I ask, did you actually *like* the movie?" She's smiling and holding her glass of wine by the stem.

Darlene looks different in real life than in the wedding photo Keisha had shown Jasmyn before. That Darlene wore no makeup on her dark brown skin. She had a short Afro and an earthy vibe. Jasmyn can't swear to it, but she's almost certain the Darlene from those photos had thicker lips and a broader nose. Maybe she'd had plastic surgery?

Everything about the Darlene across from her now is sleek. Her hair is long, black, and bone-straight with sharp bangs that end just above her brow. Her makeup is expertly applied, and there's a lot of it. It's not hard to imagine her on a runway modeling shapeless monochromatic clothes.

"I'm not sure *liking* the movie is the point," Jasmyn says. "It's like the reviews say—"

"Liking it certainly *can't* be the point," says Darlene, cutting her off again. "I mean it's hard to *like* two hours of whipping and raping and denigration, am I right?" She laughs, a high and delicate sound, a wind chime in a gentle breeze.

Keisha looks at Jasmyn and smiles bright. "Darlene has a sensitive stomach," she says.

But Darlene's not having it. "You don't need to make excuses for me. Does my Blackness require me to like that movie?"

Jasmyn expects Keisha to argue the point, to spar with her wife, but she doesn't. She looks down at her martini, presses her finger against the toothpick speared with olives.

Darlene continues on. "Do you know, I saw one review that called it *timely*? Can you imagine? Calling a movie about slavery *timely*?" She sips her wine. "Honestly, I can't fathom what that even means."

Jasmyn nudges King, wanting him to join the conversation and push back against Darlene's naivete. He makes a noncommittal sound and keeps examining his menu.

She tries again with Darlene. "It's what I was saying before. We have to be constantly vigilant or it could happen again."

"Ugh, what kind of life is that? Constant vigilance. It sounds truly exhausting. I'd rather spend all day at the Wellness Center." She sips the last of her wine. "I'm curious as to what you think, Kingston." Her voice is playful, as if this entire discussion is a joke.

King lowers his menu. "I think we need to lighten up and talk about something else," he says.

"That I agree with," says Keisha.

Jasmyn frowns over at her. If anyone else spouted the kind of nonsense Darlene is spouting, no doubt Keisha would take them to task. Keisha doesn't meet her eyes and Jasmyn finally understands the reason she isn't arguing. She's embarrassed.

"Let's move on," Jasmyn says, feeling guilty that she let the discussion go on for so long.

But Darlene isn't ready to let it go. "Those movies aren't for us," she says. The smile is gone from her voice. "They're for white people. They watch them and feel badly and tell themselves they can't be racist because of how badly they feel. Because if they were in fact racist then they wouldn't feel so awful watching Black people get the skin whipped off of them." She sips her wine. "I just don't see the point of those movies. They help no one, not Black people and not white people either."

"They exist so we don't forget," Jasmyn says, unable to stop herself from responding.

Darlene meets her eyes. "Why shouldn't we forget? Would that be the worst thing in the world?"

Jasmyn doesn't know what to say to that. Forgetting is the first step on the way to denying—to erasing—their history. *This* woman should know better. She should know the importance of remembering *especially* for Black people.

"All right, so how do you propose we tackle the problem of racism?" Jasmyn asks.

Darlene shrugs. "Slavery movies certainly aren't going to fix it. All the art in the world won't fix it." She looks at Keisha. "All the activism in the world won't fix it either," she says.

"So we should stop working to dismantle it?" Jasmyn asks. It's all she can do not to slap her hand on the table in frustration.

Darlene tilts her head back and finishes every last sip of wine in her glass. "I didn't say that. It just won't be solved in the way you think."

Jasmyn stares at her. What could she possibly mean by that?

King finally speaks up. "OK, ladies. I think it's time to talk about something else, don't you?"

"No harm, no foul," says Darlene. She raises her hand and flags down their waiter. He takes their order for appetizers and more drinks.

And, as King suggested, they move on to other topics. Darlene works in advertising and brand management, which King finds fascinating, and the two of them fall into conversation.

Jasmyn adjusts her chair so it's closer to Keisha. "You doing all right?" she asks. She keeps her voice low though the restaurant is noisy enough to keep their conversation private.

"It's all good," Keisha says, waving her off. "Every couple has their differences, right?" Keisha's eyes slide to King and Jasmyn wonders at the implication. It's true that King isn't exactly backing her up, but that's because he likes to keep things peaceful. Why argue with fools is his general philosophy in situations like these.

Jasmyn changes the subject, not because she doesn't want to pursue it, but because she can see how unmoored Keisha's feeling.

"So you remember I said I was going to try and contact those people who were in the old Black Lives Matter chapter here?"

Keisha nods.

"Take a guess what I found."

"What?" Keisha asks.

"None of them live here anymore."

Keisha's mouth drops open. "Listen, you don't think that's too much of a coincidence to *be* a coincidence?"

"Maybe they were all friends and decided as a group that Liberty just wasn't for them," Jasmyn says, dropping her voice lower. Even as she says it, she knows that explanation doesn't feel right. More than that, it makes her uneasy. Moving is a big decision emotionally and practically. What could've made a group of friends leave en masse after such a short time?

Keisha leans forward, a frown on her face. "We should ask the Sayles about it."

Jasmyn shakes her head. "The same people who didn't even tell me there'd been a Black Lives Matter chapter here in the first place?"

"Yeah, you right," Keisha says. "It doesn't make any kind of sense they didn't tell you. You think they're hiding something?"

"Probably there was some drama with the people who left and they don't want to get into it."

Keisha swirls her bourbon on the table. "Maybe they were kicked out of Liberty instead of leaving on their own."

"Jesus, I wasn't thinking all that," Jasmyn says.

"All the same," says Keisha, "we should find out why they left."

"Why who left where?" King asks. He puts his hand on Jasmyn's back.

Jasmyn smiles at him. When had he and Darlene started listening in? "Girl talk," she says.

"I'm a girl," Darlene says with a laugh.

Jasmyn waits to see if Keisha is going to fill her in on their conversation, but she doesn't. "Just gossiping," Keisha says.

"Always with the gossiping," says Darlene. Her voice is full of affection and she caresses Keisha's cheek, smiles into her eyes.

Even though she doesn't much like Darlene, Jasmyn can see how much Darlene loves Keisha.

She looks away from them and moves her chair back closer to King. He kisses her temple.

Earlier, Keisha had said that every couple had their differences. And it's true, every couple does. But Jasmyn has met couples like Keisha and Darlene before, ones who disagree on the fundamentals. And to be clear, having the same views on how to tackle racism *is* fundamental. Couples who disagree on the basics don't last.

She looks back at them in time to see Keisha lean into Darlene's touch and kiss her open palm. Jasmyn can't imagine that Keisha will ever agree with the things Darlene said tonight. From what she could see of Darlene, she can't imagine she'll change her mind, either. If their marriage was going to make it, one of them was certainly going to have to change.

17

On the Ides of March, Jasmyn wakes up tired, the all-encompassing tired of working too much, being seven months pregnant, mothering a six-year-old, and wife-ing a husband. On top of all that, her pregnancy heartburn is in overdrive.

King insists she take the day off. "Ease up a little," he says. "Work will still be there tomorrow."

It's a testament to how exhausted she is that she acquiesces.

She spends the first hour in bed reading the latest on the Mercy Simpson case. From a legal perspective, there wasn't anything new. The grand jury was still deliberating. The second hour she spends on social media reposting articles and opinion essays. She texts articles to her group chat with Keisha and Charles. She texts Tricia and her other non-Liberty friends separately.

By midmorning she feels physically better. By early afternoon she feels guilty for taking the day off in the first place. Had some other kid slipped through the system because she decided she was too tired today? Even though she promised King she wouldn't work, she spends an hour responding to emails. That done, she roams the house doing small chores—putting away Kamau's toys and loading the dishwasher. After a short while, she runs out of tasks. The housekeeper had come yesterday, the gardener the day before. She wanders into the en suite bathroom to take a shower. Her eyes skim the white marble surfaces, the gleaming porcelain of the claw-foot tub she still has yet to use. Eventually she texts King to say she's feeling well enough to pick up Kamau from school herself. And even though Kamau won't be ready for another two hours, she leaves the house, if only to have something to do.

≈

She finds a parking spot right away, but downtown Liberty is by no means empty. Every seat is occupied in both of the nail spas. Both hair salons and both barbershops are full, too. Who are all these carefree people? Don't they have jobs? You would think it was the weekend instead of a Tuesday, for all the people who are out and about.

Inside a café, she orders tea and settles into a patio chair. It's not long before she decides to do the thing that's been at the back of her mind for a few days: investigate what happened to the old Black Lives Matter chapter.

The crash happens immediately, a long screech followed by the shattering of glass and shriek of scraping metal.

Jasmyn cranes her neck to see over the hedges lining the patio. A Liberty Wellness Center delivery van has smashed into a stop sign thirty or forty feet away. The van is halfway on the sidewalk.

She walks to the patio's edge for a better look. Fortunately, the driver didn't hit anyone and doesn't seem hurt himself. He's on his phone and gesticulating wildly. The toppled stop sign lies at his feet. A few Good Samaritans offer to help, but he waves them off. Jasmyn is about to sit back down when the van's back door swings open. A handful of cardboard boxes slide out, crash to the ground, and spill their contents. A few medicine dropper bottles, the kind she'd seen at the Sayles' home spa, break. Others roll away down the street. Inside the truck, she sees cylindrical metal canisters that look like oxygen tanks. Next to the canisters are bagless IV drip stands and metal crates with what look like orange biohazard warning labels pasted on the sides.

What kind of spa equipment is this?

Jasmyn tells herself she's more curious than suspicious. She grabs her tea and finds a gap in the patio railing large enough to let her and her belly through, fully intending to get closer to the van and inspect it.

The police officer steps in front of her when she's about halfway there.

Jasmyn yelps and stops just short of running into him.

"Jesus Christ," she says, and rests a protective hand on the swell of her belly.

"Didn't mean to startle you," he says. "You're Jasmyn Williams, aren't you? Kingston's wife?"

Even though he's Black, Jasmyn knows better than to answer a random question from *any* cop. Most of the time the questions aren't random at all. Usually they're after something. Jasmyn has always thought cops should have term limits. Their job makes them mistrust the very people they're supposed to protect.

"Is there a problem, Officer?" She looks him in the eyes and uses her take-no-shit lawyer voice.

He smiles and sticks his hand out for a shake. "Officer Godfrey," he says.

His smile seems genuine enough, but like all police officers, he has cop eyes, the kind that suspect you've just done something wrong or else you're about to do something wrong.

She shakes his hand and waits for him to say what it is that he wants.

"Got to spend some time with your husband up at the Wellness Center. He's a good man."

"Sure is," says Jasmyn, because what else is there to say to a comment like that? Is this why he stopped her? To tell her that her husband was a good man, like she didn't already know that? Is he making a professional or personal judgment about Kingston's goodness?

"Well, Officer, it's nice to meet you," Jasmyn says. Her tone makes it clear she's too busy right now for small talk. She looks past him, checking to make sure the van is still there.

Instead of moving out of her way, Officer Godfrey puts his hands on his hips. "He said you were having a hard time adjusting."

She jerks her eyes away from the van. "He said what?"

"My wife was the same way, but she loves it now."

Sirens sound behind her. Over her shoulder, she watches a police car speed through the intersection and pull up to the accident. Officer Godfrey doesn't turn to look, not at the speeding patrol car or at the van.

Jasmyn steps away from him, her own suspicious nature on high alert. In her experience, cops will always run toward trouble. For him to not even glance at a fellow officer with sirens blaring? Makes no sense. The only reason he wouldn't is if he's dealing with his own emergency.

"I hear Kamau is adjusting nicely, though," he says.

It shouldn't bother her that he knows Kamau's name, but it does. King never mentioned he was friendly with a cop.

"My girl was the same way," he continues on. "Kids are just better at changing."

Jasmyn memorizes his badge number and takes another step away from him. "I have some errands to run. Nice to meet you, Officer Godfrey."

She shifts to move around him. He shifts with her. "Call me Devon," he says. "We're all family around here."

His radio crackles and then emits three loud beeps. He unhooks it from his belt and clicks a button on the side once.

Another broad smile pushes its way across his face. "Don't let me keep you." He steps aside to let her pass.

Jasmyn hurries toward the van, but there's no point. The back door is already closed. The patrol car is pulling away. The driver is back in the van.

"Goddamn it," she says, louder than she meant to.

A woman exiting a nail salon gives her a wide berth.

If only that cop hadn't stopped her. She turns back to see if he's still there and finds that he is. He tips his hat at her, says something she can't hear into his radio, and then walks away.

≈

The cop is all she thinks about on the ten-minute drive to pick up Kamau from school. Is she being paranoid? No, she's sure he didn't want her to see what was in the van. But why?

The more pressing question, though, is not about the cop's motivation, but her own. At a red light, she flips open the mirror on the car's sun visor and stares at her reflection. It's not often that she finds her own motivations to be opaque, a sullied window she can't see through. Why had she gotten up from where she was peacefully drinking her tea to go inspect the van in the first place? Was she looking for evidence? No, not evidence. That would imply that she believed there was some kind of wrongdoing happening at the spa, and she doesn't believe that, right? What she'd been looking for was an explanation. Something to account for the amount of time King and the others spend up there. But of course she wasn't going to find that in the back of a van.

Behind her, someone honks. Jasmyn looks away from the mirror to find that the light has turned green. She waves an apology to the person in the car behind her. There's no good explanation for why she got up to examine the van. She doesn't know anything about spa equipment. Probably everything in the van was perfectly ordinary.

She decides to pick up Kamau via the carpool lane instead of walking in. She's just not in the mood for smiles or small talk. The line moves quickly and Kamau gets into the car, his little face shining.

"How was your day, baby?" she asks, looking back at him as he buckles himself into his booster seat.

"It was good."

"How many thumbs up?"

He sticks both his feet up into the air and grins. "Ten thumbs," he says.

Jasmyn laughs. "You have thumbs on your feet now?" She checks her side-view before pulling away. "You like this new school, don't you, baby?"

"It's nice," he says. She thinks that's the end of it, but then he adds, "I fit in here."

She stretches up so she can see his face in the rearview mirror. "You didn't fit in at your old school?"

"Not as much," he says.

She'll never get over this aspect of motherhood, the way kids say important or profound things just by the by as if what they're saying is no big deal. He never told her before that he felt like he didn't fit in at his old school.

"That's so good, baby," she says. "So good."

She blinks away a sudden wash of tears and feels the tension in her chest soften and release. This moment, this one right here, when her little boy tells her he's found his place, is why she moved to Liberty. For this moment—for the chance to give him a strong and secure sense of himself—she can deal with any small annoyance.

Kamau prattles on for the rest of the drive, and even though he's talking much too loud, she doesn't ask him to quiet down, not even once.

Back at home, Kamau runs upstairs to his room to put away his backpack and changes into his latest, most-favorite outfit, a Miles Morales pajama set. Depending on how long it stays his favorite, she might have to get him a bigger size. She toes off her shoes, steps into her house slippers, and heads for the kitchen. Had she ever had a favorite outfit as a kid? She doesn't think so. They were all hand-me-downs from Ivy, who'd never let Jasmyn forget that they were hers first. By virtue of being firstborn, Kamau will never have secondhand clothes. And, Jasmyn admits to herself, neither will his baby brother. She'll buy him brand-new everything even if it doesn't make practical sense. She remembers that used-up feeling of wanting something to be hers alone. She remembers wanting to be the one who popped off the price tag.

Kamau bounds into the kitchen. Snack time. He pushes his step stool over to the pantry, opens the door, and buries his entire head inside it.

Jasmyn shakes her head and laughs. "Careful up there, baby," she tells him.

He pulls out a bag of microwave popcorn. "Can I have this, please?"

"Don't we usually save that for movie night?"

He sticks out his bottom lip and widens his eyes, giving her his how-can-you-resist-this-face face.

For a moment, Jasmyn finds herself overwhelmed by his innocence. He expects to be happy and for life to be fair and for the world to say yes to everything he wants.

She takes the bag from his hand and kisses his forehead. "That cute face is not always going to work on me, you know?" she says, even though she knows it will absolutely always work.

The look he gives her says he knows it, too. He pushes the stool over and together they watch the bag inflate in the microwave. "Smells so good," he says, and licks his tongue all the way around his lips three times.

Jasmyn laughs. "You know your pops makes that exact same face?"

Naturally, he does it again. "Can we watch a movie tonight?" he asks.

Ordinarily, on a school night he's only allowed half an hour of TV, but today feels special. Maybe it's because she'd had the day off or because what Kamau said in the car reminded her of exactly why she'd agreed to move to Liberty in the first place.

"OK, why not? Let's see if we can get Pops to come home early and we'll have movie night in the middle of the week."

She texts King, who, miracle of miracles, doesn't have to work late. He brings home pizza and an enormous bouquet of stargazer lilies, her favorite.

"These are beautiful," Jasmyn says, hugging him close. "You spoil me."

King kisses her. "It's my job to spoil you."

Back in the kitchen it takes her a little while to find a vase big enough, but she finally does. She rearranges the flowers, plucking away the occasional brown filler leaf and removing the powdery orange anther from the stamen. She's stained many a shirt by brushing up against them.

The first time King ever gave her flowers was on their second date. It was a much smaller mixed bouquet with only one or two lilies, but their scent lingered for days and she decided they were her favorite. King has been buying them for her ever since.

From the family room, she hears Kamau squealing. No doubt King is tickling him. She laughs to herself. They're so silly, her boys. Sometimes the best times are the unexpected ones.

She reminds herself to tell King what Kamau said about fitting in at school. He'll be so happy at this latest proof that they'd thrive here.

The accident with the Wellness Center van and Officer Godfrey edges its way back into her mind. She shakes her head, dislodging her suspicions. She'd been paranoid. She still does want to find out more about the old Black Lives Matter chapter, though, and makes a mental note to find some time to do it.

She turns off the kitchen light and heads to the family room. King and Kamau are both happy here. For the most part, she is, too. She reminds herself that people will always find one hundred percent of the trouble they go looking for.

King and Kamau are already digging into the pizza and Jasmyn plops herself down on the couch beside them. Kamau wants to watch the Miles Morales *Spider-Man* movie for the hundredth time, and they agree.

King nudges her. "Look at us being spontaneous," he says.

She grins at him. "We should plan to do it more often."

"Ha!" says King. "I see what you did there."

"Shhhhh, you're missing it," Kamau says.

"No, we're not, baby," Jasmyn says. "No, we're not."

18

The next two weeks are busy, and Jasmyn's workload is heavy with mostly drug-related cases. As tired as she is, she's grateful that, for the most part, she's been getting her clients off. The police work on one of the cases is so shoddy that the judge has no choice but to throw it out. Between work and everything else, she's barely had any time to research what happened to the Black Lives Matter chapter.

King spends most evenings working late into the night. He's doing due diligence on a huge spa chain interested in stocking Awake. "We land this one and the returns will be through the roof. We'll be flying high, baby."

"We pretty high already," Jasmyn said back to him.

He still hasn't gone back to volunteering at Mentor LA, yet somehow manages to find time for the Wellness Center. Jasmyn has to talk herself into not resenting it and being patient with him for a little while longer. She knows it's not that King is choosing the spa over serving his community. She knows that he's working hard to prove himself at his job and that he needs time to decompress. It bothers her, though, how much time he's spending with the likes of Nina Marks and Carlton Way and Catherine Vail. She doesn't know how he stands it. Still, he promises that he'll go back to volunteering as soon as his work calms down and she knows he will. It means as much to him as it does to her.

On the Wednesday of the second week, they had attended their first parent-teacher meeting at Kamau's school. The evening kicked off with a "state of the school" address delivered by the administration. For an hour Principal Harper and others talked about the previous year's achievements and about what they hoped to accomplish in the coming year. He told them that their teacher recruitment efforts had already paid dividends as evidenced by the middle and high school students having some of the best standardized test scores in the country. The next year's goals included additional extracurricular activities as well as a larger preschool play yard.

The school's entire staff stood behind him onstage while he spoke. Jasmyn marveled at the sea of shining Black faces. It reminded her of being young and in church with her grandma watching the choir perform. She'd felt the same praise and gratitude in her heart back then.

Throughout the presentation, Jasmyn squeezed King's hand over and over again. It was all so damn impressive. Kamau really was getting the best of everything. An excellent education taught in an excellent facility with excellent teachers and resources.

After the state of the school, they headed into the individual parent-teacher meetings. Kamau's Language Arts classroom was more put together and beautiful than any she'd ever been in. It was impeccably neat and bright with primary colors. The walls were decorated with book covers, famous quotes, grammar rules, student projects, etc. The teacher, Ms. Abi, was tall and thin with a short Afro and merry eyes. She welcomed them in and offered them snacks and tea. Behind her on the whiteboard the kids had all written *Welcome Parents.* Jasmyn picked out Kamau's handwriting easily.

As soon as they were settled, Ms. Abi began. "Well, your son is very bright. I'm sure I don't have to tell you that."

King laughed. "Nah, you can tell us," he said, and Jasmyn laughed along with him.

Ms. Abi continued on. She praised Kamau's maturity and his reading comprehension skills, which were well ahead of his peer group.

The rest of his teachers were similarly effusive about his attitude and abilities. The school therapist said he was shy but made friends at his own pace.

"Baby, are you getting teary over there?" King asked when they were back in the car.

"No," she said as she sniffled and laughed at the same time.

He grabbed her hand across the console and kissed it. "I feel it too, baby," he said.

She'd known of course that every one of his teachers would be Black, but it was still a joy to experience. What a relief not to have to worry if he was being truly seen. How many studies had she read that showed Black children thrived with Black teachers? That showed Black boys mentored by Black educators were more likely to attend college? Too many.

"All we need now is to get him into a sport," King said. "Liberty has a good little league."

Jasmyn laughed. "Our baby can barely catch a ball, let alone hit one."

"All the more reason," King said, and laughed too.

≈

The housewarming party is King's idea. "We been here a little while now. It's time we let folks see how we're living."

They'd been in bed when he brought it up. Jasmyn put down her crossword puzzle and side-eyed him. "Since when do you care about throwing dinner parties?" she asked. "You trying to impress somebody?"

King just looked at her. "You don't think it'd be nice to have some folks over and get to know them better?"

"And to show off a little bit," she prodded.

"Nothing wrong with being proud of what we got," he said.

She supposed he was right, even though the King she'd married didn't throw dinner parties to show off. He manned the grill at cookouts and drank Red Stripe beer with his boys.

As changes go, though, this one seemed harmless enough. Besides, Jasmyn thought, it wasn't as if she could change him back.

Keisha and Darlene are the first to arrive. One look at them and Jasmyn can tell they've been arguing.

"Girl, I need a drink," Keisha says into her ear while they're hugging.

Instead of a hug, Darlene offers her hand for a shake. "It's lovely to see you again," she says. If anything, she looks even sleeker than she did on their double date. Her hair is slicked back into a low ponytail. She's wearing a beige silk pantsuit and pale pink "barely there" makeup.

Charles texts to say that he and his wife, Asha, will be late. Most everyone else arrives over the next thirty minutes. Angela and Benjamin Sayles kiss Jasmyn on both cheeks. She resists the urge to ask them why they hadn't told her about the old Black Lives Matter chapter. Carlton Way, the Wrights, and Catherine Vail arrive within a few minutes of one another. Nina Marks gets there last.

An hour into the party, Jasmyn finds Keisha standing outside next to the bar the caterers set up.

"Can't believe you're serving French food," Keisha says.

All Jasmyn can do is shake her head. "Wasn't my idea."

She'd wanted to have a buffet-style dinner catered by the Caribbean place she and King both loved downtown. But King wanted passed hors d'oeuvres and seven courses.

"Baby," he'd said. "Let's get outside our comfort zones."

Put that way, it was hard for her to say no.

Keisha shrugs. "Food's good, though," she says. She snags a canapé from a passing server. He, like all the other servers, is white.

"They don't got Black people in France?" Keisha asks, laughing.

"Blame King," says Jasmyn. "He set this whole thing up." He'd gone out and found them a full-service caterer, who was responsible for everything from the food to the decor to music. At the end of the night, they would do the cleaning up as well.

"Anyway, never mind about all that," Jasmyn says. "You seem off to me. Why are you out here drinking by yourself? Where's Darlene?"

Keisha sips her drink and points with her chin.

Jasmyn turns to look. Darlene is standing next to the pool laughing with a woman dressed so similarly it's uncanny. "Who's that?" she asks.

"Oh, you didn't meet her yet?" asks Keisha. There's a kind of bemused laughter in her voice. "That, my dear, is Asha. Charles's wife."

Jasmyn looks back at the woman. She's tall and dark-skinned with wavy shoulder-length black hair that's either a wig or a weave. "Not what I was expecting," she says.

"Me neither," says Keisha. Her voice is flat. "Do you think they look alike?" she asks, jutting her chin in their direction.

Jasmyn studies Asha and Darlene. They look so much alike they could be sisters is what she thinks. "A little" is what she says.

Keisha gives her a look making it plain she knows Jasmyn isn't being truthful. "The fact that they use the exact same plastic surgeon might explain it," she says.

So she *had* been right. Darlene *had* gotten plastic surgery. Just as she'd suspected, Darlene's lips and nose were thinner than in the wedding picture Keisha had shown her.

"Three guesses as to who their doctor is," Keisha says.

Jasmyn looks back at her. "Who?"

Keisha points to where Benjamin Sayles is talking to Carlton Way.

"Get the fuck out," says Jasmyn. "For real?"

"For real *real*."

"Small world," Jasmyn says.

Thirty minutes later, the servers spread the word that dinner is ready. Jasmyn drifts toward the formal dining room along with everyone else. She and Kamau and King never use this room, opting instead for the breakfast bar or the cozy, less formal dining area just off the kitchen. When they'd first toured the house, Jasmyn couldn't imagine what she'd do in a house with two dining rooms, especially one this large. She'd joked maybe they could buy a long table and sit at opposite ends like one of those fancy rich white families you sometimes saw in movies on premium cable.

The dining table shimmers as candlelight bounces off the polished gold flatware and crystal glasses. Instead of a single centerpiece, the caterers had opted for three ornate gold candelabras with tall, white, tapered candles and small gold bowls with floating flower petals. Tall standing vases with orchids and white roses are scattered throughout the room. There's a string quartet in the back corner.

"Fancy," Keisha, says, laughing at her side. "Even got seat assignments."

Jasmyn laughs, too. "Another one of King's ideas," she says.

Assigning the seating was her only duty for the party. She'd once read somewhere that at dinner parties couples should be split up to encourage mingling with strangers and acquaintances. Jasmyn followed the advice but didn't put anyone too far away from their partners. King is across from her, flanked by Asha on one side and Darlene on the other. She has Keisha on one side and Charles on the other.

The string quartet begins playing as soon as everyone is seated. The servers pour water and place napkins on everyone's laps. Across from her, King smiles wide.

The first course is an amuse-bouche involving caviar and sea urchin. Vichyssoise is next, followed by escargot and then foie gras. By the fourth course, Jasmyn is already full. She spends most of the dinner talking with Keisha and Charles about the Mercy Simpson case and explaining the ins and outs of how grand juries work .

Just before the dessert course, Carlton Way clinks his fork against a glass and stands.

Jasmyn frowns over at King. Why is Carlton standing up to give a speech? This is not his house or his party.

But King just shrugs. She's going to have to talk to him about the blind spot he has when it comes to Carlton.

At least Keisha seems to understand. She leans over and whispers "The hell?" into Jasmyn's ear.

Carlton raises his glass. "I know I speak for everyone when I say thank you to Kingston and Jasmyn for welcoming us all into their magnificent home and hosting us so beautifully."

"Hear, hear," says Benjamin Sayles.

Asha and Darlene both clink forks against their glasses.

Carlton smiles and continues. "Now, I just want to take a moment to acknowledge what we have made together here in Liberty. This country being the way it is, many of us never thought we'd get to this place in our lives. But here we are."

This time it's Angela Sayles with the "Hear, hear."

"We've certainly come a long way," Carlton says. "But we still have a long way to go." He holds his wineglass higher. "Eyes on the prize," he says.

Just as they had at the Wellness Center, everyone repeats it in unison. Everyone except her and Charles and Keisha. Jasmyn wants to ask them what the prize is exactly. Even more money? Even bigger houses? Fancier French food and even whiter waiters?

Jasmyn doesn't wait for Carlton to sit before she stands. Maybe it's because Carlton and the others made Liberty feel like a place *with* Black people, but not *for* Black people. Maybe it's because come Monday morning she'll go back to working for all the people who have so little.

Jasmyn stands, compelled the way she always has been, to do what she sees as the right thing. "I have something to add," she says.

"Yes, of course. You can go ahead," Carlton says, as if she was asking for permission. He sits.

She looks around the table, making sure to catch everyone's eye before she begins.

"First of all, I am very glad to be here in Liberty with you all. And like Carlton said, I never imagined my life would take me from the projects to a place like this. We are all very fortunate," she continues. "And that is why we must give back."

"Hear, hear," says Keisha and then Charles.

"I'm not just talking about giving money. I'm sure all of you already donate to all the right causes. What I'm talking about is donating *time*. We need to get out there. Into the projects. Into the inner cities. Into the prisons. We need to mentor our kids and bring the next generation up. We need to be teaching them our history. About where we've come from and all we accomplished. About our resilience. About the beauty of our culture. We need to organize. We need to be out in the streets marching. For people like Tyrese and Mercy Simpson. We need to get out there and protest and be seen. Let them see the size and strength of us. Let them see they can't break us."

"But they *can* break us," says a voice from the far end of the table. Catherine Vail.

"I'm sorry?" says Jasmyn, confused.

"You said they can't break us. I know it's a metaphor, and I'm not an activist like you, but I never understand when people say things like 'they can't break us.' Of course they can. They can break our backs with their batons and our skin with their bullets. We are breakable. We break."

"I meant they can't break our will," Jasmyn says.

"They can break that, too," says Catherine Vail. Finally, she looks up from her glass. "Don't be naive."

Jasmyn has to fight to keep her anger in check. She breathes deeply once, and then twice. This woman has some nerve. This woman living her safe, privileged, light-skinned life really has some nerve. If every Black person felt the same as Catherine Vail, then there would've been no civil rights movement, no Black Panthers, no Black Lives Matter, no police reform, no anything. All progress for Black people was *taken,* not *given*. They'd had to *fight*.

"How you think we got here?" Jasmyn asks. She tries to keep the hot anger out of her voice, but it leaks through. "You wouldn't have your fancy house and your fancy car if it wasn't for our forefathers. They took to the streets. They put themselves in danger."

"Preach," says Keisha.

The baby kicks and Jasmyn's back is starting to hurt from standing, but she isn't ready to sit down yet. She looks away from Catherine Vail and addresses the entire table instead. "You think they would've arrested the cop in the Mercy Simpson case if folks weren't out there protesting?"

"I know that's right," Keisha says, loud enough for everyone to hear.

Charles snaps his fingers like he's at a poetry slam.

"They're not just protesting, though, are they?" Carlton says. "Don't forget the looting. Don't forget the setting fire to their own neighborhoods."

Jasmyn feels as if she's been slapped. She's too shocked to say anything. The baby kicks, reminding her again that she's been standing for too long. She sits down slowly, using the back of her chair for support. She didn't think she would hear something as foul as that here, in Liberty. She looks across the table at King, expecting to share a disgusted look, but he's staring down at his wineglass, twirling the stem between his fingers. Jasmyn wants him to say something, to push back against the obscenity of Carlton's words, but she understands that he probably feels he can't. Carlton is his boss, after all. More than that, Carlton is the one who saw King's potential, took a chance on him, made him into the success he is today. Rationally, she understands the reason for his silence. Emotionally, though, she wants him to stand up and confront the man, to draw a line with him.

"What the hell kind of Uncle Tom shit is that to say?" Charles says, taking on Carlton.

"Jesus, Charles, stay out of it," hisses Asha from across the table.

King slaps the table. "All right, that's enough now," he says. "We're all reasonable people here. As President Obama used to say, reasonable people can disagree reasonably. Let's move on."

But no one's ready to move on. The silence stretches out until Catherine Vail interrupts it.

"Did you know my brother was killed by cops?" she says. "I was thirteen. He was fifteen. Killed for being Black."

Jasmyn stares at her, shocked. How sad and how strange that Catherine and King have the loss of their brothers to police violence in common.

"I'm so sorry," Jasmyn stammers out. She says it again, not sure what else to say.

Keisha grabs her hand under the table and squeezes.

"I used to be like you," Catherine says. Jasmyn sees tears shimmering in her eyes.

And now Jasmyn's not sure how to feel. She's angry at Catherine Vail, but sorry for her too. She better understands why Catherine is the way she is. Catherine Vail is not complacent. She's traumatized and afraid. She won't fight because she already knows the cost.

Angela Sayles whispers something to Catherine and she seems to come back to herself. She brightens and looks across at Carlton. "I'm fine," she says. She looks around the table. "I promise I'm fine."

And she does seem fine now. Jasmyn can't find any sadness in her eyes.

"Well," says King, "let's keep the festivities going. I'll go let the kitchen know it's time for dessert."

"No, I'll do it," says Jasmyn. She pushes herself up.

"Want me to come with you?" Keisha whispers.

"No, no, I'm fine," Jasmyn says. She just needs a minute.

In the kitchen, she tells the catering coordinator they're ready for the last course. Instead of going back to the dining room, she heads to the family room. The lights are off and the blinds are down. She leaves them that way. The air still has that sweet plastic smell of new furniture and new paint. Jasmyn closes her eyes and presses her palms and forehead against the wall. It's cooler than she expects, and soothing, too. Turning her head, she presses her cheek against it, imagines the coolness filling her up, dousing her hot, confused anger at these people. Less than a minute later, the light flickers on. Jasmyn turns, expecting King, but finds Carlton instead.

"Sorry," he says. "Was looking for the bathroom."

She doesn't believe him, not for a second.

He leaves the doorway and enters the room. "Are you OK?"

Jasmyn stays where she is with her back against the wall. "The bathroom is down the hall," she says.

He laughs and shakes his head. "You don't like me much, do you?" he asks.

She doesn't bother denying it, no longer cares that he's King's boss. "Like Charles said, what you said out there *was* some Uncle Tom shit."

He laughs again. "I didn't mean it. Sometimes I say things to get a rise out of people."

She's not buying it. "And why would you do that?"

"Just the way I'm made," he says. He puts his hands into his pockets and turns to leave.

"You weren't really looking for the bathroom, were you?" she says.

He turns back and his smile is the widest she's ever seen it. "I was looking for you," he says. "I wanted to ask you a question."

She waits for him to continue, won't give him the satisfaction of her open curiosity.

He smiles like maybe he's guessed her tactic. "You ever think maybe you're wrong?" he asks.

"About what?"

"All of it. Maybe the solution to racism isn't to fight."

"What other choice do we have? We can't just give up."

"Not give up," he says. "Give in." He turns then and walks away.

≈

Back in the dining room, the dessert service has begun. Jasmyn watches the waiters pour ribbons of cream into hot soufflés. King meets her eyes and she reads the concern on his face. *"I'm fine,"* she mouths.

As soon as she sits down, Keisha bumps her lightly on the shoulder. "You doing OK?"

Jasmyn presses into her, grateful for the support. "I'm all right," she says.

Charles touches her back briefly. "What we need is some hemlock for these Oreos," he whispers.

Jasmyn lets herself laugh.

The rest of the dinner is fine. The soufflé is delicious and the conversation remains light. People seem to have a good time, King most of all. After dessert the waiters serve port and brandy at the poolside bar. Through it all, Jasmyn sips her lemon water and lets Charles and Keisha's banter and teasing wash over her and tries her best not to feel like a guest in her own home.

Excerpt from an interview with Carlton Way in the "Black Power" issue of *Mahogany Magazine*

INTERVIEWER: In the *New York Times*, the culture critic Walter Thomas wrote: "This movement to self-segregate is dangerous and only gives ammunition to white racists who would already like to have Black people rounded up and kept in one place." What do you say to your critics, particularly your Black critics, who push back against the founding of a place like Liberty?

CW: I don't have anything to say to them. They have their way of doing things. I have mine.

19

Despite everything, Jasmyn forges ahead with opening the Liberty Black Lives Matter chapter. To start, it will only be her, Keisha, and Charles. King says he'll join once things calm down at work. She doesn't ask Keisha if Darlene will join. She doesn't ask Charles about Asha, either.

The first meeting is supposed to take place at Charles's house on Friday, but on Thursday he texts the group chat to cancel.

Charles: Asha made us weekend getaway plans

Keisha: Oh no

Keisha: I mean good for you

Keisha: Oh no for us

Jasmyn: That will be nice

Charles: I doubt that

Keisha: Where you going?

Charles: Some spa retreat

Charles: Asha's idea of course

Charles: Says I need a vacation and to relax or align myself or some shit
Jasmyn: Is this because of what happened at my dinner?
Charles: I'm sure that has something do with it
Charles: But she's been on me to do something like this for a few weeks now
Charles: How about we meet next Friday instead?
Charles: Or you could do it without me
Jasmyn: No, it wouldn't be the same. We'll wait for you
Charles: Thanks I appreciate you
Keisha: Have fun at the spa!
Charles: Jesus
Charles: It's going to be terrible

The rest of the week is good. Jasmyn gets two different prosecutors to drop charges against boys in two of her cases. On the weekend, she and King and Kamau go to the beach. The water is entirely too cold, but Kamau doesn't mind. He can't get enough of playing chicken with the waves and then squealing his delight when the water catches him. For lunch, they get hotdogs. Before King can eat his, an enormous seagull swoops in and steals the dog but leaves the bun. Jasmyn and Kamau laugh until their stomachs hurt. The hotdog stand vendor offers them another one free of charge but King pays for it anyway.

"It's not your fault seagulls are assholes," he tells the guy.

After lunch, Kamau and King build an elaborate sandcastle complete with towers and parapets and even a moat using molds and tools from a fancy set King bought online. *How is it that there's an upscale version of even the most basic things?* Jasmyn wonders, bemused. Later, they watch the sunset and light a bonfire and roast marshmallows. On the way home, Kamau tells them, "Today was my most-favorite day ever," and Jasmyn has to agree.

The following Monday, at her pregnancy checkup, everything is progressing as expected.

On Tuesday, Keisha texts the group chat.

Keisha: How was the retreat with wifey?

Keisha: You had enough mani-pedis to last you a lifetime?

Charles: We had a medical cleansing of our touchpoints that most connect us to our essence.

Jasmyn: Hahaha, you have a future in writing luxury spa menus

Keisha: Seriously tho how was it?

Charles: It was excellent. And much needed.

Charles: You ladies should try it.

Keisha: Haha

Jasmyn: Dying to hear how it really was but I have to get to court

Keisha: Give them hell

Jasmyn: Always

Keisha texts the group chat again on Wednesday.

Keisha: I need for tomorrow to be here already. Need to see your smiling faces

Keisha: The week I'm having

Keisha: Some of these parents I swear to God

Charles: Actually, ladies, do you mind if we reschedule?

Keisha: What no why?

Keisha: I need this. I've been looking forward to it for 2 weeks.

Charles: There's a guest shaman coming to the Wellness Center tomorrow evening.

Keisha: What?

Keisha: Since when do you care about that shit?

Jasmyn: Oh I heard about that. King's going to the Saturday morning session

Keisha: Charles go to that one

Charles: I'll check in with Asha.

Jasmyn: Is Darlene going to the shaman thing too, K?

Keisha: Probably

Jasmyn: Keep us posted on what you decide, Charles

Charles: Certainly.

A few minutes later, Keisha texts Jasmyn separately.

Keisha: Something seem off about Charles to you?
Jasmyn: A little
Keisha: Asha probably slapped the pussy on him on their retreat
Keisha: Good pussy can addle the brain
Keisha: Trust me I know
Jasmyn: Hahahhahahaha

On Thursday evening, Jasmyn and Keisha get to Charles's house just in time to see some workers loading up their truck.

"Looks like he got some more art," Keisha says.

"Probably," says Jasmyn. She touches a hand to her throat, remembering how devastating the *Aftermath* painting had been.

"I was just telling Darlene last night that we should build ourselves a museum like his, too," says Keisha.

Jasmyn keeps her face neutral. "Oh yeah? What did she say?" She'd be shocked if Darlene agreed to something like that.

Before Keisha can answer, the front door opens.

"The fuck?" Keisha says, and then slaps her hand over her mouth.

Jasmyn tries not to let it show on her face, but she understands Keisha's reaction. Charles is standing in front of them, but gone are his long, beautiful locs. His head is devoid of any hair at all, not even a small Afro. To make matters worse, he's wearing a white Liberty Wellness Center sweatsuit.

"Sorry," Keisha says. "The new look surprised me is all."

"Sometimes change can do you good," Charles says. He wipes a hand over his shaved head. "What do you ladies think?"

A real sense of loss lodges in Jasmyn's throat. Without his locs, Charles seems weaker somehow. Diminished. Like Samson after Delilah's betrayal.

"You look great," she says.

Keisha makes a sound that could mean she agrees, but she doesn't say anything out loud.

Charles laughs. "I see how it is," he says. "It's all right, not everybody is ready for change right away." He steps aside and lets them fully into the vestibule. "Come on in," he says. "I set us up in the solarium."

As soon as Charles's back is turned, Keisha grips Jasmyn's arm and squeezes. "Something is going on with him," she hisses low.

"It's just a haircut," Jasmyn whispers back.

"You really believe that?"

Jasmyn glances back at the front door and then looks at Keisha. No, she admits to herself, she doesn't really believe that it's just a haircut. Something must've happened on his vacation to make him shave off his hair. Locs take a long time to form and grow. They're a commitment. All the Black men she'd known with locs wore the style as a symbol of Black pride or Black power or Black resistance. Of course, she'd never asked Charles why he wore his locs. It seemed safe enough to assume the reason. And if it was symbolic to grow them then wasn't it also symbolic to shave them off? Yes, it was. Symbolic of what, though?

Finally, they get to where Charles is leading them. "Ladies, welcome to the solarium."

"This is beautiful," Jasmyn says and means it. The room is a hexagon made of floor-to-ceiling glass, bright with light and greenery. In the center a semicircular white sofa surrounds a low marble table. Three bottles of Awake water, in different sizes, sit in the center. Jasmyn makes a mental note to tell King that the new bottle design really is beautiful enough to act as a centerpiece.

"Where the liquor at?" Keisha asks as soon as they're seated.

"Didn't I tell you? I'm doing a liver detox." He leans forward to pour her a glass of water. "Have some Awake," he says.

Keisha shoots a look so poisonous to his bowed head, Jasmyn is shocked Charles doesn't just keel over and die right then and there. She slaps a hand over her mouth to keep from laughing.

"What were those workers doing here?" Keisha asks.

Charles springs to his feet and rubs his hands together. "You'll love it," he says. "Let me show you how it's looking so far."

Jasmyn heaves herself back up to her feet and follows Charles out into the hallway. "See, I told you he was expanding the museum," she whispers to Keisha. She hears the relief in her own voice. Charles hadn't changed and his haircut was just a haircut after all.

As they get closer to the museum wing, evidence of construction is everywhere. Protective plastic tarps cover the floors. Ladders and tool chests litter the hallway.

They walk into the first gallery to find it empty. The once dark walls have been painted white and are partially covered with aqua blue tiles. Off to the left side, there's a gaping pit in the ground with some sort of plumbing being installed.

Keisha recognizes what's happening before Jasmyn does. "You're not expanding the museum," she says.

"God, no," says Charles, waving away the very thought. "We have a much better use for this space." He claps his hands together, ready for his big reveal. "Asha and I are building a spa."

He pivots and points at the pit in the ground. "State-of-the-art hot tub there." He pivots again and points to the doorway leading to the second gallery. "Ionic cleaning shower and steam room will be in there. We're still deciding on how to configure the massage and meditation spaces. Of course we'll have diffusing sconces and—"

Jasmyn interrupts him. "You're getting rid of the museum altogether?" She rubs her hand down her stomach. "I don't understand. You loved it."

"This is a much better use of this space," he says. For a second, Jasmyn thinks maybe he's teasing them, like this whole thing is a joke. But then she takes a longer look around the room at all the destruction. If this is a joke, it's an elaborate one.

She turns back to Charles. He beams so brightly, he's hard to look at. "What happened to *Aftermath*?"

"I sent it back." He claps his hands together again. "So, what do you ladies think? Can't you just picture how restful this space will be?"

The poison on Keisha's face isn't so funny this time around.

"If it makes you happy," Jasmyn says, even though she doesn't mean it. She just wants to keep the peace and prevent Keisha from blurting out whatever is on her mind.

"Why wouldn't it?" asks Charles.

The rest of the evening isn't salvageable, though they go through the motions. Jasmyn talks about what the goals for their Black Lives Matter chapter should be and whether to elect a formal leadership group with titles, etc.

"Whatever you ladies decide will be fine," Charles says.

Jasmyn is asking about membership dues, when Charles interrupts. "I'm sorry, ladies, but we'll have to call it a day. I need to meet up with Asha at the Wellness Center."

Keisha jumps up right away, like she's been waiting for an excuse to get out of there. She holds out a hand to Jasmyn and helps her to her feet.

Charles walks them to the door.

Jasmyn tries to talk to Keisha in the driveway. But Keisha walks away from her. "Not now," she says, shaking her head. She hurries to her car like she's being chased. "I'll talk to you later."

At home, Jasmyn gets caught up with making dinner and then helping Kamau with his homework. After dinner, King heads up to the Wellness Center.

She waits for his car to pull away before calling Keisha. But she doesn't pick up. Jasmyn's heart squeezes, a slow panic starting to build. She sends her a quick "just checking in" text.

Her phone buzzes in her hand, but it's not Keisha texting back. It's a notification from the group chat with her and Charles: *Keisha Daily has removed herself from the chat.*

She texts Keisha again:

Jasmyn: Why'd you leave the chat?

Keisha: Oh I'm doing more than that

Keisha: I'm telling Darlene we need to leave Liberty

Keisha: I don't want whatever happened to Charles to happen to me

Keisha: You should leave too

Keisha: Can't you see?

Keisha: Something's not right

Keisha: Something's happening to the people around here

Keisha: I'm leaving before it gets me too

PART THREE

"Look at Flint," Keisha says to Jasmyn. "Lead in the water. And they knew that shit for years." She dumps sugar into her coffee and stirs so vigorously it splashes the table. "All those babies with lead in their blood. And how many people died from that disease—"

"Legionnaires," Jasmyn says.

"Yes. Legionnaires." She points her spoon at Jasmyn. "Don't you tell me there couldn't be something in the water here," she says.

Jasmyn had called Keisha first thing this morning. It took twenty minutes of cajoling to convince her to meet for coffee. In the half an hour they'd been sitting in the café, Keisha hasn't smiled or laughed even once.

"You can't really think we're being poisoned," Jasmyn says.

"I know what I know," Keisha says, voice quiet. "You saw Charles. He was a different person."

Jasmyn sips her tea. What can she possibly say? She's as upset by the way Charles was acting as Keisha is. But it's crazy to believe there's something in the water causing him to do it.

What happened in Flint was criminal and neglectful and terrible. But, Jasmyn knows, it is also very much in keeping with the ways Black communities have always been neglected. But this is Liberty: that couldn't happen here. And besides, what Keisha is imagining isn't just institutional neglect. It's the stuff of science fiction. What kind of chemical could cause Charles to act so strangely?

"You think I'm a fool," Keisha says.

Jasmyn leans forward. "I don't think you're a fool. You're upset and confused. I am, too."

Keisha rubs the rim of her coffee cup with her thumb and looks around the café. "Black people everywhere and I never felt so alone," Keisha says.

"You have me," Jasmyn says.

"I know. But you're the only real friend I've made in the six months I've been here."

"Six months is not long," Jasmyn says.

Keisha finally smiles. "For *you* maybe. I mean you actually cringed when I hugged you that first time."

Jasmyn smiles, too. "Takes me a while to warm up to people."

"All I'm saying is six months is not long for *you*, but for me it might as well be forever. I'm not shy. I'm out there up in everybody's business. Any place but Liberty and I'd have made fifty good friends by now."

"What about the other teachers?"

Keisha shakes her head. "None of them are more than colleagues. And I'm not trying to get friendly with the parents. I mean I like you, but if I was Kamau's teacher we wouldn't be friends. I did that one time at my old job and it was a whole mess. Better for those lines not to cross."

Jasmyn isn't sure what to say. Two days ago she would've counted Charles among her friends. A new one, yes. But one with potential to last.

"Something in the water, Keisha? That just sounds—"

"Or in the air or chemical waste runoff. I don't know, but there's something," Keisha says.

"So something psychotropic or—"

"Yes," Keisha says, nodding. "You ever heard stories of people whacked out on sleeping pills? Possible side effects include murderous psychosis and rage." She laughs. "How they gonna call that shit *side* effects? Those are *main* effects. Murderous rage is not something you do on the side."

They both laugh, holding on to the feeling for as long as they can.

But their reprieve is too fragile to last. "So this . . . drug is doing what? Making folks forget they're Black?" Jasmyn asks.

Keisha sighs. "Two weeks ago Charles was James Baldwin crossed with early Malcolm. Now he's drinking cucumber water talking 'bout ionic therapies and spiritual massages or some shit. And don't forget Angela Sayles didn't even tell you about the BLM chapter that was here. Never mind Benjamin showing you his whole naked ass." She shakes her head. "I'm telling you, it's time to go."

"Come on," Jasmyn says. "You're not serious."

"Damn right I'm serious."

"You're willing to leave all this?" Jasmyn says, sweeping her hand out. At the big table in the back, six brand-new mothers are having a mommy meeting. At another table, a group of teenagers are laughing the way teenagers laugh, which is to say too loud and too long. No one is giving them dirty looks.

"It's just the money turning him bougie, Keisha. Swear to God money and property and status will make people forget themselves."

Keisha looks at her with something close to pity. "You go ahead and believe what you want," she says. "But me and Darlene? We leaving."

≈

King and Kamau are playing Monopoly at the coffee table in the family room when Jasmyn gets home.

She plants kisses on both their heads. "Who's winning?" she asks.

"I don't like this game," Kamau says.

King leans back against the couch. "Don't give up on it because you don't understand it. Give it time."

"Can we play Uno instead?" asks Kamau.

King sighs, but he pushes the Monopoly set to the side and deals the Uno cards.

"How's Keisha?" King asks.

"Tell you about it later," Jasmyn says, not wanting to talk about it in front of Kamau. "Deal me in," she says.

Later doesn't happen until Kamau is in bed. They settle down on the backyard couch after King lights the firepit and turns on the pool waterfall.

"Keisha wants to move out of Liberty. Back to the city," Jasmyn says.

King frowns. "Darlene loves it here."

"*She* may love it, but Keisha's not happy," Jasmyn says. She tells him what happened with Charles. How he got rid of his museum. How he wasn't interested in starting the BLM chapter anymore. "He's different," she says.

"You hardly know him. Maybe this is who he is," King says.

Jasmyn grips King's shoulder and shakes him lightly. "Baby, come on. You know I have good instincts for our kind of people. He wasn't no Uncle Tom. He was fierce. I told you what he said about sending white people out to sea." She lets go of King's shoulder. "I can't understand it. People don't change overnight like that."

"I agree with you," King says. "Which is why I'm saying he must've always been this way."

"And what? He was pretending? For what?"

King shrugs. "I don't know, baby. You know people don't always make sense. Maybe he was just talking the talk to fit in with you and Keisha."

She drops her head into her hands. Why would Charles pretend? Why would he feel like he needed to play a role for them?

King is right about people not making sense, though. One of the first things she'd learned as a young public defender was that there's nothing more mysterious than other people and their motivations.

"Still," Jasmyn says. "People around here are not like I expected."

King tilts his head back and drains his beer. He puts the bottle aside and opens another one. "You know what's funny about what you just said?" he says with a little laugh.

"What?"

"You doing the same thing white people do to us. You're stereotyping, thinking we're all the same."

"That's not—"

He shakes his head. "Yeah it is," he says. "We always insisting to white people that we're not a monolith. That we don't all think the same. But the minute one of us thinks something different we're quick to call him Uncle Tom and race betrayer."

Jasmyn turns to him, watches the firelight flicker across his face. "Why are you defending him?" she asks.

"I'm not defending him," King says. "I'm just saying we can't expect all Black folks to be the same as us."

Mildly irritated now, she turns away from him. Of course he's wrong about how she expects all Black people to be the same as them. To have the same sense of kinship, community, and solidarity. She stares into the fire and remembers the first time she understood this. She was a freshman in college. The class, held in one of those enormous lecture halls, was introductory biology or chemistry or some such. She'd scanned the room and sat down next to one of the few Black girls she could find. Jasmyn can still picture the way the other girl shrank into herself and never looked her way even once. It took Jasmyn a couple of semesters to realize that some Black people like to be the only Black person in a room. One Black person is special, uniquely gifted maybe. Two or more Black people—especially if they are sitting together?—well, surely affirmative action was at play.

King brings her back to the present. "So what does Charles have to do with Keisha wanting to move?"

Jasmyn shakes off her irritation and explains Keisha's theory about something being in the water. In the air.

King laughs. "I guess we don't know Keisha as well as we think we do," he says. "I mean, what kind of crazy talk is that?"

Saying it aloud to King does make it seem even more ridiculous.

Jasmyn pinches the bridge of her nose and sighs. Keisha might be a little out there because of this theory of hers, but it doesn't change the fact that Jasmyn doesn't want her to leave. Keisha is her friend. The only one she's made in Liberty. The thought of her leaving fills Jasmyn with a low-level panic. Who else will help make her feel grounded? Who else will make her feel like she's part of a community? No one else even seems to understand what being in community means.

King takes a long sip of his beer. "Anyway, I don't care about all that," he says. "What I want to know is, are *you* unhappy? You want to move back to the city, too?"

Is she unhappy? Not so much unhappy as disappointed. Across the yard, she watches as the waterfall cascades into the pool. Waves ripple across the surface before dissipating into nothing at the edges. King had told their landscape architect that he wanted the backyard to be an oasis, someplace to retreat from the world.

King nudges her shoulder with his. "Baby, if you're not happy here, we can leave."

She leans into him, laces her fingers with his. "Really? You would move?"

He kisses her forehead. "We moved here to make our lives better. No point in being here otherwise," he says. "Besides, if you're not happy, I'm not happy."

"I'm just impatient," she says. "Let's give it a few more months." There are so many things she likes about Liberty. The Black excellence. The sense of physical safety. Psychic safety. The way no one follows her around a store when she's shopping. The way no one crosses the street or clutches their purse or locks their car door when King walks by. The way Kamau is thriving.

Charles will come to his senses, and if he doesn't, he'll be the one missing out. Keisha's not really going to leave. Together, they'll get the BLM chapter going. Anything worth having takes effort and time.

Jasmyn's willing to give as much effort and as much time as it takes.

2

Keisha: Talked to Darlene last night.

Keisha: She wants us to stay until summer

Keisha: Something about selling the house and property taxes blah blah

Jasmyn: What about taxes?

Keisha: For real? Who cares?

Keisha: Only thing I care about is getting out

Keisha: You talk to King?

Jasmyn: Yeah

Jasmyn: But I'm going to give it a few more months

Keisha: A few more months and maybe you'll turn into Charles too

Keisha: I'm not waiting until summer

Keisha: I already found a real estate agent

Keisha: If we lose money, we lose money

Keisha: Meantime imma get in touch with some reporters I know

Keisha: See if we have a Flint situation up in here

3

On Sunday morning, Jasmyn opens her front door to find Nina Marks on the other side of it. The woman smiles bright and extends a hand for Jasmyn to shake.

"You probably don't remember me. I'm—"

Jasmyn frowns. What's Nina Marks playing at? Less than a month ago, she'd been at their dinner party. And before that, they'd talked for over an hour at the Wellness Center. "Of course I remember you," she says.

"Wonderful. I was hoping I could—"

"King's not here," Jasmyn says.

"I'm not here to see King," Nina Marks says. "I promise I won't take too much of your time."

Jasmyn tries one more time to forestall the other woman's entry. "If you're here to offer me a spa membership, I'm going to have to decline," Jasmyn says.

"Oh no. I would never offer you a membership," says Nina Marks.

Jasmyn's mouth drops open slightly. The gall of this woman.

Nina Marks clarifies. "Unless I've misjudged your interest?"

It takes Jasmyn a second to understand that Nina hadn't been trying to insult her. "No, you haven't misjudged," she says.

"Very well," Nina says with a nod. "I'm here because Kingston thought maybe you'd be able to help me with a project." She glances down at a briefcase Jasmyn hadn't noticed she was carrying. "May I come in?"

Jasmyn wants to say no, to tell Nina that she's too busy at the moment. It wouldn't be a complete lie. She spent the entire morning catching up on some work and the news. But her curiosity, and the fact that King had volunteered her in the first place, convinces her to let the other woman in.

In the kitchen, Jasmyn considers not offering Nina something to drink. She doesn't want her to get too comfortable and linger. In the end though, it feels too impolite not to at least go through the motions of being hospitable. She offers Nina a cup of coffee, which she accepts before settling herself into a chair at the breakfast table.

Jasmyn takes a seat opposite her, clasps her hands on the table, and straightens her posture the way she does in court. She's not going to make the mistake of relaxing in Nina Marks's company again. "How can I help you?" she asks.

"Do you remember at the spa we spoke about some of the work I do surrounding trauma?"

"Yes," says Jasmyn. That work was part of why Jasmyn had liked her initially.

"A year or so ago my colleagues and I were awarded a grant to document the deleterious psychological and physiological effects of racism on the Black psyche. Our working title is 'Memory and Trauma.' As a country, we often talk about the judicial and financially punitive effects of racism. We spend less time focused on the mental health ramifications of living in a racist society." Now Jasmyn remembers that Keisha had mentioned something about this project before.

Jasmyn unclasps her hands and drums her fingers on the table once. "Huh," she says, not hiding her skepticism. "I have to say I'm surprised."

"Why is that?"

She meets Nina's eyes. "How do you reconcile a project like this with what you said to me at the spa?"

"Aha," Nina Marks says with a nod. "You're upset that I said Blackness is a problem."

It's uncanny, Nina Marks's ability to guess what she's thinking. Still, Jasmyn doesn't confirm for Nina just how aggrieved and disappointed she'd been by that comment. Instead of responding, she deploys a tactic she sometimes uses with reticent clients: she folds her arms across her chest and waits in silence.

A few seconds pass before Nina capitulates and continues on. "I'll admit I could have put it more elegantly. But you can hardly deny that Blackness is perceived as a problem in this country. Whiteness is good, fair, attractive, intelligent. It allows for individuality, a multiplicity of being. Blackness is its opposite. Bad, unfair, ugly, unintelligent. Not to mention the extent to which all of us Black folks are perceived as being the same."

Jasmyn almost laughs at Nina's phrasing. Academics are something else. Why use one word—racism—when one hundred words will do? Still, the project does sound interesting. "Why do this?" she asks. "Certainly we, Black people at least, already know the effects of racism."

"Yes, but we're attempting to open a new field of study." From her briefcase, Nina Marks unearths something that looks very much like Jasmyn's sleep bonnet, except it's attached via an electrical cord to a slim black box with a single toggle that reads RECORD ON / OFF.

She hands the contraption to Jasmyn. "That device monitors brain activity," she says. "One of the things my colleagues and I know from our work with soldiers suffering from PTSD is that trauma lights up specific parts of the brain. Using that device, we're hoping to prove *scientifically* that—"

Jasmyn finishes her thought for her. "You're trying to prove that being Black in America is like being constantly traumatized."

"Yes, that's exactly right," says Nina.

Jasmyn examines the bonnet. It's dark blue and just her size. A network of flat wire receptors crisscross the interior. "What a world," she says. "We can figure out where harm resides in the brain, but not how to prevent the harm from happening in the first place." She sets the bonnet down on the table. Despite her wariness, Jasmyn finds herself leaning in, intrigued. "How does this all work?" she asks.

Nina explains. She's asking participants to wear the monitoring device while recording every racist incident they can remember experiencing, starting from early childhood and continuing through to their present day.

"As soon as you turn it on and start recording, the data is automatically uploaded to our servers. We made it as easy as possible to use," Nina says.

"I see," Jasmyn says with a nod. "And what are you going to do with the information once you have it?"

"Hard data backed by rigorous study is hard to deny. We can use it for advocacy—"

"Not just that," Jasmyn says, interrupting Nina as her mind races through the legal implications. "You can use the data to prove harm." She fast-taps her fingers against the table. "And if you can prove it, you can litigate it. And if you can litigate it, you can be compensated for it." Imagine, Jasmyn thinks, if racism cost the perpetrator as much as it cost the victim. Of course money alone could never be enough to make up for all the harm, but it was a start.

"Yes, exactly," says Nina. "I hoped you'd be as excited about this as I am," says Nina.

Jasmyn looks at her. On the one hand, she doesn't much like Nina Marks. The weirdness at the spa is too much to let go of. All the same, Jasmyn can't deny the project's merit.

"What would you need me to do?" she asks.

Nina touches the bonnet of the device. "Record all the racial trauma you can recall. Be as vivid and specific and detailed as you can. No incident is too small to document. And even if you aren't sure an incident was racially motivated, record it anyway."

"And it would be safe for me to do all this with the baby?" Jasmyn asks.

"Yes, absolutely. Of course, you should take good care and pace yourself as you go."

"OK," Jasmyn says with a nod. She looks back at the device and huffs. "You understand how long it will take, right? To record *all* my racial trauma?"

"It takes as long as it takes," says Nina. She sips her coffee. "What do you think? Will you help me?"

The glimmer in Nina Marks's eyes tells Jasmyn that the other woman already knows what Jasmyn's answer will be. It's possible she knew Jasmyn's answer even before she asked. Nevertheless, this project is too good a cause for her to pass up.

"OK," Jasmyn says. "I'll help."

"Wonderful," says Nina. "Just wonderful."

4

"Welcome to the Black Beverly Hills," Keisha says as she parks the car.

Jasmyn laughs. "Fancy," she says.

With a 70 percent Black population, Baldwin Hills is one of the largest Black communities in Los Angeles. The largest is, of course, Liberty, at 100 percent.

"Why do they call it that anyhow?" Jasmyn asks.

"Tina Turner used to live here. Ice Cube, too," Keisha says. She looks out the driver's-side window. "What do you think?" she asks, meaning the two-story house she's set to tour today. "I know it's . . . modest."

Jasmyn knows that by *modest* Keisha means small. Of course it's really only small when compared with the houses in Liberty. Even the homes at the base of Liberty Hill are bigger than this one.

"Are you sure you want to do this?" Jasmyn asks. "We could go have an early cocktail instead."

But Keisha's not having it. She pushes open the car door. "I'm more than sure."

The real estate agent, a Black woman with light brown skin and shoulder-length braids, guides them through the tour.

The house is fine. Three small bedrooms and two bathrooms. The kitchen is newly remodeled and the backyard has a small pool. Keisha doesn't say much, but her disappointment is obvious.

"Why are you looking to leave Liberty?" the agent asks Keisha once they are back outside.

"Just not for me," Keisha says.

The agents nods. "Funny enough, I applied for a job at their brokerage firm but I didn't get it."

Jasmyn watches Keisha's attention prick up. "They say why?" she asks.

"You know, I was so disappointed I even called back and asked the woman if there was something I could've done better during the interview process. She said I just wasn't what they were looking for."

"What's that mean?" Keisha asks. Her voice is too loud. Jasmyn puts a hand on her shoulder.

"To each his own," the agent says with a shrug.

Back on the sidewalk, an older Black couple in their late sixties or seventies wearing matching blue sweatsuits walks by. "This is a good neighborhood to live in," the man says with a smile and a wink.

"We raised all three of our boys here," adds the woman. She smiles too and they walk on. Jasmyn watches them until they turn the corner onto the next block.

When she and King were still newlyweds and she imagined raising a family and growing old, this is the kind of neighborhood she pictured. Modest. Friendly. The house they just toured is what she pictured, too. But now, compared with the expansive splendor of the houses in Liberty, it seems quaint and shabby. Jasmyn wishes, just for a moment, that she could see it with her old eyes.

Back in the car, Keisha starts the engine, but doesn't pull away. "Costs too much for what it is," she says. "Darlene will never go for it."

Jasmyn touches her arm. "I know you said you were sure, but maybe you should reconsider all this. Like you said, Darlene won't—"

Keisha cuts her off. "No. I'm doing this." Her voice is loud and hard.

"All right, Jesus," Jasmyn says, throwing her hands up as if to ward her off.

Keisha grabs both of Jasmyn's hands in her own. "I'm sorry. I'm sorry," she says. "I know you don't understand all this."

Jasmyn tugs her hands away, places them in her lap. "I just don't want you to leave is all."

"We'll still be friends. You can't get rid of me. You're the best thing I found there and I'm not giving you up," Keisha says and then sighs. "Besides, it's only a matter of time before you realize I'm right and want to hightail it out of here, too. Maybe we'll end up being neighbors."

Before they came to look at houses, it felt to Jasmyn that Keisha could still change her mind. Now, though, she can't deny that she really is going to leave.

Keisha grips the wheel and stares outside the window. "You ever feel like you and King are living in different worlds?" she asks.

The question is rhetorical. Jasmyn waits for her to continue.

"Used to be that me and Darlene saw everything in the same way. Things started to change after she switched jobs and got all those promotions and started making the kind of money I never even knew to dream about."

The similarities between their situations is striking. Thankfully, King hadn't changed too much.

"Anyway, no point in looking backwards. Have to forget about the way things used to be." Keisha shifts the car into drive. "We best get going," she says. "Don't want to be late for the next one."

A few blocks later, they pass by the older couple they'd seen before. They're holding hands. The woman is laughing and the man is watching her laugh.

Seeing them, Jasmyn can't help projecting herself into the future. By the time she's their age, she and King will, hopefully, have lived in Liberty for thirty or forty years. All her reservations about it will be long gone. They will have formed deep friendships and meaningful community. Their family will have made memories in every corner of their house and on every block of their neighborhood. At the edge of her periphery, Jasmyn sees it: some gorgeous Christmas morning in their home years from now. Kamau and his younger brother and their spouses and their children will be there. Oh, how wonderful it'll be to have grandkids to love. Both living rooms will have Christmas trees and they'll be littered with tinsel, discarded wrapping paper, and bows. From outside she'll hear the sounds of pure happiness, her children's children laughing and splashing and making new memories. The kitchen will be warm and suffused in scent. Trays of haphazardly decorated cookies and one too many pies will line the countertops and both ovens will be filled with roasts and stuffing and mac and cheese and the adults, tipsy from boozy eggnog, will chat and reminisce and plan and all of it will be too much and, too, just enough.

Jasmyn comes back to herself feeling lighter than she had before. She imagines it. Kamau and the new baby grown. And with kids of their own. It almost feels like a memory, this vision of what her life could be. It's exactly what she needs to ground herself. One day, in the very near future, she knows she'll look back on this day and be unable to remember what her old friend Keisha had been so afraid of.

5

Jasmyn hovers her finger over the RECORD switch. With King working late and Kamau long asleep, her plan is to spend the rest of the evening documenting racist encounters for Nina Marks. Certainly it's going to take a lot more than one session to catalog the litany of experiences she's had. Should she, for instance, document every time she'd been followed around a store as if she was going to rob it? Or every time someone had tried to touch her Afro without permission? Or every time someone assumed the only reason she was in an honors class or an advanced college seminar or even law school was because of affirmative action? And so what if it was affirmative action? Historic wrongs needed to be redressed. Never mind that white people had been benefiting from their own form of affirmative action since the days of forty acres and a mule. Should she record every single time she's had to debate someone—usually white, usually a man—who was "just playing devil's advocate" about the ongoing need for affirmative action? The devil, she sometimes informed them, didn't need any more advocates.

The baby moves and Jasmyn rests her hand on her stomach. "Quit partying in there," she says. She picks up the bonnet part of Nina's device and puts it on. Just as she'd suspected, it fits perfectly.

The more she considers where to begin, the more she realizes just how long this process will take. Should she record the racist things that happen not to her, but to the people she loves? Those incidents affect her, too, after all.

Jasmyn remembers the night King first told her about what happened to his brother. They were exclusive but still at the beginning of their relationship, at the stage where they were starting to reveal their secrets, the ones kept intentionally and the ones that you only remember in the telling. That night, they'd just made love. They were cocooned together in the afterglow, drifting through the stories of their lives. Idly, Jasmyn told King some silly anecdote about her older sister. She'd expected King to laugh, but he didn't.

"I need to tell you something," he'd said.

Here it comes, thought the part of her that loved him too much already. The part of her that knew what they had couldn't last and that he couldn't be as wonderful as he seemed. But he didn't tell her about an estranged wife or a child he'd abandoned. He said, "I used to have a brother. His name was Tommy. A cop killed him."

King cried as he told her the story. One minute he'd had an older brother that looked like him and spoke like him and walked through the world the same as him. An older brother that played ball with him and sometimes let him win. An older brother who protected him from their mother's rages and excesses. An older brother who understood—same as him—how unlovable she sometimes was but—same as him—loved her anyway. One minute King had been ignorant of the ways in which the world not only inflicted damage, but demanded that you survive it, and the next minute he was not.

"I never tell anyone that story," he said when he came to the end.

"Thank you for telling me."

"I love you," he said. It was the first time he'd ever said the words.

"I love you, too," she said, and knew in that moment that she'd marry him.

As she fell asleep, Jasmyn felt she'd understood something essential about King. There was a wounded and innocent place inside him that she'd always be able to sense, but never locate. She'd be able to feel its contours, but be unable to map its terrain. To be with him would be to accept that a part of him was closed and unknowable. But, she told herself, we all have soft and damaged places that need protecting, and she would safeguard his as long as he needed her to.

Now Jasmyn pulls herself back to the present. This is going to take forever. Not only will she have to record the things that happened directly to her and those that happened to people she loves, but she'll also have to include the racism that finds its way into her orbit. The viral videos of racist incidents that flood social media daily. The articles quoting some racist politician or television personality. The seemingly constant news cycle about yet another police shooting. These things don't happen to her, but they affect her. Every headline or viral video simultaneously depresses her and raises her blood pressure. No wonder even well-off Black people don't live as long as their white counterparts. The unrelenting stress of racism kills just as effectively as any bullet.

Jasmyn decides to start with the first time she'd been called the N-word. She takes five long, slow breaths and stretches her neck from side to side, the same ritual she uses before making an opening statement in court. Then she presses the button.

She'd been a freshman in college. It was a late night, unseasonably cold for early fall but otherwise ordinary. She and three other girls had just left a party. She remembers wishing she'd worn more than a mini skirt and a tank top.

The three boys walking toward them were your standard-issue drunk white boys with their baseball caps and their dangerous boredom that so often veered into cruelty. Just as they passed, one of the boys said he'd heard that n***** girls liked to put out. The other three laughed and leered.

Leah, the only white girl in Jasmyn's group, spun back to face them.

"What did you say?" she demanded. Her voice was loud, equal parts shocked and outraged.

Jasmyn pauses the recording. She shivers, suddenly as cold as she'd been that night. She pulls on a sweater and marvels at the power this old memory has over her.

She continues recording. Jasmyn and the other girls had grabbed Leah by the arms and dragged her away. The boys followed them for another block, calling Leah a n*****-lover. Eventually they lost interest and took off, like a passing storm.

Later that night, Leah said, "How dare those boys talk to us like that?" But the other girls knew better. Knew that boys like that dared things all the time and got away with it. After that night, their foursome became a threesome. Leah made new friends, white ones.

After the first recording is done, Jasmyn moves on to the time when she was thirteen and the white security guard at the mall followed her and her sister around all day. At first Jasmyn had been scared and wanted to leave, but Ivy had been defiant. She'd insisted they stay. Together they'd faked loud laughter and pretended for all the world that they were having a good time.

Then on to the time her mother had given her a white baby doll for Christmas. "They don't make Black ones as nice looking," she'd said and laughed. "A whole shelf of them just sitting there and ain't nobody buying them, not even Black folks." It'd taken years of self-examination and years of African American history classes in college to get over her secret fear that she wasn't as pretty as white girls.

Then on to another security guard, this one at the drugstore. He accused her of stealing lipstick and forced her to empty her purse onto the counter. He found nothing because she'd stolen nothing. She'd been so angry, incandescent with it. She'd wanted to pull the shelves down, smash every bottle, smear the ground with so much lipstick they would never get it out. But of course she couldn't do that. She'd left feeling stained and empty, like something had been stolen from *her*.

Then on to her first and only date with a white guy. It'd been a setup by one of her coworkers. Jasmyn had known he was white but was trying to be open-minded. He'd spent a good portion of the appetizer course talking about how he'd never dated a Black woman before and how his parents wouldn't approve. He acted as if being on a date with her made him somehow virtuous. Afterward she'd joked with a girlfriend that maybe sometimes it was better to keep your mind closed. She turned him down for a second date.

Jasmyn checks the time. 10:30 p.m. She texts King to see when he'll be home. *Another hour*, he texts back. *Give you a back rub when you get here*, she promises him.

She pulls the bonnet off and stands. Her neck and shoulders are tight with the kind of tension that will take days to dissipate. It's not easy, this excavating of long-buried hurts. Something about it makes her feel insubstantial, like a specter haunting her own life. She imagines her data making it to Nina Marks for parsing and analysis. She knows the other woman is interested in the science, which part of the brain is triggered by which type of memory. But there are so many other things to be learned. Did most participants have the same kinds of stories? Which were the most prevalent? At what age did they start experiencing micro- and macroaggressions? How many had loved ones they lost to drugs, or poverty, or gang violence, or police violence, or poor health care, or poor education? Who had they lost and when?

Over the next hour Jasmyn records four more incidents, each of them making her feel more hollowed out and vulnerable than the last. She simultaneously feels the need to stop and the need to carry on. She rests her forehead on her desk and reminds herself that, no matter how painful this process is, it's for a good cause. Doing the work is never easy, but always worth it. A new energy washes over her. She picks her head back up, puts the bonnet on, flicks the RECORD switch and continues recording, for the good of Black people everywhere.

PART FOUR

King has been working so much and so hard that when he suggests they take Kamau out of school for a couple of days and have a long weekend getaway, Jasmyn agrees despite the number of cases on her docket. At work, her boss is surprised at her request. The last time she'd taken time off, outside of the usual holidays, was for maternity leave with Kamau.

The resort, perched on a cliff overlooking the Southern California coast, is extravagant. They are greeted by name, offered champagne, and escorted to their three-bedroom oceanfront villa by their personal butler.

King and Kamau immediately rush out to the patio to take in the view.

Jasmyn hangs back, wandering through the rooms, running her fingers over the surfaces of things, her emotions swinging between awe, gratitude, and guilt. Awe because the resort and their room is undeniably beautiful. Gratitude because she gets to be here with the people she loves most in the world. Guilt because how is this her life? Why should she have so much when others have so little? How many people are being unfairly sucked into the system while she's here?

"Incredible isn't it?" King says when she joins him on the patio.

And it is. The air smells of brine and tastes of salt. The Pacific Ocean, splayed out before her, glitters silver and blue.

Jasmyn puts her arms around King's waist and presses herself into the warmth of him. "How'd you hear about this place, anyway?" she asks.

"Carlton," he says.

Of course. Jasmyn forces herself not to say anything disparaging. How long will King's hero worship last?

"You know we're not billionaires like him, right?" she says.

King pulls her in closer and smiles down at her. "Stop worrying," he says. "We can afford it."

Jasmyn looks back out over the ocean. "We should increase our charity donations."

"Which one?"

"All of them," she says.

≈

On the first day, instead of the beach, they go to the family pool. It has a lazy river and four water slides. But Kamau refuses to swim. He sits at the pool's edge, his skinny legs dangling just above the water. When Jasmyn asks him why, he says he's not feeling it today.

Ordinarily she wouldn't prod him to get into the pool, wouldn't ask King to push him to get in, but Jasmyn can sense the guests—the white guests—watching them. She feels that strange multiplying that she always does in predominantly white spaces: she's aware of who she is, and of who they think she is, and of who she thinks they think she is.

A dark-haired white woman is looking their way. She's wearing sunglasses, so Jasmyn can't be sure she's watching them. Still, she imagines that the woman ascribes Kamau's reluctance to swim to an inability to swim, and that inability to swim to Blackness. Jasmyn remembers a story she'd heard about a Black boy in the Jim Crow south. Somehow he'd ended up on a little league baseball team with all white teammates. At the end of the season, the team won the league title. To celebrate, they went to a public pool. But back then Black people were forbidden to swim in public pools for fear their Black skin would contaminate the water. The pool workers denied the boy access. For most of the day, he was forced to sit outside the pool and watch his teammates celebrate without him. Eventually one of the coaches worked out a compromise with a pool attendant. All the white people were asked to leave the pool for a few minutes. The pool attendant allowed the Black boy to board a float. The worker then pushed him—once—around the pool, all the while admonishing him not to get any of his body parts into the water. If he did, the pool would have to be drained and refilled, effectively ending the swim day for everyone else. The little boy didn't touch the water.

It hurts Jasmyn to think of it. To think of the confused devastation that little boy must've endured. How small he must've felt. She knows in the deepest part of herself that he never recovered from that wounding, that it was a scar he returned to day after day for a lifetime, turning it over, running his finger along the raised keloid, pressing down on it, as if it'd just happened, as if it was always already happening.

How can she protect Kamau from such a wounding? *Can* she protect him?

She knows, of course, that this situation with Kamau isn't the same. For one thing, he's choosing to sit where he is. For another thing, he's *allowed* in this pool. They've paid for him to be able to choose whether to enter. They've paid for his right to be here.

But *why* is he choosing not to enter? Is it because the other kids in the pool are all white and blond? She wonders, briefly, if her efforts to make Kamau more comfortable in his own skin have made him uncomfortable with other people's. It seems to Jasmyn that it doesn't matter what Kamau's reason is. Not being allowed versus not feeling welcome. Maybe they're not so far away from the Jim Crow south after all. There are still so many ways to restrict Black movement.

"Go help him," she says to King. Her voice, she knows, is shrill.

King looks at her, a question on his face.

She doesn't have an answer for him. "Help him," she says again.

Half an hour later Kamau and King are in the pool together playing. The resort staff doesn't drain the pool.

Later, she texts Keisha to ask about her house search. It's been only a few weeks of looking, but Jasmyn knows Keisha's probably getting antsy. A part of her wants the search to be going well for Keisha's sake. Another part of her, though, wouldn't mind if it dragged on long enough for Keisha to come to her senses and realize she's being paranoid about Liberty. Maybe she'd even realize that it's better for her to stay and help get some of their neighbors on board with helping out Black folks less fortunate than themselves.

Jasmyn: How's the search going? See anything good?

Keisha: Not a one

Keisha: But never mind about that right now. Guess what I'm doing?

Jasmyn: What?

Keisha: Taking a vacation!

Jasmyn: That's great! To where?

Keisha: No idea! Darlene's surprising me. Planned a whole thing. Even got Principal Harper to give me a couple of days off.

Jasmyn: Fabulous!

Keisha: Right?

Keisha: It's just a few days but time away from this place is just what we need.

Keisha: Maybe I can even get her to come around to my POV on leaving Liberty

Keisha: And don't forget: vacation sex is the best sex

Jasmyn: Hahahahahah

Jasmyn: Have a good time

On the second day of the trip, when she goes down to the pool, Kamau's already in and playing with an Asian American boy who looks to be his age.

"He finally found a friend," King says.

The boy's parents are in the cabana next to theirs. The wife's name is

Christina. She's thin and muscled and wearing a bright pink one-piece. Both she and her husband are attorneys, but "nothing noble like the work you're doing," the woman says. She just made partner in one of the big mergers and acquisitions firms. Her husband, who is "taking a quick call in the hotel room," is the lead in-house attorney for a massive hedge fund. They talk about the things they have in common—law school and the bar exam and raising a little boy.

"We're one and done," Christina says, looking at the boys as they race from one end of the pool to the other. "We're both so busy. And we like our lifestyle the way it is. Who wants to go back to diapers?" She takes in Jasmyn's stomach and blushes. "I'm so sorry! No offense!"

"No worries," Jasmyn says, laughing. "I'm not looking forward to diapers, either."

Finally they get to talking about Liberty.

"Oh, you live *there*?" Christina says.

Jasmyn takes a breath, ready to defend Liberty. *We're not excluding other people, we're simply prioritizing ourselves.*

"I've heard incredible things about that place. The houses. The schools. Vincent and I were even joking the other day that it might be worth it to turn Black just so we can live there."

Jasmyn can see from the slight widening of her eyes that the woman realizes her mistake. This time she doesn't offer an "I'm sorry" or a "no offense." As if by not apologizing she can fool herself into thinking there's nothing to apologize for.

This, Jasmyn thinks, is the thing about being Black in America. Any conversation with a non-Black person could take a turn at any time. You think you're talking about one thing, but the other person is always somehow talking about your Blackness.

Might even be worth it to turn Black. Jasmyn examines the phrase from all angles and knows there's no good way to take it. In it, there's the idea that Blackness is a costume with certain benefits that you can slip into when it suited you. But she'd said "*might* be worth it." Jasmyn supposes that the *might* contains a kind of tacit acknowledgment of just how hard it is to be Black in America. In the end, the woman had concluded that not even the perceived benefit of *becoming* Black in order to get into Liberty was worth actually *being* Black. Then, too, there was the issue of what it would mean to "turn Black." Did the other woman think Blackness was just a matter of pigmentation? Didn't she know that it was more than that?

Silent minutes pass as Jasmyn turns the phrase over in her mind.

The other woman settles back on her lounge. "How *does* Liberty work actually? Is it all copacetic, legally I mean? Can Asian people live there?" she asks with a laugh. "I wouldn't mind getting away from all the white people myself. We're victims of racism, too. We should band together."

"Liberty is about more than victimhood," Jasmyn says.

"Of course," says the woman. "I didn't mean to imply otherwise."

Jasmyn slips on her sunglasses and leans back on her lounge. The other woman says nothing more.

In the pool, Kamau and his new friend are throwing a beach ball back and forth. Jasmyn watches as water streams from their hair, washes over their eyes, slips across their thin shoulders, rolls across their skinny, not-yet-muscled arms before it reenters the pool. The boys laugh and splash and dunk their heads beneath the water.

Each time they come up, Jasmyn thinks of the purity of baptism. She thinks about that poor boy who hadn't been allowed in the water for fear he would contaminate it. She tries to imagine Kamau in that little boy's place, but her mind refuses to make the substitution. Even in her imagination, she can't inflict that horror on him.

At the other end of the pool, two little white boys are playing a game similar to Kamau's. Jasmyn watches as they dunk their heads under. She watches as the water baptizes them, too.

Excerpt from *The Brooklyn Informer* newspaper:

Grand Jury Declines to Indict Brooklyn Cop Who Killed a 37-Year-Old Unarmed Black Man

Officer Charles Easton fatally shot Byron Way outside of a convenience store in the Brownsville section of Brooklyn. The officer reportedly believed that Way matched the description of a suspect involved in a series of armed robberies in the area. According to police, Officer Easton's attempt to stop Way resulted in an altercation followed by a chase. Way allegedly reached into his waistband, which led the officer to shoot him. However, Way was unarmed.

Way's wife decried the rulings. "My husband is dead because he was profiled, because every white cop in this city thinks every Black man is a suspect. He didn't look anything like the person they were looking for and now my son doesn't have a father. My son no longer has a father because a white cop claims he made a mistake. He made the mistake, but me and my Carlton are the ones paying for it."

2

The days after their vacation are hectic—Jasmyn is extra busy at work to make up for the time off. At her thirty-two-week pregnancy checkup, Jasmyn's doctor asks when she'll start maternity leave. Jasmyn tells her she wants to wait as long as possible.

"Take it easy," the doctor says. "The world's problems will still be there when you get back."

On Wednesday night, just after she finishes recording a few more incidents for Nina Marks's project, Jasmyn texts Keisha, figuring she must be back from her trip.

Jasmyn: My vacation sex was great. How about yours?

No doubt, Keisha will have something outrageous to say to that. What Jasmyn really wants to ask is if she's changed her mind about leaving Liberty, but she doesn't want to aggravate her in case it's a sore subject. Hopefully, she and Darlene had a good time and reconnected the way she wanted them to. Hopefully, their reconnection made Keisha decide to stay.

By Thursday afternoon, she still hasn't heard back from her. She sends her a quick text:

Jasmyn: Drinks later? Dying to catch up

Two hours later, Jasmyn is about to ping her again when she hears a commotion from the break room. In the hallway, she spots one of the newer public defenders. She's young and Black. Her eyes are rimmed red.

Jasmyn stops the young woman, touches her arm. "Are you all right?"

"You haven't heard?" the woman asks.

Jasmyn waits for her to continue.

"They didn't indict the cop."

Jasmyn feels the news in the closing of her throat. She'd known it was possible, but the emotional distance between possibility and reality is vast.

The young woman pulls her into a long hug. "I'm leaving for the day," she says. "You should, too."

Jasmyn watches her stride the length of the hallway until she turns a corner and disappears from view.

In the break room, a few of her colleagues—all of them white—are watching the wall-mounted television. A legal expert on CNN defends the lack of indictment from a legal perspective. "This case comes down to the technicalities. I understand that for a lot of Black folks out there this will feel like a slap—"

Jasmyn tunes out. These experts talk about laws as if they weren't written by people. As if the laws and all their technicalities were somehow impartial. Why is she even watching this farce? She knows exactly how the next few days of news coverage will go. The cable channels will each have their own civil rights expert. They will recite the names of the Black men and women lost to police violence in recent years. The news anchors will listen and nod, masks of solemnity on their faces. *Powerful stuff*, they'll say before cutting to a commercial break. Then some other legal expert will come on and explain why, in this *particular* case, the policeman was allowed to get away with murder.

Jasmyn feels tears prick behind her eyes, but she'll be damned if she cries in front of anyone here. Her young colleague had it right. She should leave.

Back in her office she has a sudden mad urge to sweep everything off her desk, to pluck her diplomas from the wall and shatter them against the ground. What is the point of her work, what is the point of a justice system that doesn't believe in justice for all?

She wipes her eyes with the back of her hand. She needs to talk to King. She tries calling but can't reach him. Then she calls Keisha, who picks up right away.

"You saw the news?" Jasmyn says. "They didn't indict."

Keisha is silent for a long time.

"How come you're not saying anything?" asks Jasmyn.

Keisha sighs. "What's there to say?"

It's a fair point. "I was thinking we should go out to a protest," Jasmyn says.

"Is that a good idea?" asks Keisha. "It's going to be a mess out there. You're pregnant. God forbid something happens to you or the baby."

Jasmyn looks at the news page on her laptop screen. All the headlines are about the case. A news conference from the NAACP is expected within the hour in front of the hospital where Mercy Simpson is still fighting for her life.

"You're probably right," Jasmyn says. "What about you? You gonna head down there? BLM is calling for a march to city hall."

"I can't. Darlene and I have plans tonight."

Jasmyn frowns at her phone. She fully expected Keisha to say yes. "You can't cancel or reschedule?"

"No," Keisha says. Her voice is flat.

Jasmyn straightens, suddenly alert. She waits for Keisha to elaborate or explain, but she does neither.

What kind of plans could be more important than marching herself down to city hall and making her voice heard? Jasmyn wonders. *What could be more important than getting out there and fighting?*

She's about to ask one or both questions when she reconsiders. Why is she about to pick a fight with Keisha? It's OK that she has plans. Keisha is not the one she's angry at. She understands her anger over the lack of an indictment is making her unreasonable.

After she and Keisha hang up, Jasmyn stares at the phone for a long time. She remembers how, after her grandmother had died and her sister had moved out, her mother liked to rearrange the furniture in their small apartment. Sometimes it was something big, like moving the TV cart closer to the window. Or the side table from one end of the couch to the other. Most times, though, the thing her mother moved was small. The little wood carving of the Three Wise Men from the shelf table to the coffee table. The stack of gossip magazines from above the coffee table to below it. On those days, Jasmyn would get home from school and know something was off, but she'd be unable to pinpoint exactly what was wrong. This is how she feels now. Like there are changes all around her, but she can't say exactly what they are.

Excerpt from the *San Antonio Examiner*:

Civil Rights Lawsuit Filed Against San Antonio Medical in Case of Black Woman Who Died Hours After Childbirth

The widower of a woman who died from internal bleeding just hours after childbirth is suing famed hospital San Antonio Medical alleging she was given inferior care due to the color of her skin. Otis Marks (pictured above with now-deceased wife Gwendolyn Marks, and their child Nina Marks) and his attorneys allege that San Antonio Medical has a rampant culture of racism that leads to inferior care for Black patients.

"My wife would've received the attention she needed and would still be alive if not for the color of her skin," Mr. Marks commented at a news conference announcing the lawsuit.

3

In the end Keisha is right about the protests turning violent. By the end of the first night, social media is alive with videos. Here are police pepper spraying protestors. Police shoving folks to the ground and kneeling on their backs before cuffing them. Here are burning cars and smashed-in storefronts and boarded-up businesses with freshly constructed BLACK LIVES MATTER signs.

But the image that goes the most viral—getting even more views than the original shooting—is a seven-second clip of a little Black boy hugging a white cop. The boy is small, with a shaved, round head and cheeks that are as chubby as Kamau's used to be. His head is bowed, eyes closed, against the cop's chest. His arms are wrapped around his neck. For his part, the cop is down on one knee. Both his hands are splayed across the boy's back. His eyes are open. His baton and gun are holstered. An armored wall of cops in riot gear blockading protestors forms the backdrop. Jasmyn has already read five think pieces about the video. Some people, mostly white ones, are saying how beautiful and hopeful the video is. There's talk of redemption and forgiveness. Jasmyn sucked her teeth in anger when she read that one. Whose redemption are they talking about? And why should Black people ever forgive white people for all that they'd done? All they are still doing?

The protests grow larger in size every night. More cops. More arrests. More violence. There's talk of a curfew and bringing the National Guard in. The media tallies the cost of property damage. Activists tally the cost of police brutality and systemic racism. Politicians call for peace.

On the sixth night of protests, while she and King are lying in bed together, Jasmyn shows him another viral video. This one is of a Black woman, an activist, angrily describing America as a rigged game of Monopoly where, for four hundred rounds, Black people don't get to play. Then, for the next fifty rounds, Black people do get to play, but if they start to do well, America burns their cards, burns their money, burns their game.

"She's right," King says. "But she should know by now that nothing will ever change."

Jasmyn rests her head on his shoulder. "Baby, that's just your anger talking. You don't really believe that," she says. "We're not out here working this hard for nothing." As cynical as she is about the state of America, Jasmyn still has to believe in its capacity for change. Otherwise, there's no hope for Kamau. For the new baby.

King closes the video. "She's good," he says. "Makes me sick to think of all the things she could accomplish if she didn't have to spend all her time fighting racism."

Jasmyn nods. "It's like that Toni Morrison quote about how the function of racism is distraction."

King frowns. "Which one?"

"Let me find it," Jasmyn says and does a quick search. "OK, here it is. She said: 'The function, the very serious function of racism is distraction. It keeps you from doing your work. It keeps you explaining, over and over again, your reason for being. Somebody says you have no language and you spend twenty years proving that you do. Somebody says your head isn't shaped properly so you have scientists working on the fact that it is. Somebody says you have no art, so you dredge that up.

Somebody says you have no kingdoms, so you dredge that up. None of this is necessary. There will always be one more thing.' "

"That's right," King says, suddenly energized. "That's exactly right."

"Yes and until we get to a world without racism, we don't have any choice but to fight," says Jasmyn. "In the meantime, we need people like her and you and me."

King leans over and kisses her forehead. "You're still the same," he says. "After all this time, you're still the same."

Jasmyn puts her phone away on the nightstand and turns off the lights. "Of course I'm the same," she says into the dark. "Who else would I be?"

King shifts down into the bed, kisses her temple again. "I'll start back up with Mentor LA tomorrow," he says.

≈

It's been two weeks since their respective vacations and Jasmyn still hasn't seen Keisha. The last two plans they made fell through, once because of Keisha and once because of Jasmyn. Tonight, though, they're finally managing to make it work.

Jasmyn gets to the restaurant first. As soon as she slides into the booth, she toes off her heels, leans her head back into the seat, and closes her eyes.

Her peace doesn't last.

"Fancy seeing you here," says a voice from above her.

Jasmyn opens her eyes to find Charles smiling down at her. The area under his eyes is bruised purple and green. Medical tape extends across the bridge of his nose to his cheekbones.

Jasmyn snaps her head forward. "Jesus, what happened to your face?"

"You should see the other guy," he says with a grin. His bruises stretch and crease. Jasmyn winces. Doesn't it hurt him to smile so broadly?

He slides into the booth across from her. "Fantastic to see you," he says.

Was it? Both she and Keisha had gotten the impression he didn't want to see either of them anymore.

Like the last time she'd seen him, Charles is wearing a white Liberty Wellness Center sweatshirt. His head is still shaved. His nails are trim and polished. Manicured.

"Nice to see you, too," Jasmyn says, cautiously, hearing the uncertainty in her own voice. Which version of Charles is she getting today? The one she'd initially met, who she'd wanted to be friends with? Or the one she met later, who'd destroyed his museum, shaved his head, and seemed to want nothing to do with her or Keisha? The one who'd changed so drastically he made Keisha want to leave Liberty? It'd be nice to have the first version back.

Jasmyn touches a hand to her own face. "What happened?" she asks again.

He gives her yet another too-wide smile. "Long story," he says.

Jasmyn waits for him to continue. He doesn't. Instead, he flags down a waiter and orders a gin and tonic. Does he mean to sit there and drink it? She glances over his shoulder toward the door. Seeing him sitting in their booth will just put Keisha in a foul mood.

"Listen, I'm meeting someone," she says.

Charles gives her a small, puzzled frown. "Keisha invited me to join you all. I can leave if you need some girl time," he says and starts to slide back out of the booth.

Jasmyn tries to keep the shock off her face. Unless something drastic had changed that she didn't know about, Keisha hates Charles. Why would she invite him? And without telling her?

"No, stay. I just didn't know is all." Hopefully the smile she's giving him doesn't look as skeptical as she feels.

"How you been?" Charles asks. "Still rocking that 'fro, I see."

When and why had Keisha decided to give him a second chance? She was surely going to be disappointed.

Before Jasmyn can respond, Charles holds his hands up, palms out. "Just teasing," he says.

Jasmyn doesn't know what the joke is.

Across the way, the restaurant door opens. A woman that reminds her vaguely of Keisha—if Keisha got rid of her Afro and straightened her hair and traded her bright, loose clothes and big jewelry for a form-fitting ecru pantsuit and pearl earrings—walks through the doors. The woman's eyes land on Jasmyn. She grins, waves, and strides over.

"Lord. The day I've had," the woman says. "Sorry I'm late." She playfully shoves at Charles until he slides over to make room for her.

Jasmyn is aware her mouth is hanging open, that she hasn't yet greeted Keisha back. She tries to set her glass down but misses the table. It shatters against the floor. Water splatters over her legs, her shoes. "Shit. Shit. Shit," she says.

"Sweetie, it's all right," Keisha says. "It's just a glass."

Jasmyn has an urge to get down on her knees and run her hands over the ground in search of shards. Maybe one will slice deep into her fingertip and she will bleed and, because of the blood, she will have an excuse to leave.

"What is it? Are you all right?" Keisha asks.

She reaches out for Jasmyn's hand, but Jasmyn flinches away.

This person isn't the Keisha she knows. This person is a stranger.

A waitress is suddenly there at the table, promising that someone will clean up the spill. A few seconds later, someone does come over. Jasmyn uses the interruption to will herself to calm down. She watches as the man sweeps up the glass and mops the floor dry, all the while telling herself not to panic, not until she's certain there's something to panic about.

The waitress drops off a new glass of water. Keisha orders a bourbon.

Jasmyn looks at her. At her hair. Maybe it's just a wig. Something to change up her look. "Your hair," she says. Her new bone-straight style is short, flat, sleek, and sharply cut on the bias.

Keisha claps her hands together. "I *know.* Do you love it? I *love* it. Look, I can do this now." She runs her fingers through the strands and smiles. Is that specific ability—the ability to run her hands through her hair unencumbered—one she'd coveted?

"So it's not a wig?" Jasmyn asks, though she can tell from Keisha's hairline that it's not.

Keisha shakes her head. Her hair pendulums around her face.

"You don't like it," Keisha says. Jasmyn can hear the hurt under the accusation. "Darlene said you wouldn't."

Of course she doesn't like it. And the Keisha from a few weeks ago wouldn't have liked it, either.

"It's not that—"

But Charles cuts her off. "I think it looks great," he says.

"Thank *you*," Keisha says. "A little change never hurt anybody." She turns her body to face Charles. "How's your spa coming along?"

Jasmyn presses her back into the booth. Is she hearing what she thinks she's hearing?

Minutes pass and the spa construction talk shows no sign of letting up.

Jasmyn interrupts them. "Starting to sound like you want one, too, Keisha," she says. Her voice isn't as casual as she wants it to be.

"Oh, I'm getting one. I didn't tell you? Construction starts next week."

Jasmyn presses her hands flat against the table. She knows the burning sensation at the base of her throat is more than pregnancy heartburn. It is fear. "What happened to leaving Liberty, moving back to the city?"

Keisha waves her off. "I changed my mind about all that. I was just overreacting. Darlene set me straight. Why would I move back to all the mess the city brings?" She shakes her head. "Everything I need is right here." Her tone is mild, as if leaving Liberty was a silly notion she'd once had, some long time ago.

But just a few weeks ago, Keisha had dragged Jasmyn along to tour houses in Los Angeles. A few weeks ago, Keisha had confessed that Darlene had changed and that their marriage had changed. A few weeks ago, Keisha had thought there was something in the water, in the air, in the food, changing Black people with a capital *B* into black people with a lowercase one.

Where had that Keisha disappeared to, and why?

4

Kamau is asleep when Jasmyn gets home from happy hour, but she checks on him anyway. He likes to sleep with the shades open, and tonight's moon is bright and washes his face in silver light. She bends to kiss his forehead. He's warm, a little bit salty and a little bit sweet. His cheek is leaner than it used to be, baby fat melting away.

Looking at him, Jasmyn thinks maybe it's possible to feel time as it's passing, like a creeping shiver that charts the length of you. Yes, he would always be her baby, but one day he would be a man—a Black man—in America. At what age would he stop being perceived as sweet and cute and innocent and become seen as a threat? Has he passed that age already? Has she missed it?

She sees herself old and dying, in some other room and some other time, some other moonlight casting blue on her skin. Their roles will be reversed. It'll be Kamau who hovers and soothes. Kamau who asks the world to be merciful and to let her live another day, year, lifetime. Will her boy live long enough to tell her goodbye?

In the shower, she forces herself not to think about Keisha and Charles. A brief respite is all she needs before deciding what to do next.

She finds King out in the backyard drinking a beer.

"How was Mentor LA?" she asks.

"It was fine," he says. "His name is Deshaun. Got the usual history. You know how that shit goes."

She's immediately angry. "Your first night back and this is the attitude you're sporting?"

King looks at her, shocked. "Jesus, I didn't mean anything by it. Cut me some slack."

She eyes him hard. "You sound resigned, like you're ready to give up on him already."

"All right, I'm sorry. I didn't mean for it to sound like that. Truly, I didn't mean anything." He pats the couch. "Come on. Sit down."

She sits, lets out a long sigh, and tries to tamp down her anger. What King said upset her, but he's not the one she's angry at, not really.

At the edge of the pool there's a small, foreign piece of plastic trash, the lid to something. Maybe it blew in from the neighbor's bin or from a garbage truck. Jasmyn imagines her own detritus in someone else's yard. What of theirs had the wind deposited elsewhere? What has it brought to them that she can't yet see?

All at once, she needs the lid to be gone, for everything to be in its proper place.

She stands and makes her way over to it.

"Where you going?" King asks.

"Just getting rid of this trash," she says. As she bends to get it, a sharp pain lances through her abdomen. She cries out, wobbles, and almost pitches forward into the pool.

King is at her side immediately. He wraps his arms around her, holding her steady. "Jesus, baby. You OK?"

She presses her hand to the underside of her belly. The pain is already gone. "I'm fine," she says, but her voice is shaky.

"What were you doing?"

"Trying to get rid of that," she says and points at the lid.

King frowns at her. She knows he's confused by the urgency in her voice. She's confused by it herself.

He walks her back to the couch and throws the lid away. "Baby, what's going on?" he asks.

"Something's different about Keisha," she says after he sits.

King looks at her. "Different how?" he asks. There's something in his voice. Something tired and watchful. She imagines what he's thinking. They'd had this conversation before. A few weeks ago she'd said the same thing about Charles.

Still, she tells him how Keisha had invited Charles to happy hour and how they talked about their home spas and how no one had brought up how the cop hadn't been indicted, not even once.

"And she doesn't want to move out of Liberty anymore, if you can believe that."

King swigs his beer.

Jasmyn looks at him. "You not surprised?"

"Nah," he says. "I was surprised when you told me she wanted to move away in the first place. Now she just seems flighty to me." He takes another sip of beer. "I thought you'd be happy she's not leaving."

Jasmyn slaps her thigh. "You're not listening to me. She's *different*."

A few hours ago she would've been thrilled that Keisha was staying. But now? She would rather have lost her as a neighbor than the way she's losing her now.

"How's she different?" King asks.

"She relaxed her hair," Jasmyn says. "No more 'fro."

King looks at her. "When did you get to be so Blacker-than-thou?"

It's not the first time she's been called that, but it's the first time King has called her that.

"I'm not—"

"Sure acting like it," he says. He nudges her shoulder with his. "You the Black police? You going to arrest her for changing her hair?"

Jasmyn isn't sure how to feel. Put that way, her feelings seem absurd. Still, though, it isn't like Keisha did something as simple as wear different color lipstick.

King nudges her shoulder again. "People change, baby."

"You keep saying that to me, but everyone here changing in the same way. Make that make sense."

"You're talking about two people who you barely know in the first place."

But she does know Keisha. Doesn't she?

Jasmyn sighs. "It doesn't even look good on her," she says. "Looks like she's trying to be somebody else."

King shrugs.

"You want me to relax my hair?" Jasmyn asks.

His answer is immediate. "No, of course not. What kind of question is that?"

"You sure?" she asks.

"You're the most beautiful woman in the world. You know I think that."

And it's true. She does know it.

She kisses his cheek. "I love you," she says.

"I love you, too."

"Maybe I'll get braids. Just for a change. Braids are still Black."

"Whatever makes you happy," King says.

Excerpt from the *Charleston Post Gazette*:

A Call to 911 Led to the Death of an Unarmed Black Teenager

Police in South Carolina responded to a 911 "breaking and entering" call. Upon arrival, they encountered a man matching the description provided. According to police, the man, 19-year-old Darren Vail, ran toward them. One of the officers opened fire, killing Vail.

Vail was unarmed. Further investigation revealed that Vail, a food service delivery worker, had mistakenly arrived at the wrong address.

5

Maybe Jasmyn had worried for nothing. Keisha texts her during the week and she almost seems like her old self. They chat about this and that. There's a new movie Keisha wants to see. Things with Darlene are good since their vacation. The one time Jasmyn brings up the lack of indictment for the cop, though, Keisha offers a simple "same as it ever was." The exchange leaves Jasmyn feeling tentatively hopeful. Maybe she hadn't lost her friend after all.

On Wednesday Jasmyn heads downtown to meet Tricia for happy hour.

"Look at your huge, beautiful belly," Jasmyn squeals when Tricia arrives. "You're what, around twenty-eight weeks now?"

Tricia nods and then strikes a pose with her head tossed back and a hand cradling her abdomen. "Can you believe how big I am? *Essence* needs to come put me on their cover."

"You look fantastic," Jasmyn says, laughing.

"I know, right?"

Already, Jasmyn can feel herself relaxing. A night out with Tricia—someone who, unlike Keisha, she's sure she knows—is exactly what she needs.

"This place is still tacky as fuck," Tricia says as they settle in their booth.

The bar is an old favorite of theirs from their college days. It's Hawaiian themed, meaning coconut bras, grass skirts, and tiki torches.

Jasmyn grins. It really is awful but she kind of loves it, too. They both order virgin mai tais.

"How've you been?" Jasmyn asks. "Not having morning sickness anymore, right?"

"It went away the day the second trimester hit, but, funny enough, now all I want to eat is chicken liver and cookies-and-cream ice cream at the same time."

Jasmyn pulls a face. "Ugh, what a combination."

Tricia shrugs. "The child wants what it wants."

They spend the next half an hour talking all things baby. Jasmyn still feels bad about the way she behaved the last time they saw each other. Tricia tells her that she and Dwight are almost done with their nursery. They painted it green to push back against those "dumb gender norms" although she couldn't resist buying the cutest pink onesies she's ever seen.

They're on their second round of drinks before they get to talking about the Mercy Simpson case. Tricia brings it up. Jasmyn feels relieved and vindicated simultaneously. *Of course* they'd talk about it. After all, they're two Black women—Black mothers and mothers-to-be—living in America. The strange thing is *not* bringing it up. *Not* talking about it.

"Can I ask you something?" Jasmyn asks. "It might sound weird."

Tricia nods. "I could feel something was on your mind."

"You think I overdo things?"

"Depends on what we're talking about," Tricia says with a laugh.

"King said something to me last week. Said I was 'blacker than thou.'"

Tricia puts her drink down. "King? That doesn't sound like him at all."

Jasmyn has been so focused on what King said, she forgot to consider whether it was strange that he'd said it.

Tricia is right. It doesn't sound like something King would say. But Jasmyn doesn't think he's changed. She would've noticed that. And he definitely hasn't changed in the way Charles has. The way Keisha seems to have. Still, if she's being honest with herself, he's been different ever since they moved to Liberty.

"You remember me telling you about the teacher at Kamau's school, Keisha?"

Tricia nods.

"She used to have this big old Afro. Kinky as all get out. I just saw her the other day. She relaxed her hair."

"Wait, I'm confused," Tricia says. "What does her hair have to do with what King said?"

"He said the 'blacker than thou' thing *after* I told him about Keisha's hair."

"All right, I'm with you now," she says. "I don't agree with what he said, but I take his point about the hair."

Jasmyn doesn't understand. "You don't think a Black woman relaxing her hair after years of wearing it natural means something?"

"I'm saying it doesn't have to mean *everything*. Maybe she likes the way it looks."

"She only *thinks* she likes the way it looks. She doesn't realize she's been taught to think that white hair is better than Black hair. That's what's so insidious about the whole system."

Tricia smiles. "Careful there. You sounding a little—"

"Blacker than thou?"

Tricia laughs and shakes her head. "When I was in high school back in Brooklyn, I used to have to pass by these Nation of Islam brothers. All day they'd stand on the street corners talking 'bout how we all need to get back to Africa. I remember thinking they were ridiculous. We are Americans. What we know about Africa?"

"What are you saying?"

"Maybe hair doesn't need to make a statement."

Jasmyn is struck by what a naive thing it is for Tricia to say. She's struck by how ahistorical it is. "One of the first things they did to Africans on slave ships was to shave their heads—"

Tricia stops her. "I don't need a history lesson. All I'm saying is the woman has her reasons. You know how hard it can be to maintain a big Afro. I used to rock mine back in the day, but I don't have time for all-day wash days anymore. Why you think I have braids now?"

"Why didn't she jump to braids then?"

"You're going to have to ask *her* that one," Tricia says. She twirls the straw in her drink. "My turn to ask you something. You ever wonder who we would be, as a people I mean, without our history? Without slavery and racism?"

"History is who we are, Tricia," says Jasmyn.

"But aren't we more than trauma and all the things they did to us?"

"Of course we're more," Jasmyn says. "We're *survivors*. After all they did to us, we're still here."

Tricia sighs. "Lately, Dwight and me have been talking about the things we're going to need to teach little Marina about being Black."

Jasmyn claps her hands together and smiles. "I didn't know you picked out a name."

Tricia grins at her. "You like it?"

"It's perfect," Jasmyn says. She offers her glass up for a toast. "To Marina Gates, may she thrive."

"And sleep through the night so her moms can rest," Tricia says.

Jasmyn laughs. "That too," she says. She finishes the last of her drink before asking: "You and Dwight come to any conclusions about what you're going to teach her?"

"Well, I'm going to start with the good stuff," she says. "I mean, what is this country without us? Just start with music. From gospel to rap to rock 'n' roll to blues," she says, ticking each off on her fingers. "Without us, the food is bad, dance is bad, art is bad. The whole culture is *us*. We invented cool." She sighs. "And there's the more serious stuff, too. For instance, how many other groups benefited from our push for equality and the civil rights movement?"

"All of them," Jasmyn says, nodding.

Tricia leans back and sighs. "You know what's funny, though? Even me sitting here listing all the good things about being Black and about Black culture feels weird to me. Like, can you imagine white people sitting around listing all the good things about white culture?"

"Of course I can," Jasmyn says, eyeing her with a smirk. "I got three letters for you: KKK."

"Ha! My bad," Tricia says, laughing. "I mean, you're one hundred percent right. But I'm talking about regular degular white folks, the ones we'd be friends with. I'm sure they don't feel any need or compulsion to list all the good things about themselves as a people. They don't have to go out of their way to teach their kids to be proud of the color of their skin."

"Yeah, well you don't have to teach fish what the water is, right?" says Jasmyn. "They lay claim to everything good and they stay trying to erase us and our contributions. And then it's up to us to set the record straight over and over and over again."

Tricia stirs the ice in her glass, solemn for a moment. But then she looks up and smiles. "You know what I love most about us?"

"What?"

"How hard we go for each other. Not all of us, mind you. But most of us. We love each other. We look out for our own."

"Truth," Jasmyn says. "Truth."

Tricia presses a palm flat against the swell of her stomach. "Having said all that, I know I have to teach her the truth about what this world, what America, will be like for her. I have to teach her about slavery and about cops and racism and how to be resilient in the face of all that. I know I do." She sucks in a long breath like she's gearing up for something. "But the real truth of it is, I wish I didn't have to. I wish I was bringing her into a world that wasn't so meager in its love for Black people. I want to tell her that no one would ever harm her for something so trivial, so *inessential*, as the color of her skin."

Now Tricia presses both palms against her stomach. There are tears in her eyes. "I want to tell her that if she loves the world, the world will love her back without any reservations." She looks at Jasmyn. "Isn't that what any mother wants?"

To Jasmyn's surprise, she finds herself tearing up, too. It is painful to compare the world that *should be* with the world that *is*.

Tricia stretches across the table and squeezes Jasmyn's hand. "I'm sorry. I didn't mean to make things so heavy," she says.

"It's all right," Jasmyn says.

Tricia squeezes her hand again and then steers them on to lighter topics. "Cloth diapers or regular disposable ones?" she asks.

"That's easy. Disposable," says Jasmyn.

"That's what I say. Dwight's the one going on and on about being eco-friendly and saving the planet. I don't even understand where all that is coming from."

Jasmyn laughs. "He'll change his mind soon enough," she says. "But listen, Dwight's going to change a little bit on you, you know that, right?"

Tricia frowns. "Change? How?"

"I don't even know how to describe it. It's like all that modern, civilized stuff goes away and they turn into little cavemen," Jasmyn says.

"Girl, what are you talking about?"

"No, it's true. I saw it with King. When Kamau was a baby we'd be walking down the street with our stroller and it was like he would puff himself up looking out for dangers. Like he'd put his own body in between us and an oncoming train."

It was also the time when King decided he needed to make more than a teacher's salary to take care of them properly, but Jasmyn doesn't say that part to Tricia. Why bring up the disparity in wealth between them? Tricia and Dwight seemed happy with what they have. King's attitude wasn't modern or feminist, but Jasmyn found she didn't mind it. It was nice to be protected.

They're having such a good time catching up that Jasmyn texts King to say she's going to stay out later than she planned. He tells her to take as long as she needs. He and Kamau are having a fun boys night in.

"All right, real talk, what are the first weeks after the baby is born like?" Tricia asks.

"Lord, where to begin," says Jasmyn. She tells Tricia about the too-awake, sand-in-your-eyes feeling of not getting enough sleep. The uncertainty you have in your ability to keep this precious new life alive. The constant worry that your baby is not getting enough food.

But the thing Jasmyn remembers most from those first nervy days is that they're shot through with small joys. The soft, sweet smell of Kamau's skin and the awestruck look in King's eyes, and the silly sleep-deprived arguments. She remembers the three of them cocooned in their old apartment and how helplessly in love they all were.

She tells Tricia that there aren't words to describe that time, there's just a feeling of the world expanding and your heart expanding and how it turns out that there's no limit to how much you can love another person.

"That's beautiful," Tricia says, tearing up.

Jasmyn tears up, too, and then they are both crying. "Look at what these damn hormones are doing to us," Tricia says.

"It's terrible," Jasmyn says, smiling through her own tears.

Another hour passes with more silly tropical mocktails. Jasmyn feels a part of her she hadn't known was empty fill back up.

At the valet stand, Jasmyn hugs Tricia for a long time and tells her how much she loves her. "I'll see you soon," she says.

On her drive home, Jasmyn thinks about what Tricia said about Blackness being about more than just trauma. She tries to imagine an America where slavery didn't happen. An America where racism doesn't exist. What does it mean that she can't conceive of who she would be in that world? What does it mean that she can't conceive of that world at all?

Once, when she'd been eight, maybe nine, she'd gone to the corner store with her mother to get lottery tickets. The jackpot was at a record high and the line had been long. Together, they imagined all the things they'd do with the money once they won it. A big house with so much land you couldn't see the end of it. No more working. Private jets and chauffeured limos and champagne for breakfast. Jasmyn imagined her new bedroom. Everything in it would be a shade of purple. A new backpack, and a new pencil case, and new clothes with the tags still on so she could pull them off herself.

Two days later, she found her mother drinking coffee in the kitchen, torn-up lottery tickets on the counter next to her.

Jasmyn rushed in, picked up the pieces. "Why'd you do that for?" she asked. "How are we gonna show them that we won?"

"I know I didn't raise a fool," her mother said. "I know you didn't really think we were going to win."

Jasmyn clutched the torn pieces tightly in her fist and willed herself not to cry. She *had* believed that they could win. At the stove, her mother banged the frying pan and jabbed at the eggs as she made breakfast. As she watched her, Jasmyn understood that her mother had also believed they could win, and that she was angry she'd allowed herself an emotion as frivolous as hope. Quietly, Jasmyn crossed the room, dropped the tickets into the garbage can, and made sure to bury them underneath the other trash.

Even after that, her mother still bought lottery tickets and Jasmyn still took the walk to the store with her. On the way home, they still indulged in their fantasies, but Jasmyn never again made the mistake of believing in a world that would never exist.

Excerpt from *The Missouri Sun Times*:

St. Louis Board of Education Settles with Family of Girl Who Committed Suicide After Racist Bullying

The Board of Education of the City of St. Louis has agreed to settle for an undisclosed sum with the family of Marie Sayles, 11, the girl who took her own life. The Sayles family filed a lawsuit against the board alleging that their daughter had been subject to racist bullying by students and teachers alike and that months of complaints went unaddressed. The St. Louis City Council approved the settlement and released a statement acknowledging the tragedy. "We hope this resolution will bring a sense of closure to all involved."

The Sayles family did not respond to our request for a comment.

6

Jasmyn digs her nails into her palms as she watches Keisha and Catherine Vail laugh together on the other side of the schoolyard. She sucks in a breath, tries to swallow down her rising confusion and jealousy. *When had Keisha become so friendly with Catherine?* The answer comes to her. The Wellness Center.

Watching them, Jasmyn remembers how Keisha had once told her that Catherine Vail was missing a real, working heart. How she'd let Jasmyn know that Catherine had mocked her for crying over the Mercy Simpson video.

Keisha laughs again and touches Catherine Vail on the upper arm.

Jasmyn looks away. It's a ridiculous feeling, juvenile even, this sudden notion Jasmyn has that she's being replaced.

Jasmyn makes her way over to the slide. "Time to go," she says to Kamau.

"Moms, can I get just one more?" he begs.

A little girl with two cute Afro puffs makes big eyes at Jasmyn. "Please, Kamau's mom, can he go again?"

How can she say no to that? "OK, but just one more," Jasmyn says.

He's off before she even finishes her sentence.

Jasmyn moves to the perimeter to watch them and wait. In her purse, her phone buzzes. Mindful of the school's "no phones on campus" policy, she ignores it. She watches Kamau make his way up the ladder to the slide. Her phone buzzes again once and then twice.

She opens her purse and peeks down at the screen: News Alert—Mercy Simpson Dead.

For a few seconds, Jasmyn loses her sense of the world. A hazy light eclipses her vision. Sound drops out. She's sensationless. Bodyless.

But her reprieve is brief. And then she feels as if she's been invaded. Her blood feels thicker, infected. It seems to Jasmyn that each new racist horror compounds all the old racist horrors. That these kinds of woundings change a person at the cellular level. She's a different person now than she was a few seconds ago. Even her skin feels changed. Raw. It feels to her as though her insides are exposed, like she has no skin to protect her from the world and its outrages.

The baby kicks once and hard. Jasmyn presses one hand over her mouth, the other against her stomach. It can't be true. Mercy Simpson was eight years old. She had a life yet to live. Eight-year-olds don't die from bullet wounds. Eight-year-olds don't get shot in the first place.

Jasmyn swipes at the alert and reads. "Mercy Simpson succumbed to her injuries at MLK Hospital." She can't make it past the first line. She's going to be sick. She presses her palm over her mouth. Briefly, she realizes that this is yet another incident she'll need to record for Nina Marks's project.

She clicks on another article about the mayor's press conference. He offered condolences. He called for peaceful protests. Jasmyn thinks of what she knows of the mayor. He has two children. Girls. Did the parent in him expect people to be peaceful? In the face of this horror? If someone ripped Kamau's small body apart with bullets, Jasmyn would burn the city down. The mayor shouldn't be calling for peace. He should be calling for revolution.

Keisha is suddenly next to her and touching her shoulder. "Hey, what's wrong?"

But Jasmyn can't make herself say the words. She hands the phone to Keisha.

Some warning instinct tells Jasmyn to pay attention to what happens next. What she sees on Keisha's face is almost as devastating as the news itself. What she sees is *nothing.* No rage at a world that allows children to die at the hands of those who should protect them. No grief. No despair.

Nothing.

Keisha stares at the phone for three seconds before handing it back. "That's awful," she says. But mildly, like someone tasting too-bitter coffee.

Jasmyn steps away from Keisha's touch, drops the phone into her purse.

"That's awful," Keisha says again. "But you really can't let that stuff get to you too much, you know?"

Jasmyn has heard a version of these words before. From Catherine Vail. The day she watched the video of Tyrese Simpson being killed.

"You really should come up to the Wellness Center," Keisha says. "It will wash all your cares away."

Jasmyn feels Catherine Vail's eyes on them. The same warning instinct that told her to watch Keisha's reaction to the news tells her to smile now. She won't confront Keisha. Won't demand to know how she can be so apathetic in the face of so much horror. Keisha *had* changed and it wasn't just her hair. It was more than cosmetic. She'd changed in the same way Charles had. If Jasmyn stays in Liberty, will it happen to her and King and Kamau, too?

"I need to get going," she says to Keisha. Jasmyn doesn't wait to hear her response. She strides over to where Kamau is waiting in line for another turn on the slide. "Baby, we're going now," she says and grabs his hand.

"But I got next," he says, trying to pull away from her.

She holds on to him and he yells out in pain. "Ow, that hurts."

Jasmyn looks at him, confused. Did she squeeze him too hard? "Baby, we need to get going." Her voice is too loud. She can hear the anger and fear in it. The others can too. Their eyes are on her.

Keisha calls her name. There's *something* in her voice. Something both confused and full of affection. Something lost, too.

But Jasmyn does not have time. She has to save herself. Her family. She pretends not to hear Keisha calling and scoops Kamau up.

"Moms, I can walk by myself," Kamau says.

But she doesn't put him down until they get to the car. In the rearview, she spots Catherine Vail watching her from the sidewalk. Her cellphone is pressed to her ear. Jasmyn runs several stop signs before she forces herself to slow down. She doesn't want to get stopped by a cop, even a Black one.

It's time now. Time to admit to herself, finally, that something *is* happening to the people in Liberty. And that, whatever it is, she and King don't have much time left.

PART FIVE

King's not home when she gets there. She calls his cell and then his office line, to no avail. What is she even going to say to him? That she wants them to leave Liberty, that very night if they can? That something in this town is taking people's Blackness away?

She makes her way upstairs to her bedroom as quickly as her belly allows. By the time she makes it to the walk-in closet, she's breathing so hard she can feel it in her chest. She pulls out their largest suitcase and hoists it up onto the bed. What does she need to pack? A few days' worth of clothes. Toiletries, of course. Everything else they can come back for. No. They're not coming back here. They'll send someone to get the rest of it.

She opens her chest of drawers, grabs handfuls of underwear, socks, and a pair of pajamas and dumps them into the suitcase. What else? What else? She needs her hospital go bag and essentials for King and Kamau, too.

"Kamau, baby, can you come in here?" she yells. She'll just get him to pack his stuffed animals and whatever else he wants into the suitcase himself.

Kamau doesn't answer. Where is that boy?

She hurries to the bedroom door and yells again. "Kamau, where are you? Answer me."

She remembers the dream she had after her trip to the Wellness Center, the one where she couldn't find King or Kamau no matter how much she searched.

Now at the top of the stairs, Jasmyn clutches the banister and yells so loud her throat hurts. "Kamau, baby, where are you?"

That's when she hears it, the theme song to Kamau's favorite show, playing entirely too loudly.

She almost collapses with relief. Jesus. *Jesus Christ.* She holds tight to the handrail and makes her way down the stairs and into the family room.

Kamau is there, safe, sound, and happy as can be, sitting on the carpet with a bowl of chips in front of him.

"Baby, you didn't hear me calling you?" she asks, working hard to keep the panic out of her voice.

He turns down the TV volume. "Sorry, Moms," he says before turning back to his show.

Jasmyn stands there staring at him. He's fine. *Of course* he's fine. Why had she been so worried?

She sits down on the couch and waits for her heart rate to slow to normal. "Come sit next to me, baby," she tells him.

He plops down next to her. "Moms, are you OK?" He tilts his head and raises his eyebrows just the way King does when he's concerned about something.

"I'm fine," she tells him and kisses his forehead.

Kamau snuggles close and stuffs another handful of chips into his face, leaving crumbs all over his cheek and chin.

She chuckles and kisses him again. He's all right. She holds him close and thinks about the Mercy Simpson news and Keisha's reaction to it. Could it really be possible that something was stripping people of their

Blackness? But it's not possible to strip people of their identities, right? And what would it mean to lose your Blackness anyway?

She thinks of that white woman, Rachel Dolezal, who'd pretended to be Black for years. She'd worn Black hairstyles and dark makeup, been president of an NAACP chapter and a college-level instructor of Africana studies, and alleged herself to be the victim of racist crimes. After it was revealed that she was born to white parents, she claimed herself to be "trans-Black," said that the "essential essence" of her was Black, that she felt Black internally, and that whiteness had always felt foreign to her. Basically, she was Black because she *said* she was.

Jasmyn remembers being both fascinated and repulsed by the story. Why did Dolezal do what she did? Was it for sport, or entertainment, or cultural relevancy, or some other thing? How dare she play dress-up with Black identity, especially when she could just change her hair and makeup and go back to being privileged? Practically speaking, how dare she take away jobs—NAACP chapter president and instructor—from actual Black women?

But perhaps the thing that confused Jasmyn the most was how the woman had managed to fool so many people for years, especially the Black ones. She remembers laughing about the whole thing with Tricia. "Best believe," she'd told Tricia, "I would've known right away. Black is Black is Black," she'd said.

A couple of hours later, she still hasn't heard from King. Where could he be?

She heats up leftover fried rice for her and Kamau but can't bring herself to eat it. Kamau asks her if she's all right no less than fifty times. She promises him that she is. "Mommy is just tired," she says.

"Maybe you should go to the place where Daddy goes," Kamau says. "He always feels better after."

She looks at Kamau, surprised. Even he knows about the Wellness Center.

Jasmyn's scalp prickles, like tiny needles being pressed carefully into the delicate skin. She remembers the scream she'd heard as if someone were being gutted.

Does the change happen at the Wellness Center? Are they brainwashing people there, making them become apathetic? And who is "they" and how are they doing it? Can it, whatever *it* is, be undone?

How long before it starts happening to King?

One unanswerable question just leads to another unanswerable question. Jasmyn slaps the table, frustrated.

Kamau stops chewing and looks at her with wide eyes.

"Sorry, baby. Sorry," she says.

"How come you're not eating?" he asks.

"I'm eating," she says, and forces a spoonful of rice down past the lump in her throat.

A terrible thought occurs to her. She remembers one of those trite memes about living in the moment. The wording of it had struck her. *Live in the now because you never know when your lasts are.* The hug you're giving could be your last. The *I love you* you're saying. The meal you're eating. Only when it's too late to go back do you realize that you should've hugged longer, said *I love you* louder.

"I love you, baby," Jasmyn says now to Kamau, looking him over. He's definitely grown another inch or so over the last few months. She leans in and inhales the scent of him. He smells like school, like hand soap and permanent markers and sun and sweat and himself. She kisses his forehead once, twice, three times. He's such a good kid, such a mama's boy. She loves the way he sits still, lets her love him up. She kisses his forehead again. She tells herself that this—this moment right now—is not the last time she'll ever say it.

"I love you, too, Moms," Kamau says.

An hour later King finally calls her back. She can't say all she needs to say to him, not on the phone. She tells him they need to talk. When he presses, she admits that she wants to talk more about Keisha and Charles and their changes.

King doesn't say anything for so long she thinks they got disconnected, but no. "All right, baby," he says. "I'll be home as soon as I can. In the meantime, relax. I love you."

"I love you, too," she says.

It's only after they get off the phone that she realizes she forgot to mention Mercy Simpson's death, and that he had too.

Kamau is unusually tired, so she starts his bedtime routine—bath and two stories—earlier than she normally does. He falls asleep in record time.

Back in her bedroom, she eyes the half-packed suitcases. Maybe they don't have to leave tonight. She imagines waking Kamau up and hurrying him into the car. He'd be so confused and scared. Also, she still needs to explain everything to King and convince him to leave. She closes the suitcase. They won't leave tonight. They'll leave tomorrow. By the weekend at the very latest.

She heads downstairs, makes some tea, and heads up to her office. While she waits for King to get home, she'll do what she should've done months ago: find out just exactly who her neighbors are.

It doesn't take her long to find Angela Sayles's Instagram page. Nothing she sees is surprising. Exotic photos from exotic vacations with Benjamin. Here are pictures of her enormous house, too-long descriptions of her skin-care routine, admonitions on the importance of sunscreen, exfoliants, and self-care. More photos: newspaper profile clippings, professional awards, post-surgery selfies of herself in scrubs. Jasmyn doesn't find a single social justice post, not even from the summer when everyone was paying attention to Black lives and why they mattered.

Jasmyn scrolls back in time until she gets to Angela Sayles's first post. It's from the day she and Benjamin moved into Liberty. They're standing in front of their house, arms raised high with triumphant smiles. The caption read Made it.

Jasmyn leans back, rubs at her temples. She'd been hoping to see what Angela Sayles's life was like before she moved to Liberty. Where had she lived? Who were her friends? Was she always the woman Jasmyn knows now?

Benjamin Sayles's social media account is very similar to his wife's, although his includes more before-and-after photos of his plastic surgery clients. Invariably, there'd be a comment from the client with praise for Benjamin and praise for their changed selves. Some of his posts simply extol the mental health benefits of plastic surgery. Why look like one thing when you can look like this other, better, thing? Like Angela's, there are no social justice posts. Like Angela's, his first post is of the day they moved to Liberty.

Jasmyn tosses her phone onto her desk. What kind of evidence is she hoping to find? Evidence of what, exactly?

The back of her neck throbs from staring down at her phone for so long. She closes her eyes and tilts her head from side to side, trying to ease the soreness. Her eyes fly open on a dark thought: she could really use a massage. She straightens herself up, flips open her laptop, and types Angela Sayles into a search bar.

After another hour of clicking on links for various women named Angela Sayles, she finds a photograph. At first, she thinks the woman in the poorly lit photo is not the Angela Sayles she's looking for. But something about the woman is familiar. Jasmyn clicks on the photo and follows the trail to the defunct Our People page of a medical practice in New York. Angela Sayles, Internist, reads the caption. The photo is probably misattributed. The woman in the photo resembles Angela Sayles but couldn't possibly *be* her. It's the skin color that gives Jasmyn pause. This woman has significantly darker skin than the Angela she knows. The Angela she knows passes the paper bag test. The woman in this photograph fails it.

Jasmyn aligns this photo alongside Angela's most recent selfie. It's as if someone chiseled the new Angela from the old one. Her nose and lips, even her jawline, are narrower. Obviously, she'd had plastic surgery. Obviously, the changes were meant to make herself look more stereotypically Eurocentric. Those changes are bad enough, but the depth of self-loathing Angela Sayles must have to lighten her skin color is astonishing. It is frightening.

A similar search on Benjamin Sayles doesn't turn up anything like what she found with Angela. Both Catherine Vail and Carlton Way's Instagram accounts are private. They don't seem to have any other social media presence.

She thinks back to her dinner party. Hadn't Keisha said that both

Darlene and Asha, Charles's wife, had had plastic surgery, and that Benjamin Sayles had been their surgeon? What does it mean that they all had the same kind of surgery, the kind that gave them Eurocentric features? Neither Darlene nor Asha was anywhere as pale as Angela. And from what she remembers of Keisha's wedding photo, Darlene's skin color is unchanged.

Back on her phone, Jasmyn finds both Darlene's and Asha's Instagram pages. They are remarkably similar to Angela's. No social justice posts. Like Angela's feed, there are no posts from before they moved to Liberty. It's as if their lives before they moved to Liberty didn't matter. That, or they were trying to hide their previous lives.

It occurs to her then that she should check Keisha's Instagram feed. They'd been engaging with each other on the platform since becoming friends. Jasmyn had even looked through her posts going back a few years to get a better sense of her. Mixed in with the usual friends, family, and food photos, Keisha'd had plenty of social justice content.

Jasmyn types Keisha's name, but hesitates before hitting SEARCH. There's an impossible theory taking shape in her head. Right now—this moment before clicking the SEARCH button—there's an order to the world, a sense to it. There are things that are possible. And there are other things that are not.

She clicks SEARCH to find out which world she lives in.

Keisha's feed has been purged.

Gone are the #sayhername and #blacklivesmatter posts.

Gone are the calls to action, the pictures of raised fists and the Malcolm X and James Baldwin and Toni Morrison quotes.

Gone are the infographics highlighting racial disparities.

Gone are the photos of the latest victims of police brutality.

Only seven photos remain. Six of them are selfies showing off her new hair and clothes. The earliest is from two weeks ago, when she'd gotten back from vacation. She and Darlene are standing next to the WELCOME TO LIBERTY sign with smiles as bright as they are wide.

It's not that Jasmyn needs more confirmation that *something* is happening in Liberty. Keisha's reaction to Mercy Simpson's death was confirmation enough. But now she has something tangible to show King. Not conclusive evidence, but enough for him to realize that they're in real danger here.

Jasmyn tries to stand but the surrounding air feels suddenly thin. She presses her palms flat against her desk. Her breath is coming too fast. A panic attack isn't good for her or the baby. She rests her forehead on the cool of her desk and exaggerates her breathing: a slow, long inhale through the nose and a slow, long exhale through the mouth. But breathing this way reminds her of yoga or meditation, which reminds her of self-care and the strange malevolence of the Wellness Center. Her heart rate kicks up again. She forces her thoughts elsewhere. Instead, she pictures Kamau's face from earlier in the evening asking her if she's OK. She imagines King reassuring her that everything will be OK.

It's another few minutes before she's calm enough to get up and get ready for bed. She slides the suitcase to the ground and slips under the covers. As exhausted as she is, sleep doesn't come. She feels simultaneously wrung out and on high alert, the way you do after a nightmare. She turns her bedside lamp to the dimmest setting, props herself on her pillows, and waits for King to come home. Together, they'll figure out what to do.

2

Jasmyn is still awake when King finally gets home.

He drops a kiss on her forehead. "You're still up," he says.

"We have to leave Liberty," she says. "In the morning I can find us a rental and get us some movers. We can be gone by the end of the day."

King sits at the edge of the bed, drops his head into his hands. "We really doing this again, baby? Is this what you called me about tonight?"

"Just listen. I found out some things."

"Baby, I'm tired," he says.

Jasmyn glances at the clock. 10:50 p.m. But she can't worry about that now. Who knows how much time they have left?

She moves closer to him, puts her hand on his shoulder.

He shrugs her off, keeps his head in his hands.

"What are you so mad about?" Jasmyn asks.

It's a few seconds before he responds. "What am I mad about? You about to keep me awake because Keisha's hair not Black enough for you.

You think I don't see the suitcase in the corner? You want to take our son out of the school he loves, us out of this house and neighborhood that I work myself to the bone for, all for what?"

"Let me show you all I found," Jasmyn pleads, reaching for her phone. "I keep telling you this is about more than hair—"

King springs up, spins to face her. "Bullshit," he says. "You ready to revoke the woman's Black card over some fucking relaxer."

Jasmyn's mouth drops open. She can count on a single hand how many times King has sworn at her. She looks at him. In his eyes, there's something hard and remote, something she can't hope to soften or even reach. All night she's been thinking they have to leave Liberty *before* it's too late.

But what if it is *already* too late?

He isn't as far gone as Charles and Keisha, but what if this outsized reaction is a sign that he's changing?

King rubs his hand down his face, squeezes his eyes shut. "I'm sorry, baby. Forgive me," he says. "I'm tired, that's all it is." He sits back down on the bed. "What did you want to show me?"

Jasmyn scrutinizes his face. The remoteness is gone, but he still seems wrung out.

"It can wait until morning," she says, even though she's already reconsidering her decision to stay the night. What she really wants is for them to finish packing that suitcase together, grab Kamau, and steal away from this place and never look back. "It can wait," she says again. When she touches King's shoulder again, he doesn't flinch.

"You sure you forgive me?" he asks.

"Of course," she says. "We'll talk in the morning."

≈

But there's not enough time in the morning. While she's still in the shower, King tells her there's some emergency at work that he needs to go in for. "I'll be home early so we can talk," he says.

"Promise me," she says, and he does.

When she gets out of the shower, she sees he's written *I love you* in the condensation on the medicine cabinet mirror.

"I love you, too," she says.

Her day goes steadily downhill from there. On the way to school, Kamau complains of a stomachache. Hoping it will pass, she takes him in anyway. It doesn't. Midmorning, the school calls and asks her to pick him up. He'd vomited and was running a low-grade fever. But she's scheduled for court, so King is the one to take him home for the remainder of the day. One good thing about him taking the rest of the day off is that at least he's guaranteed to be home later so they can talk.

She eats lunch in her office and reads the news. After everything she'd found out about Angela and Keisha and arguing with King, she'd almost forgotten about Mercy Simpson. Overnight, the governor imposed a curfew and called in the National Guard. According to him, the guard would be in the streets, "ensuring the peace." Jasmyn scrolls through her social media wanting to see what she'd missed. There's video of one group of protestors wearing funeral black and carrying a child-sized coffin to the main steps of city hall. Another photo is of a group of women carrying signs pleading PLEASE STOP KILLING OUR BABIES. Others were more defiant: A LIFE FOR A LIFE. More than one article makes her cry at her desk.

An hour before she's due in court, she decides to check Keisha's feed again. Maybe, by some miracle, her truncated feed had been a technical glitch. Jasmyn recognizes this thinking for what it is: wishful and magical. Still, seeing only the seven photos sends a slow, dark shiver snaking down her spine. She stands, puts on her suit jacket, and tries to shrug her disquiet away, but it covers her like a shroud. There are too many unanswered questions. Why would Keisha get rid of her old photos as if her life before Liberty didn't exist? What would happen if Keisha were ever to leave Liberty?

Do people ever leave Liberty?

A thought occurs to her. Their realtor had mentioned that they were the second family to live in their house. Even then, Jasmyn had thought it strange that the previous family had stayed in Liberty for less than a year. What if they'd left Liberty for the same reason Jasmyn wants to leave now? What if they'd seen the same kinds of changes? What if they'd left before it could happen to them? She needs to find that family and talk to them. They can confirm that she's not imagining things, that she has reason to be afraid.

She finds the realtor's phone number and calls.

"Mrs. Williams, how can I help you? Are you and your husband ready to make an offer on the Beverly Hills compound?"

Jasmyn frowns. "What are you talking about? What compound?"

The woman doesn't say anything for a full two seconds. "I'm sorry, Mrs. Williams. I see now that I was looking at a file for another family."

"You're sure?" Jasmyn asks, staring down at her phone. There's something like panic in the woman's voice.

"Very sure," the woman says. "I made a mistake, that's all."

Jasmyn presses a hand to her heart and takes a breath before continuing on. "Listen, I'm calling because I want to get in touch with the previous owners," she says.

"Why would you want to talk to them?" the realtor asks.

The forthrightness of the question strikes Jasmyn as strange, suspicious even. Is she being paranoid? She decides to press. "I'm just curious as to why they left after less than a year."

A too-long pause from the other woman and then: "Unfortunately, the wife's mother was diagnosed with cancer. They wanted to live closer to her. In fact, I found them a lovely new home within walking distance of her."

Jasmyn knows she's being lied to, but *why* is she being lied to? What is this woman hiding and why is she hiding it?

"Thanks for that," Jasmyn says, keeping the skepticism out of her voice. "I'd still like to be in touch with them, if that's all right," she says.

"I'm afraid for privacy concerns I can't give you that information," the woman says. "If you'll just tell me what this is about, I'm happy to pass along your questions."

Why not offer to pass along Jasmyn's phone number instead, and leave it up to the other family to get in touch with her?

"Never mind," Jasmyn says. She thanks the woman, hangs up before she can respond.

There's more than one way to get the information she needs. She calls a cop friend of hers—one of the few police officers that she trusts—who puts her in touch with a private detective the department uses. She'd met the man once: he was white, middle-aged, and even more suspicious of people than most of the cops she'd come across.

Just before she has to go to court, he returns her call. Jasmyn fills him in on all she knows. The people she's looking for lived in Liberty and moved out within the year. She mentions the sick mother and how the realtor found them a new place. She tells him the name of the realtor, and that she suspects the woman was lying.

"Everybody lies," the detective says. "Is this official county business?" he asks.

"No, this is just for me," Jasmyn says. She gives him her credit card number and asks him to call as soon as he knows anything.

At court, her client doesn't show up. The judge adds Failure to Appear in Court to his list of charges and issues a bench warrant. Outside on the courthouse steps, she leans against a column, taking a minute to swallow her disappointment. The frustrating part is, Jasmyn is sure she would've been able to get the kid off. The evidence against him was circumstantial at best. Now, though, he's almost certainly going to do some time and be part of the system forever.

The detective calls back at 4:00 p.m. "Got some preliminary info for you."

"Go ahead," Jasmyn says. He has her on speakerphone. Her voice echoes back at her.

"Husband and wife. Three kids, all boys. He's a lawyer. She's a stay-at-home mom. Their names are Clive and Tanya Johnson."

The detective keeps talking, but Jasmyn doesn't hear anything after Clive and Tanya Johnson. Aren't they the couple who helped found the Liberty chapter of BLM?

She scrolls back through her texts with Keisha. Yes, there it is. Clive and Tanya Johnson. They founded it together.

Jasmyn tunes back in to hear the detective ask if she'd like to see pictures of the family.

"Yes, please," she says. "Do you know where they moved to?"

"Now, here's where it gets tricky. I can't find them."

"I don't understand," says Jasmyn.

"You and me both, sister," he says.

Jasmyn pinches the bridge of her nose, suppresses the urge to tell him she's not his sister.

"It's the damnedest thing," he says. "It's like they disappeared. And, before you ask, they're not dead. Or, if they are, they didn't die in the state of California."

"I suppose they could've left the state or moved overseas," Jasmyn says, rubbing at her forehead. That would be a lot of moves, too many in fact, for a family in just two years. It doesn't make sense.

"I didn't see any evidence of a move. One more thing I should mention. That realtor you talked to. She said she found the Johnsons a new house after they moved out of Liberty, right?"

"That's right."

"I went digging through all the records where she's listed as both the buying and selling agent. I think I found the house she sold them. Thing is—and this is where it gets even trickier—the Johnsons never moved into it."

"What do you mean?" Jasmyn asks.

"As far as I can tell, the house sat empty for about two months, and then another family—not the Johnsons—moved in. Husband, wife, and three kids."

She's about to ask for their names when a contraction hits. She cries out, more from surprise than pain. She's at thirty-seven weeks, which is full-term, but still a couple of weeks earlier than Kamau had been. Instead of breathing through the contraction like she's supposed to, she grips the edge of her desk and clamps her mouth closed. After it passes, she caresses her stomach. *Hey there, baby boy,* she thinks. *You getting ready to come out?* If this labor is anything like it was with Kamau's, it'll be a long time before he's really and truly ready to come into the world. She rubs a small circle over her stomach again. *Moms has to take care of some stuff. Just give her a little more time.*

"You all right over there?" the detective asks. It's clear he's asked a couple of times already.

"I'm fine," she says. "Listen, can you text me those names and the address?"

"Not a problem."

A few seconds later, the notification chimes on her phone.

"So, you want me to keep trying to find the Johnsons?" he asks.

"Yes. Please."

"No chance they could be in witness protection or anything like that, right?"

Jasmyn hesitates. Is that possible? "I don't think so," she says.

"Don't mind my asking, but why are you looking for them?"

But of course, there's no answer she can give him that will make sense. Jasmyn just tells him to call her whenever he finds something.

She opens the detective's first text and looks at the photo of the Johnsons. The five of them are posed like they sat for a family portrait. They look like any other young Black family. Tanya Johnson has a round face and short braids and a nice smile. Clive Johnson is clean shaven, bald, and thin. His smile is as nice as his wife's. The children show all their teeth. Jasmyn had always meant to get one of these portraits done for her and King and Kamau.

His second text has the names of the family who moved into the house the Johnsons supposedly bought when they left Liberty. Brandon and Jessica Wainwright. They have three children. There's no photo of the family.

The detective asked about witness protection. Is it possible that the Johnsons and the Wainwrights are the same family? Not that the Johnsons are actually in a witness protection program, but what if they'd changed their names, hidden themselves?

What if they don't want to be found?

And if that's the case, can the reason be the one Jasmyn suspects? That they discovered something off about Liberty? And if so, what are they so afraid of? What would make them go to such lengths to stay hidden?

Jasmyn maps the address of the house on her phone. It's a forty-five-minute drive. If she leaves now, she might be able to find someone at home. Maybe if she can convince them that she's on their side, they'll tell her the truth.

She closes her laptop, slips her phone into her purse. Before she leaves, she picks up the photo of King and Kamau that she keeps on her desk. It's one of her favorites. Kamau is eight or nine months old and wearing only a diaper. King is holding him up in the air above his head and blowing raspberries on his tummy. If Jasmyn concentrates, she can still hear Kamau's helpless giggles. Love has a sound, and it is the sound of her son laughing.

She doesn't like lying to King, but she tells him she needs to work late. If things go the way she hopes they will, she'll have proof of everything she's been saying and he'll forgive her for this little, white, lie.

3

It took Jasmyn twice as long to get there than she'd planned. In anticipation of more protests, most major streets had been blockaded, sending her down detour after detour. In her life, she'd never seen so many police cruisers, heard so many sirens. So many Black people were going to get hurt and arrested tonight.

On the radio, the mayor and governor gave a joint press conference. The governor moved the curfew an hour earlier, to 9:00 p.m., for most counties.

Now, in the car, Jasmyn slams her hands against the steering wheel, willing the red light to turn green. She needs to find the Johnsons/Wainwrights, talk to them, and go home to King so she can convince him they need to leave. What she doesn't need is to get caught up in the police violence that will inevitably erupt on a night like this. The light turns green and, thankfully, she doesn't run into any more detours.

The neighborhood she ends up in is an up-and-coming one just south of Wilshire Boulevard in the Miracle Mile section of the city. The streets have speed bumps and signs that read DRIVE LIKE YOUR KIDS LIVE HERE.

The houses are older but well maintained and done in the Spanish style, with red brick roofs and archways. She sees two young white families and a Black one out for a stroll.

Jasmyn cruises by the address. Instead of parking right in front of it, she parks half a block away on the opposite side of the street.

A contraction, smaller than the previous one, hits her. She checks her watch. An hour between them. Really, she needs to be getting ready to go to the hospital, but she has to do this, has to go talk to the Johnsons/Wainwrights. An hour between contractions still gives her enough time.

On the walk from her car to the house, she plans her strategy. First, she'll explain who she is and where she lives. Maybe just mentioning Liberty will provoke a reaction in whoever she's talking to. Depending on what the reaction is, she'll decide what to do next.

Jasmyn rings the doorbell.

The woman who opens the door is white. Against her hip, she's holding an infant, also white.

Jasmyn swallows her disappointment. She'd known her theory that the Johnsons and the Wainwrights were the same people was a stretch, but she'd hoped she was right. She'd hoped that there were answers to be found here.

"Hello," the woman says. "Can I help you?"

Jasmyn looks past her into the house beyond. Inside, she can hear boys laughing. On a mantel, she spies a family portrait. They look like any other white family.

"I'm sorry," Jasmyn says. "I think I have the wrong house. I was looking for Tanya Johnson."

The woman smiles. "You're in the right place," she says. "I'm Tanya Johnson."

At first, Jasmyn thinks she made a mistake and said the wrong name. She checks her phone. No, she has it right. Tanya Johnson is the name of the Black woman who used to live in her house in Liberty. She and her husband started the BLM chapter.

Jasmyn looks up from her phone.

The woman backs away from her. Horror spreads across her face. "I meant to say I'm Jessica Wainwright. You have the wrong house." She takes another step back and slams the door in Jasmyn's face.

Jasmyn looks between her phone and the now-closed door, trying to make sense of what happened.

Another contraction racks her body. Her water breaks.

She hunches over and half breathes, half groans through the pain. Fluid, warm and sticky, pools in her underwear, coats her inner thighs. She wants to ring the doorbell again, to ask the woman to use her restroom so she can get herself cleaned up. But that's not a good idea. In her marrow, she knows she can't trust that woman. The woman who may or may not be Tanya Johnson.

What she needs is to go home to King and Kamau. She needs to save them and the baby.

She turns and hustles as fast as she can away from Tanya Johnson/ Jessica Wainwright's doorstep. With every step, more fluid slips down her thighs, but she doesn't let it slow her down. By the time she's back at her car door, the fluid has seeped into her heels. As soon as she sits down, it will smear across the seat. Hopefully it won't stain. Even so, they'll probably be able to get it out. Jasmyn takes off her suit jacket and lays it across the driver's seat.

Somewhere in her head, she knows her thoughts aren't making sense. But it's easier to think practical thoughts—how to clean herself up, how to clean her car—than to think about what had just happened.

What *had* happened?

Jasmyn's mind flinches away from the truth as if it were the point of a blade.

There are some things too cruel to contemplate.

But she's not allowed to look away, not from this.

Back when Tanya and Clive Johnson and their three boys had lived in Jasmyn's house in Liberty, they were Black.

Now they are white.

That is the impossible truth.

And it *is* impossible. A Black person can't turn white. There's no plastic surgery for that. And it would entail so much more than plastic surgery.

It isn't possible. Except that it obviously is possible.

Jasmyn flashes to the family portrait on their mantel. Even their kids are white. The baby on her hip, with his wispy yellow hair and pale blue eyes, is white.

Another contraction and Jasmyn rests her head against the steering wheel.

How does it work? Her instincts say everyone from the Wellness Center is involved. Carlton Way and the Sayles and Catherine Vail and Nina Marks. Her lawyer mind needs to piece the whole treacherous scheme together.

But for now, she needs to get King and Kamau out.

She presses the START ENGINE button but doesn't pull away. It's not safe to drive in her condition. Not her physical condition, but her mental one. She closes her eyes and sucks in as long a breath as she can manage and breathes it out again. She turns the radio to her favorite jazz station. Another slow, deep inhalation. Another slow and deep exhalation. One more breath and she'll be able to pull away.

She opens her eyes to find an angry white man staring at her from the driver's-side window.

The man—is it Clive Johnson/Brandon Wainwright?—punches the car window with the side of his fist. "Who are you? Why did you attack my wife?"

Jasmyn screams and tries to pull away. In her terror she forgets to disengage the parking brake.

Clive Johnson/Brandon Wainwright punches the window again. "I called the police." Another punch to the window. "You're going to jail."

Jasmyn screams again. She puts the car in reverse and floors the gas. Dimly she thanks God that there are no other parked cars behind her. Half a block later the street dead-ends, forcing her to do a three-point turn in the cul-de-sac. Clive Johnson/Brandon Wainwright sprints toward the car, forcing Jasmyn to swerve up onto the sidewalk to avoid hitting him.

Across the street, Tanya Johnson/Jessica Wainwright isn't angry or gesturing the way her husband is. She watches Jasmyn with a steady calm. All the horror is gone from her face. She's on the phone. And in her gut, Jasmyn knows that whoever that woman is calling, it's someone scarier than the police.

4

The night is a chaos of sounds. Police helicopters and sirens and the distant chants of protestors. Most businesses are boarded up, with plywood serving as both protection and as canvas. Jasmyn sees some version of BLACK LIVES MATTER and REST IN POWER, MERCY and #SAYHERNAME #MERCY SIMPSON spray-painted on almost all of them. Across one lonely stretch of wall, there's a poorly painted mural of Mercy with angel's wings.

Because of the street closures, the car's GPS has rerouted Jasmyn four times now. Why tonight of all nights?

She's called King three times. His cellphone goes straight to voicemail. Each time, she leaves him a message that's some version of "Baby, it's me. Where you at? Listen, some stuff happened I need to tell you about. And my water broke. Call me when you get this."

She calls the house phone, too, and leaves the same message. Where is he? He should be home taking care of Kamau.

A text notification icon appears on the car's touchscreen. It's from King. Jasmyn touches the icon to listen.

Hey, baby, Kamau is feeling better. We're up at the Wellness Center. Why don't you meet us up there?

No. No. No. He must not have heard her messages.

She calls back but, again, his phone goes to voicemail.

Another contraction hits just as she's pulling into their driveway. That's twenty minutes between contractions now. And now she remembers once hearing that sometimes second babies come faster than firsts.

"Hold on, baby boy. Just a little longer for Mama," she says.

Except for the porch light, the house is completely dark.

Inside, she cleans herself up and grabs her pregnancy go bag from their bedroom closet.

She calls King again. Nothing.

Back in the car, Jasmyn grips the steering wheel tightly in her hands, knowing she has no choice about where to go next.

A passing truck holds her briefly in a beam of light. She's flooded with the same terrifying feeling she'd had last spring with the white cop: that the direction of her life is not up to her. Maybe it had never been.

Jasmyn turns the car on and begins the long uphill drive to the Wellness Center.

5

She sees them as soon as her car crests the hill. They are standing shoulder to shoulder in a single line between the two white columns of the Wellness Center. They are, all of them, waiting for her.

Carlton Way; Nina Marks; Catherine Vail; Angela and Benjamin Sayles; Keisha's wife, Darlene; and Charles's wife, Asha.

And Kingston Williams.

King walks toward the car with a hand outstretched. Even with the windows closed, the grate of his shoes against the gravel is too loud.

"Open up, baby," King says.

A part of her is screaming. Another part of her is sure that there has to be an explanation for why King is here with those people.

Jasmyn opens the door. "Where's Kamau?" she asks. Her voice is so quiet, she barely hears herself.

"Don't worry, baby. He's safe," King says.

"Safe," Jasmyn whispers. What can he mean? Of course he's not safe. None of them are safe. The others are here. The others who—

Another contraction hits, even more intense than the last. Jasmyn drops her head back against the headrest.

King takes her hand. "Remember how we do. Breathe through it, baby. Just breathe."

Jasmyn's dimly aware of movement outside. Of the Wellness Center doors opening. Of the others walking inside. Of a man she's never seen pushing a wheelchair toward her car.

She and King breathe together until the contraction passes.

"Let's get you inside," he says into her ear.

She swivels her head to him. "Where's Kamau? I want my son."

"He's inside, baby," King says. "Come on inside with me."

Jasmyn scours his face, trying to discern what the truth is. King loves her. She knows it in her bones. He loves their family. There's an explanation for all this. Something other than what she thinks is going on. King would never hurt her.

Jasmyn allows him to help her out of the car and into a waiting wheelchair. They are halfway to the door when she twists back to look at him. He is crying. She's only seen King cry twice before: when he first told her what happened to his brother and when Kamau was born.

"I want Kamau," she whispers.

"I promise you he's all right," King says. But his voice breaks on *promise.*

King wheels her through the high white-and-gold doors of the main spa, through the labyrinth of corridors and rooms she'd seen on her visit. The air smells like lavender and ozone and carelessness. They arrive at the blond-wood door where she'd heard that terrible scream the last time she was here. The only time she was here.

She tries to push apart the chair's foot braces so she can get her feet on the ground and press herself to standing, but they're locked in place. She turns to look at King. "Let me out of this chair." She tries to make it a demand, but her shattering fear keeps her voice weak and low.

King doesn't respond. He enters a code into the security panel next and wheels her through the door.

It's a hospital room.

Jasmyn moans low as her eyes take it all in. The gurney. The IV stand. Oxygen tanks. Other medical equipment she doesn't know the names of. Those bright blue medicine dropper bottles. Awake water. Diffusers on the wall. The smell of lavender in the air.

She grips the chair's arms and pushes back against the seat. "Let me out," she says again, voice no firmer than before.

King stops moving the chair and walks around to the front.

Jasmyn looks up at him, tears already in her eyes. His face is solemn and tender. "King, tell me what's going on," she pleads.

"Baby, you already know," he says.

Jasmyn closes her eyes. "They're turning people white."

He waits for her to reopen her eyes before answering. "Yes," he says.

Jasmyn had almost drowned once. It'd been one of the few times her mother had taken her to the beach in Santa Monica. She was so afraid; she couldn't get enough air into her lungs even to yell. Inexplicably, she'd tried to grasp the water to push herself up. That's how she feels now, like she can't get purchase, like she's trying to hold the very thing trying to kill her.

King drops to his knees in front of her. His eyes are full of love. "It won't be so bad," he says. "And you won't remember being anything else."

"No," she chokes out. She feels as if she's been kicked in the chest, as if there's no air left in her lungs. "No, you would never do this. Not to me. Not to us."

But looking at him, she sees the truth. The gutting pain in her chest *knows* the truth.

"You planned this," she says. "This is why we moved to Liberty in the first place." It hurts to speak. Every word is a fresh wound.

"Yes."

"You knew what was happening to Keisha and Charles."

"We call it 'tempering.' It takes a few months of drinking Awake and using the lavender diffusers to help prepare the body for the final process."

Keisha had been right after all. Something *was* in the water. In the air.

Jasmyn frowns. "But you didn't want me drinking it—"

"Because of the baby," King explains. "We never gave it to anyone pregnant before. We decided to wait until after the baby came, but you figured it out before we could get there." He smiles. "You're always the smartest person in the room."

This isn't real. Soon she'll wake up and tell King about the terrible dream she had and he'll kiss her forehead and comfort her until she's OK again.

She bows her head, squeezes her eyes shut. Dimly, she understands that King is talking, explaining something. He's telling her that one person in each family is the Sponsor. Darlene is Keisha's Sponsor. Asha is Charles's. Tanya Johnson was Clive Johnson's.

"And I am yours," he says. "The Sponsor is like a guide, helping their spouse through the steps—"

She snaps her head up, opens her eyes. "How can you call yourself a *guide* when the spouses don't know they're being led?"

He concedes the point with a faint smile. "I know this is a shock," he says, voice gentle.

Tears stream down her face. "I don't understand," she says. "You wouldn't do this."

"Baby, can't you see I'm doing it for you?" he pleads.

How is it possible to hurt this much and still be alive?

"I don't want this," she says, choking on the words.

He puts his hands on the arms of the wheelchair. "Just let me explain it to you. Let me help you understand," he says. "When the tempering is done, we move on to erasing. Then the rest of the surgeries until the whole family is turned. After that, they get relocated with new identities."

Jasmyn feels as if she's trying to breathe water instead of air.

"You going to do this to Kamau? To our beautiful boy?"

Now King is weeping, too. Impossibly, Jasmyn can feel how much he loves her. How much he *thinks* he loves her.

He puts his hand on her face. And the terrible truth is that she leans into his palm, her body not yet understanding that there's no comfort or safety to be found in his arms anymore.

"We've been preparing Kamau for this. It made him sick a few times, but our boy is strong. He pulled through."

Jasmyn jerks her face out of his hands. Hot rage burns away her fearful sorrow. She slaps him. Hard. Her hand is wet with his tears.

King straightens and rubs at his cheek. He doesn't look angry. Just sad. "I didn't want it to be like this," he says. "I was hoping you'd come around on your own."

Jasmyn shakes her head over and over again. "Tell me you're lying to me. Tell me you didn't experiment on our baby," she says, voice low and raw.

This is not real. What's happening right now can't be real. King would never betray her, betray their marriage and all the love they've shared like this. He would never hurt her or the baby or Kamau. He would never put them in danger. He protects them. It's all he's ever done.

She sees their entire life together. When they first met at the bar, him with his cheesy pickup line. The second time they'd made love, instead of the first. Their wedding. How they'd each written their own vows and said them at city hall. Then cried unabashedly at how lucky they were to have found each other. The night Kamau was born. How she'd understood how eclipsing love could be.

"Baby," she pleads. "We love each other. You love me. Don't do this."

His sadness turns to resolve. He stops rubbing his face. "Like I said, you won't remember. He won't, either."

"What about you?" Jasmyn chokes out. "Will you remember?"

"We Sponsors only undergo the physical changes. We keep our memories. We have to, in case something goes wrong." He gives her a small shrug. "It's a small sacrifice for all we're getting in return."

Behind her, a door opens. King rises to his feet and turns her wheelchair so that she can see.

It's the others. Some of them at least. Carlton Way is first, followed by Angela and Benjamin Sayles, Catherine Vail, and Nina Marks. They are all dressed in surgical scrubs.

Raw terror rises in her. She tries to stand, but King puts his hands, firmly, on her shoulders. He will not let her leave.

She looks back at him. Somehow she has to make him see reason. "Blackness is not something you can erase. It's more than just skin color. It's who I am. It's in my blood. In my culture. In my memory," Jasmyn says.

Except, she knows she's wrong. They've figured out how to erase all of it somehow. Clive and Tanya Johnson are evidence of that.

Nina Marks is the one to respond. "Part of becoming white is cosmetic, to be sure. But that isn't all there is. It's a cutting away—a judicious paring—of history."

Jasmyn covers her mouth with one hand, clutches at her throat with the other.

Oh, God. What had she done?

She remembers the hours she'd spent using Nina Marks's device to record all her racial trauma. She remembers that Nina Marks used to be a brain surgeon. She'd given Nina Marks a precise map of her brain, a guide she could use to hack away at her roots, to destroy her foundations.

The rest of the scheme comes together in Jasmyn's mind. Angela Sayles specializes in skin grafts for burn victims. Benjamin Sayles specializes in reconstructive plastic surgery. Catherine Vail specializes in diction.

Carton Way speaks next. "You know your history, so you know that back in the day Black folks with pale enough skin used to pass for white. The first time I ever heard about passing, I couldn't understand it. Of course I understood *why* a person would pass if they could. What I couldn't understand was, what *exactly* it was that made a person Black in the first place? I mean, if their skin was pale enough for them to look white and be called white, what was it that made them Black? All my life I'd been thinking about that. I was fifteen when I—"

He stops talking. Something like grief passes over his face. It's there for a moment and then gone.

"I was fifteen when they killed my father. It took me years to figure out just exactly what I was going to do about it. You activists are forever talking about 'doing the work.'" He touches his hand to his chest. "This is *my* work. This is *my* underground railroad. This is how I lead my people to freedom."

In her life, Jasmyn has never closed her eyes to horror. It is important, after all, to bear witness. But some things are too offensive, too barbaric to look at. She turns away from Carlton.

"Tell me why," she says to King.

He gets back on his knees in front of her. "Every single one of us in this room has a story to tell. Carlton lost his father. Nina lost her mother. Catherine and Angela each lost a brother. Benjamin lost his sister. We all lost somebody. They've been killing us for four hundred years. It's enough now. Baby, don't you see? White people are never going to change. *We* have to be the ones to change. It's the only way to get free," he says. "I'm tired of the struggle," he says. "I'm tired of worrying that one day a cop will put bullets in Kamau. Just like they did to Mercy Simpson. Just like they did to Tommy."

Tommy.

This has always been about Tommy. His murder condemned them all, foreclosed on all their futures.

Jasmyn thinks of that secret place inside King that devastation and grief had created. *This*, this horror, is what had grown wild and unchecked and poisoned in there, laying waste to who he'd once been.

But maybe he's still in there somewhere. Maybe she can still reach him.

She sucks in a shuddering breath. "Nothing will happen to our babies. I promise. You and me. We're working so hard. Aren't we? We can change things. We can protect them." She touches his cheek and he nuzzles into her palm. "Don't do this. Please."

But she can see the resolve hardening on his face.

"I'll forgive you," she whispers, lying in her desperation. "I promise.

You and me and the baby and Kamau, we'll walk out of here. We'll find another way. Please, baby," she begs.

King shakes his head. "I was hoping I could make you understand," he says, sorrowful. "This is the only way," he says. "Can't you see we still in chains? We still fighting every damn day. Still protesting every damn day. Still struggling every damn day. No more." He slices the air with his hand. "No more begging not to be killed. No more scrounging for scraps. I don't want any more talk about reform and equity and fairness and history." He bows his head. "And I want more than the basics for us. I want us to be free, baby. When Kamau walks into a room, I want no one—not white people, not Black people, not anybody—making assumptions about who he is based on his skin color. I don't want his humanity, all the possibilities about who he might be, to come down to the pigmentation of his skin. It's not right. It has to end."

King lets go of Jasmyn's hand. He stands. "This is the only way," he says again.

Jasmyn shakes her head. "You don't believe that. We have to stay who we are. We keep on fighting. We're going to get to the mountaintop."

He smiles down at her. "I love your spirit," he says. "I've always loved that about you." He looks over at Carlton Way and nods.

Carlton Way looks at her. "This is not giving up," he says. "It's giving in."

Jasmyn bends over, trying one last time to stand up and escape somehow, but it's much too late.

The others advance on her.

King stands back and lets them take her.

"King," Jasmyn screams, hugging her stomach. "What about the baby? What about our baby boy?"

"Try not to worry," Nina Marks says. "We'll deliver the baby, and then we'll get started. We'll take good care of you. You'll be all better in a few months."

"Don't you see?" King says. "I'm giving us a fighting chance in this country. I'll see you on the other side. I love you."

Ever since they'd moved to Liberty, some essential part of herself had been clanging, had been trying to warn her that she'd end up here in this white room, unable to get away from these people? Why hadn't she listened to it? To the voice that told her that these people, Black though they were, were not her kind?

Jasmyn Williams screams and screams until her throat is raw. Until she has no voice left.

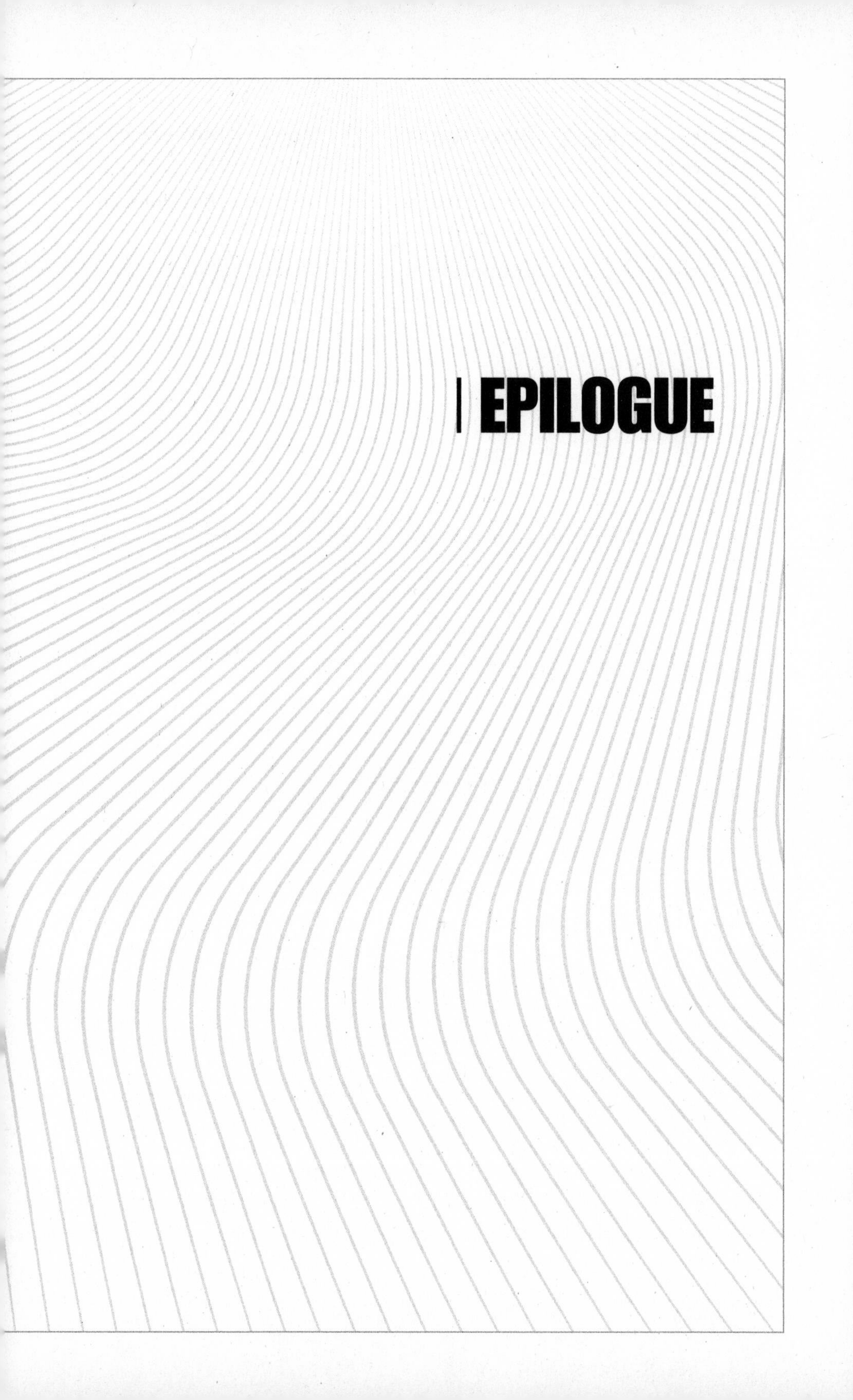

EPILOGUE

The white woman who used to be Jasmyn Williams walks into her pediatrician's office with her six-month-old and her seven-year-old son. She checks in and sits down in the waiting area.

"You have a beautiful family," says the Black woman across the way from her.

The white woman who used to be Jasmyn Williams smiles an overly friendly smile at the Black woman. "Your baby is adorable. How old is she?"

"Five months," says the woman.

"Oh yeah? Mine is almost seven months."

The white woman who used to be Jasmyn Williams nudges her son. "See how cute that baby is? You used to be that small."

Her little boy—Chase is his name—doesn't look over.

The white woman who used to be Jasmyn Williams gives him a stern look. "Wave hello," she says, low. She doesn't want it to seem like she, or her son, is racist.

Chase rolls his eyes but does as she asks.

A TV screen mounted to the back wall displays a breaking news alert. Police had killed a Black man the night before. The broadcast cuts to images of the protest that broke out in the aftermath. She sees signs denouncing white supremacy and blaming systemic racism and calling for the abolition of police. The white woman who used to be Jasmyn Williams doesn't agree with any of that. Not that she is allowed to say such things. Not publicly, anyway. The news cuts away to the dead man's mother. She's crying and clutching a picture of her dead son. The white woman who used to be Jasmyn Williams clucks her tongue. *That's too bad,* she thinks.

She looks away from the TV and chances a glance at the Black mother. There are tears in the other woman's eyes. She's pressing both her hands to her heart. There's something so familiar about the woman's gesture, but the white woman who used to be Jasmyn Williams can't put her finger on it. Maybe one day it'll come back to her.

Across the way, the door that leads to the doctor's office opens. "Mrs. Gates?" the nurse calls out. "Tricia Gates?"

The Black woman, Tricia, wipes her tears before standing. "Nice to meet you," she says before turning to follow the nurse.

"You as well," says the white woman who used to be Jasmyn Williams.

Against her chest, her infant coos. She looks into his wide, innocent blue eyes and coos right back at him. "Everything is all right, baby," she says.

All at once she remembers she meant to make herself a massage appointment at the fancy spa that just opened close to their new house in Beverly Hills. She takes out her phone and navigates to the site. She doesn't look back up at the television, not even once.

ACKNOWLEDGMENTS

This is a story of tragedy. I wrote this book from a place of despair and anger and, also, from a place of hope. Authors are often asked what they want readers to take from their work. My dearest wish for this book is that Jasmyn's profoundly tragic fate inspires you to have thoughtful conversations inside your circles and outside of them as well. Thank you for taking this journey with me. I hope that it has meant something to you.

There are, as ever, so many people to thank for shepherding this book into the world. First, my brilliant editor, Caitlin Landuyt, who made this book deeper, richer, and sharper in every way. Thanks also to Sareeta Domingo for her insightful editorial notes. Thank you to my agent, Jodi Reamer, who champions me and championed this book when it was barely even a book.

Books are written in isolation, but they're certainly not published that way. Thanks so much to the brilliant team at Knopf for their tireless care. Special thanks to my publisher, the legendary Reagan Arthur; publicist, Julie Ertl; marketer, Lauren Weber; production editor, Melissa Yoon; production manager, Marisa Melendez; text designer, Debbie Glasserman; jacket designers, John Gall and Kelly Blair; copy editor, Shasta Clinch; and proofreader, Nicholas LoVecchio.

Thank you to my immediate and extended family, and to my found family, David Jung and Sabaa Tahir, for all the laughs and all the love.

Thank you to my little girl, Penny, for showing me exactly who I am.

And, finally, thank you to my husband, David Yoon. David reads every draft of every book and without his insight and encouragement, none of them would exist.

Both David and Penny give me the kind of joy I didn't know was possible, and for which I can never thank them enough.

ABOUT THE AUTHOR

Nicola Yoon is the number one *New York Times* best-selling author of *Instructions for Dancing*; *Everything, Everything*; *The Sun Is Also a Star*; and a co-author of *Blackout* and *Whiteout*. She is a National Book Award finalist, a Michael L. Printz Honor Book recipient, a Coretta Scott King–John Steptoe New Talent award winner, and the first Black woman to hit number one on the *New York Times* young adult best-seller list. Two of her novels have been made into major motion pictures. She's also the co-publisher of Joy Revolution, a Random House young adult imprint dedicated to love stories starring people of color. She grew up in Jamaica and Brooklyn, and lives in Los Angeles with her husband, the novelist David Yoon, and their daughter.